Book One in the Legacy Series

Amelia's Legacy

Betty Thomason Owens

Amelia's Legacy

© 2014 Betty Thomason Owens

ISBN-13: 978-1-938092-70-1

ISBN-10: 1938092708

Scriptures are taken from the Holy Bible, New International Version®, NIV®. Copyright © 1973, 1978, 1984 by Biblica, Inc.™ Used by permission of Zondervan. All rights reserved worldwide. www.zondervan.com

Published by Write Integrity Press, P.O. Box 35, Holly Springs, GA 30142.

www.WriteIntegrity.com

Printed in the United States of America.

Dedication

For my Robert.

Acknowledgments

Amelia's Legacy began years ago with a very rough story written by someone who knew very little about the art of professional writing. That someone was me, of course. I dragged it out of the mothballs, in part, because I needed something to send through ACFW's critique loop, and also because I loved the story.

As the "captain" of the main critique loop at the time, Fay Lamb held my hand through some devastating moments along the way. She kept encouraging me to "not give up--you're a good writer," as any leader worth her mettle will do. I held on, sometimes by the skin of my teeth. When the long process had ended, I bundled it up and sent it to an editor who was familiar with the story. I think I heard her groan all the way from Florida to Kentucky. Thank you, Fay Lamb, editor extraordinaire, for all of your hard work and encouragement.

Thanks also to the many fine critiquers on both my Scribes' Loops, especially Jennifer Hallmark who always tells the truth no matter how bad it hurts, Connie Cortright, Christina Rich, Shirley Connolly, Jean Thompson Kinsey, Nike Chillemi, and Amy Blake.

My deepest apologies if I've forgotten anyone.

Chapter One

"Nancy Sanderson, what have you to say for yourself?"

In Grandmother's office, Nancy endured yet another long drawn out lecture dealing with her recent behavior at school. Her back rigid, she sat on the edge of her chair. Her gaze wandered past Grandmother's stern expression into blue sky outside the window. Grandmother's voice receded as Nancy drifted into oblivion.

Handcuffs pinched her wrists. The cold barrel of a Derringer pressed into her ribs. Nancy lifted her chin and stared down her beautiful nose at her accusers. "I will never betray my friend."

"So you are in collusion with the miscreant?"

Nancy wracked her brain. What did collusion mean?

"Are you listening to me, young lady?"

Nancy snapped to attention. No Derringer digging into her ribs but a more formidable force in front of her. "Yes, ma'am."

Grandmother clasped her hands and peered at Nancy through tortoiseshell spectacles. "I don't think you were, but I haven't the time to fool with you. I've business to attend. You've earned your punishment. Go to your room at once. I won't see you until breakfast."

"Yes, Grandmother." Nancy tiptoed to the door, but once through it, she ran for the stairs and her room—her sanctuary. She got right to work, so she'd be free to join Nate Conners when he came for her after midnight. Picking up a large, black Bible, she thumbed through the worn pages to find "… every scripture on respecting one's elders" and "a list of the benefits of such behavior." She frowned into the ancient tome. But scripture or no scripture, she'd never be remorseful over her actions. She'd stood up for what she believed was right.

Elena Newcombe, one of her classmates, had bobbed her hair and had been dismissed. What a nest of vipers Elena had unleashed with that simple act.

Nancy twirled a strand of her own hair and stared out the window. She and several of her friends dared to stand up in open defiance of the dismissal. They'd been reprimanded and had received demerits on their records. Of course, the worst for Nancy came later when she delivered the headmistress's letter to Grandmother.

The clock on the bedside table ticked away the minutes. She glanced at it and gnawed her lower lip. If she finished her homework before ten o'clock, she'd have time for a nap before Nate came for her.

A soft knock at the door interrupted Nancy's struggle to finish her grammar homework. She knew who it was before she heard the whisper, "Miss Nancy?"

With an exasperated sigh, she crossed to open the door. "Yes, Sissy?"

Sissy offered a napkin-wrapped bundle. "I brought you a sandwich." A frown creased her dark skin. She pressed her ample lips together and shook her head. "It ain't right, old as you are. She treats you like a child."

Nancy glanced around outside her door, expecting to see her grandmother's stern countenance. "Thank you, Sissy. You'd best get on with your work before she catches you."

"Good night." Sissy cast the words over her shoulder as she sped down the hall to the servants' stairs.

Nancy unwrapped the sandwich and took a bite, chewing as she sat back down at the desk. So much for Grandmother's punishment. She smirked at her reflection in the dressing table mirror. "I have the staff's sympathy. They always side with me."

A pebble struck the window. Nate arrived right on time, as usual. Nancy grabbed her jacket, pushed open the sash, and climbed out. It took only a moment to lower the window. Then she moved soundless as a cat to the edge of the roof. Dangling her legs over the side, she stretched her arms toward the limb of the old maple tree.

Nate grabbed her legs to lower her to the ground. "You're a regular monkey."

She took off across the grass. "Let's get out of here before we're seen."

Seated in his car, Nancy glanced at his handsome face. In the semidarkness, she could just make out his profile. She'd met Nate Conners, a sophomore at the local college, at a friend's party. He leaned forward, catching her gaze. "Mind if I smoke?"

She gave her head a shake and crossed her arms over her chest to calm her nerves. Tonight they were going to a place he'd told her about—a forbidden place—a roadhouse. The mere thought of the word sent a thrill racing down her spine. She loved Nate's wild side. He seemed to like her too. She grinned into the darkness. The fact that her grandmother would never approve of him made him even more interesting.

They rounded a corner and there it stood—the roadhouse, a rough-looking place, windows darkened to the outside world.

Nate rapped on the door. It opened a crack, revealing only a dark interior. He whispered something, and the door opened just wide enough for them to squeeze through.

Inside, they followed a portly gentleman down a wooden staircase. Another door at the bottom opened into a dank cellar full of cigarette smoke, the clinking of glasses, and low chatter. Sultry jazz filled the thick air. At the bottom of the stairs, Nate pivoted and moved toward the back. As he slowed, he whispered to Nancy, "The proprietress," then halted in front of a woman. "Hello, Lena."

Lena glanced past Nate to Nancy. She sniffed and shook her head.

The woman had the reddest hair Nancy had ever seen. It had to be fake. Pancaked makeup, dark lipstick, and rouge plastered Lena's rough complexion. Her eyes bore into Nancy. "I warned you about this, Nate." She poked a ruby red fingernail at his chest. "You can't bring her in here. She's underage."

He leaned close to the woman. "Lena, Lena, we won't stay long. Just one itsy-bitsy drink?"

Nancy stood ready to fly away at the first hint of Lena's disapproval. She was not one to stay where she wasn't wanted. She turned away and tried to tune out their conversation. Her eyes swept over the crowd of faces. A tremor skipped down her spine as she came to the realization she could be recognized by some of these patrons and reported to her grandmother.

"What I'm telling you is that you won't stay at all"—Lena shot a quick nod toward Nancy—"with that child on your arm. What do you think would happen?" She punctuated each point with a slap of her hand on the well-polished bar. "At any time, there could be agents on the premises. We never know when. I could go to prison. Now get on out, and don't bring any more babies back in here."

"All right. All right. We're going." He blazed a trail through the sea of people as the two of them headed for a back entrance. Over his shoulder, he called to Nancy, "Let's make tracks. We've been given the bum's rush."

She followed him through the rear door, which opened into a long, dark tunnel. Another door led out to the riverbank. Once there, he pulled her aside, and they turned to look back at the entrance.

"What'd you think of it?"

She peered into the darkness. Not even a sliver of light showed around the door. She sniffed. "Seemed interesting."

"One of the better joints. I came prepared either way." He stepped to a row of low bushes and held up a couple of amber-colored bottles. "The best money can buy, just like I promised." He jerked his head to the side. "Come on over here."

She followed him along a moonlit path to a grove of willow trees along the riverbank. Here, water tumbled over dark rocks.

Nancy sat down beside Nate on a fallen tree by the water's edge.

He opened one of the bottles and tested it then grimaced, catching his breath. "Great stuff." When he held it out to her, she leaned away from him. He pushed it closer. "You said you wanted to try it."

Yes, she'd once expressed the desire to taste the brew, but now she hesitated. She'd heard the wild tales from the other girls at school. She could get into so much trouble. After a few more minutes' hesitation, he pulled back with a shrug. "All right then. Have it your way."

Grandmother's disapproving face floated before her, and in that split second, Nancy snatched the bottle and touched it to her lips. After a brief pause, she squeezed her eyes shut and tipped. The flaming liquid hit the roof of her mouth then the back of her throat. The taste repulsed her. She coughed and lost most of what she'd taken in.

Nate laughed and patted her back. "It takes some getting used to, like smoking. You gotta take it slow at first." He opened the second bottle and raised it to his lips, took a drink, and swallowed. "Ah." He shot a sideways glance at her.

She giggled as she tried another sip. Not so bad the second time, perhaps because she expected the fire. A few minutes later she relaxed and leaned against the tree.

She didn't mind being kicked out of the speakeasy. She enjoyed this little rendezvous more because now they were alone. Not many minutes passed before Nate became the funniest person she'd ever met.

"Miss Nancy, wake up. What's the matter with you?" Sissy shook her again and tugged the covers off her. The whole bed shook. "Land child, you'll get me in so much trouble if you're late to breakfast. Are you all right?" She laid a wrist across Nancy's brow. "No fever. What could it be?"

Nancy moaned, rolled over, and sat up on the edge of the bed.

Sissy took a backward step. "Oh my. Girl you look like my ole grandpappy when he'd been—oh my stars and garters. Don't tell me."

Nancy held up a shaky hand. "All right, I won't—if you'll just be quiet. Help me get to the bathroom. I can take it from there."

Never, never again. Closing her eyes, she sucked in a deep breath to settle her stomach. She struggled to make herself presentable. After Nancy scrubbed her face and brushed her teeth, Sissy helped to pin up her hair then left her to dress.

When Nancy managed to end up at the table only five minutes late, her grandmother's eyes registered disapproval.

Nancy focused on her plate. Her stomach lurched. "I apologize, Grandmother. There's no excuse for my tardiness."

"Obviously, you were up too late trying to finish your work. From now on, perhaps you will accomplish it in a timelier manner."

Nancy kept her head down. Throbbing pain made her eyes water. "Yes, Grandmother." Sissy set a cup of black coffee in front of her.

Grandmother shook out her napkin. "That's a very good idea, Sissy. Thank you for thinking of it."

Sissy backed out of the room, her big brown eyes on Nancy's face.

Nancy scowled back.

Near the end of the meal, Grandmother glanced up from the newspaper. "I need you to come straight home from school today."

Nancy's mouth hung open as she met her grandmother's gaze. *What?*

"As soon as you get home, go change out of your uniform and into something more appropriate for entertaining guests. Then you may join me in my office." She folded the newspaper and laid it aside. "There will be someone here I'm most anxious for you to meet."

Cryptic. Nancy's curiosity quickened. But she didn't want her grandmother to know. "Yes, Grandmother," she said while rising to make a quick exit.

The family driver, Kip, had the car waiting so Nancy got in and sat down. She had a lot to think about on the short trip to school. Only two more weeks until graduation, then the summer trip to Europe. Afterward, she'd be off to university, and freedom. Or at least a measure of it. She'd be out from under Grandmother's thumb and away from this town where everybody knew her business. "Small town," she scoffed.

"Miss Nancy?" Kip asked. "You say something?"

She peered at Kip and shook her head when he glanced over his shoulder. Had she spoken aloud? "Just, um … memorizing … something. For class."

Kip flashed a luminous smile. "Okay, Miss Nancy."

Small town, indeed. If she sneezed, they published news of it in the newspaper.

Nancy Sanderson, granddaughter of Amelia Woods-Sanderson, suffered a sneeze last week while walking down Main Street. This reporter overhearing it said she may have taken cold while—

A painful bump in the road jarred Nancy back to the present and Grandmother's strange request. Who is this mysterious person Grandmother wanted her to meet? She pressed her fingertips against her temples. Just thinking about it made her head ache even more.

Chapter Two

Tired and suffering a splitting headache, Nancy barely endured the school day. She wanted rest, and plenty of it. Of all times for Grandmother to spring a meeting on her. Fingers of dread closed around her heart as she walked into the house after school and trudged up the stairs. In her room, she loosened the laces of her shoes. After she kicked them off, she changed out of her uniform. Pleated gray wool skirt, navy coat, and plain white blouse. Soft silk suited her so much better.

She tied the sash of her favorite day dress, slipped on a pair of brown pumps, then adjusted the combs in her hair. On the way out the door, she paused to look with longing at her bed. If only she dared take a short nap first. Better not.

She continued to berate herself for her spinelessness as she descended the stairs. Outside the study door, she stood for a moment listening to the voices inside. She suppressed a groan. One of them was Uncle William, Grandmother's attorney. Boring. She knocked softly and waited for the summons.

Grandmother sat at her desk, facing her guests. Only one of the men was truly a guest in Nancy's opinion, as Uncle William was so often in attendance. He was not truly her uncle, but a trusted family friend.

The two men stood as she entered.

Her grandmother nodded. "There you are. We've been waiting."

"Good afternoon, Nancy," Uncle William said.

Grandmother introduced the younger man. "Mr. Robert Emerson, my granddaughter, Miss Nancy Sanderson."

Robert faced Nancy. "How do you do, Miss Sanderson?"

"Very well, thank you," she answered, peering up at him. He seemed vaguely familiar to her, but she couldn't place him. Probably met him at one of Grandmother's dull parties.

"You may sit, Nancy." Grandmother rang for tea.

While they waited, Uncle William made small talk in his usual boring way. She tried hard to concentrate, refusing to let her eyes glaze over from boredom. She sat up straight, with her legs crossed at the ankles and tucked beneath her chair, exactly as she had been taught.

Sissy entered and set the tea tray on the side table. She cast a sideways glance at Nancy, who lifted a brow and met her gaze.

"You may go now," Grandmother addressed Sissy. "Nancy will pour the tea." Though her grandmother spoke softly, Nancy understood quite well. She was on display. But why?

She glanced from her grandmother's face to Robert Emerson's before turning to the task at hand. Quite adept at the social graces, she even managed to enjoy them sometimes as they kept her hands busy. This was different. Perhaps it was due to the lingering effects of the night before or the constant chaffing of her grandmother's ordering her about. She struggled to keep her hands steady as she poured the tea and handed the delicate cups to the guests. Somehow she managed not to spill a drop.

Returning to her chair, she sat in silence, sipping her tea.

"Mr. Emerson, William tells me you graduated magna cum laude?" Grandmother began to speak in the grand tone Nancy knew so well.

"Yes, ma'am."

Nancy positioned herself so she could watch Mr. Emerson's face. He was an ordinary looking man with dark eyes set beneath a strong brow and a not-so-large nose. His wide mouth, now upturned in a crooked smile, revealed straight white teeth and a single dimple in his right cheek. She figured him to be about twenty-six. Old.

"Mr. Emerson is a recent graduate of Harvard Law and will soon take his place at the Boston Emerson Law Firm," Grandmother spoke to Nancy.

The color rose in Robert's cheeks as he cast a quick glance her way.

Nancy blinked. Had he actually blushed? Her gaze returned to Grandmother, who seemed to be testing his ability. Perhaps she was interested in engaging his services at some future date.

Nancy frowned into her teacup.

A momentary lull in conversation seemed a good opportunity for her to offer refills. Robert continued to answer the questions her grandmother addressed to him, holding up well to Amelia Woods-Sanderson's scrutiny. Nancy admired him for it.

"My granddaughter and I will be leaving in a month for Europe. Have you ever traveled abroad, Mr. Emerson?"

"Actually, no, Mrs. Sanderson. I had the chance but opted for a summer of service instead."

Nancy turned her head to look at him full on. *Really?* Of course her grandmother would be impressed.

Grandmother sat forward on her chair. "A summer of service?"

"Yes, I did some volunteer work in a poverty-stricken area of West Virginia. My experience was quite interesting."

Grandmother's long fingers were busy folding and refolding her linen napkin. "And rewarding, no doubt. The service must have improved your perspective."

"Indeed," Uncle William said. "That's the kind of dedication that assured him a spot with our firm. We didn't just allow him a place because of his father."

Nancy had paid little attention to Uncle William up to this point but now noticed the streaks of silver in his dark hair. Funny how she hadn't noticed it before. She fidgeted with her skirt, rearranged it, and re-crossed her ankles. At Grandmother's scathing glance, she relaxed and gave Robert Emerson her undivided attention.

As he spoke of the abject poverty and the faces of the children, his face showed genuine emotion. He was so serious he could have been pleading their case before the Supreme Court. He didn't drone on, however, but kept it short and to the point. He glanced in Nancy's direction often as if to include her in the conversation. When he finished speaking, his piercing gaze bore into Nancy.

She squirmed.

He turned back to her grandmother. "You're not concerned about the continued unrest in Europe right now, Mrs. Sanderson?"

"Just what I asked her." William gave a slight shrug. "She's a stubborn woman, though—as you'll soon learn."

"Posh!" Grandmother said. "You don't want to get me started on labor unions, young man. My connections in France and England assure me the situation is well under control for the time being. We'll be safe enough. Besides, Nancy's been looking forward to this for some time. I wouldn't wish to disappoint her."

Nancy darted a glance at her grandmother. Really?

Finally, her ordeal ended when William Boston rose from his chair. He smiled. "Thank you, young lady, for your kind attention." He turned to her grandmother. "Amelia, thank you for your gracious hospitality."

Mr. Emerson stood and strolled over to Nancy, who'd risen from her chair. "Very nice to meet you, Miss Sanderson, though I believe we've met before."

She forced her lips into a polite smile. "I thought so, too, though I don't remember where it may have been."

He flashed a toothy smile. "One function or another, no doubt. Perhaps a long-ago birthday party? Our families are socially connected, after all. We will no doubt meet again." His eyes warmed to hers. "I look forward to getting to know you better."

She swallowed hard and managed a nod before he swung away and followed Uncle William and her grandmother from the room. "I'll be in touch," her grandmother said.

The front door closed, and Grandmother returned to the study.

Nancy frowned as she gathered the cups and saucers and placed them onto the silver tea tray.

Grandmother touched her hand. "Leave that. Sissy can clean up." She turned aside, facing the window. "Thank you for your forbearance. I know you found it difficult to sit still for so long a time. But I very much wanted you to meet Mr. Emerson."

Thank you? Nancy swallowed. Was she being sarcastic? Grandmother never thanked her for following orders. Her head throbbed. "May I be excused now, Grandmother? I have … homework."

Grandmother waved her away. "Certainly, of course, go."

Nancy frowned as she trudged up the stairs. If only Nate would come tonight. Sometimes he would surprise her—ping her window with a pebble.

Once in her room, she sat at her desk and removed her textbooks from a leather valise. Just a few more days of homework.

In the car on the way back to the office, Robert turned to William. "What was that all about?"

William smiled. "I told you yesterday. She just wanted to meet the newest member of the firm." He eased the car onto Main Street and headed for the courthouse.

Robert blew out a breath. "Right."

William leveled his gaze at the younger man. "You don't believe me?"

"No, I don't. It felt like an interview or a slave auction. I'm surprised she didn't check my teeth."

William chuckled. "If anyone was on display, it was Nancy."

Robert frowned as the truth of William's statement sank in, followed by suspicion. Was the old lady trying to make a match? But her granddaughter was still so young. Not that he hadn't thought about her. He had.

William parked the car and turned off the engine. "Not convinced?"

Robert gave him a sideways glance. "I keep coming up with the same question—why?"

"All you need to know right now is, if Amelia Sanderson wants something from you, she'll let you know. I suspect you will be hearing from her. Soon."

Robert ran his fingers through his hair and donned his hat. William knew something. He was almost certain of it.

William opened the door and got out. Robert followed and walked with him into the building. "So what are you not telling me?"

William stopped in front of his office door, his hand on the knob. He grinned and shook his head. "Can't tell you what I don't know."

Three days later, Robert had a call from Mrs. Sanderson's secretary.

"Mrs. Sanderson would like a meeting with you. Can you come to her office Friday morning, say—ten o'clock?"

Robert consulted his calendar and finding nothing, agreed to the time. After hanging up the phone, he made a note then drummed the desk with his fingers. What did she want with him? Had she set her cap for him? He chuckled but quickly sobered. Most likely, she wanted him to court her granddaughter, as William had intimated.

He stood and crossed to the window, thrust his hands in his pockets and concentrated. As a boy, he'd coveted this office with its view of the town square and the hulking courthouse. He'd set goals and achieved them all. He'd planned his life to this point and then ...

His phone rang again, jarring him out of his reverie. Time to get back to work. Whatever Mrs. Sanderson wanted from him would have to wait until Friday at ten o'clock. Maybe it wasn't what he thought. Maybe it was something entirely different.

Thursday, May 22, 1924

The young women's preparatory school Nancy attended didn't wear the mortarboard hat for graduation. They wore white dresses, white silk stockings and white slippers. Each graduate carried a budding rose, stripped of its thorns.

Nancy clamped her jaw shut to stifle a yawn. She scanned the platform where each one of their instructors sat along with two of their classmates. She supposed Grandmother was disappointed she hadn't made valedictorian. She had tried, but the competition proved brutal.

Her gaze travelled from the platform to the bright blue sky. She closed her eyes and tried to imagine herself wearing the cap and gown of Jennings College, two years distant. Perhaps then she could be on her own, truly free. Able to live her life as she wished, what would she do?

Her young classmate's words drifted into her reverie. "We stand poised to begin our careers as wives and mothers ..."

Nancy sniffed. Not everyone. *Some of us prefer to have a different kind of career.*

She tried to imagine Nate in the role of companion to a businesswoman. It didn't fit. He lacked something she couldn't quite put her finger on. But he was wildly exciting and so much fun.

When the last speech ended, Nancy took her place in line to file forward and receive her diploma. As she accepted it, her gaze rested on Grandmother's face. Was that a flash of pride in the old woman's eyes? Had she finally done something her Grandmother approved?

"I wish your father could be here to see this," Grandmother said as they walked across the garden to the street where Kip awaited them. Once they were in the car, she turned to Nancy. She held a black velvet box in her hand. "I've kept this for you since your ... mother passed."

Nancy gazed into the older woman's eyes. Something of her mother's?

Grandmother cleared her throat. "Your father gave this to her on their wedding day."

With careful fingers, Nancy opened the box to find a large garnet set in gold and fastened to a delicate chain. "It's beautiful."

"Your father had good taste. He was especially drawn to beautiful things." Their gazes held for a moment until Kip stopped the car.

They had arrived at their destination. *The Breakfront*, the finest restaurant in Springfield. Grandmother was full of surprises today.

Amelia's Legacy

Chapter Three

Robert Emerson entered the offices of Woods-Sanderson and Associates at nine fifty-five on Friday morning. After the perky young woman at the front desk took his coat and hat, she asked him to take a seat on a nearby divan. "I've informed Mrs. Sanderson's secretary of your arrival. She will call for you soon."

Robert sat down. It was quiet here in the executive offices, unlike the busy clamor of the work areas on the first floor. He was glad to be away from the constant buzz of the switchboard and din of voices, mixed with the clatter of the steno pool. As he waited, he mentally rehearsed the impressive list of business interests included under the Woods-Sanderson umbrella. The latest, in an important castling move, Mrs. Sanderson had acquired a fledgling oil company.

Robert's watch showed five past ten when a door to his left opened, and a well-dressed middle-aged woman approached. Robert recognized Edith Reynolds, Mrs. Sanderson's personal secretary. He stood.

"Mr. Emerson, sorry to keep you waiting. Mrs. Sanderson will see you now. Please follow me."

With a polite nod to the receptionist, Robert followed Edith. The short corridor she led him down was bright and airy, decorated with marble topped tables and healthy philodendrons. Edith opened a door and stood aside for him to enter. He was vaguely aware of the door closing behind him. Mrs. Sanderson sat at a large mahogany desk flanked by high windows.

She welcomed him with a pleasant smile. "Mr. Emerson, so good of you to come." She gestured toward one of two plush velvet chairs.

As he lowered himself into the chair, he took in the rich navy and red decor before centering his attention on her.

"May I have Edith bring you something—a cup of coffee or water—perhaps?"

"No, thank you. I'm fine."

She gave him a moment to settle in. "I've asked you here today to discuss a matter of grave importance. I'm quite impressed with your single-minded pursuit of your goals."

Robert internalized his surprise at this remark and kept his gaze trained on her face.

She removed her spectacles and laid them on the desk. "As you know, my granddaughter will soon be of marriageable age." She paused.

Here it comes. Had he been right? *Concentrate. Keep your mind on the present.*

"Since she is my sole heir, I feel duty-bound to make provisions for her in case of my—*any* unplanned event that would leave her in responsible charge of my estate. She is an emotional young woman and I am concerned, not only for her personal safety, but ..."

She sat forward, drew a slow breath, and exhaled. "She does not always make good decisions in her choice of friends, Mr. Emerson. I hope you understand my meaning."

"Yes, Mrs. Sanderson. I understand." And he did. He'd heard the gossip around town, that Nancy preferred the company of a certain football player—a roguish type—a bad boy.

Mrs. Sanderson nodded. "What I am looking for, Mr. Emerson, is someone to step into a leadership role in my granddaughter's life. Perhaps friendship would be a better term. I'd like you to befriend her, gain her trust, and gently prod her into compliance."

Mrs. Sanderson's smug smile sent a chill through Robert. He gripped the arms of the chair as he sought the proper response. What exactly was she asking?

She smoothed the creases from a sheet of notepaper on her desk. "I see I've shocked you. I'm making a proposal only. There's no need for an immediate answer. Please give it some thought. That's all I ask."

He nodded. "If I understand you correctly, Mrs. Sanderson, you're concerned that your granddaughter will align herself with the wrong people. In your absence, should anything happen to you, she could be persuaded into a less than desirable marriage and put the company, and all of its assets, at risk."

She nodded her consensus. "There is more to this than simply guiding my granddaughter through dangerous waters, Mr. Emerson. I am interested in having you as my personal liaison attorney."

Robert sat forward. "I thought Mr. Boston—"

Mrs. Sanderson lifted her hand to stay his objection. "I have discussed this at length with William Boston and your father." She pushed away from her desk and rose to her feet.

Robert also stood, facing her. Had their meeting ended?

She beckoned for him to join her at the window. "Come, Mr. Emerson. Tell me what you see."

Robert moved to her side and gazed out the window. A narrow alley separated the building they were in from a row of warehouses spanning an entire city block. Near the river, redbrick smokestacks filled the sky with dark smoke. Inside each one of those buildings, laborers worked throughout the day and night. The first word that came to his mind was money. He pushed that aside and found a better answer. "The life's blood of this town, Mrs. Sanderson. That's what I see."

She gave him an admiring nod. "Good answer, Mr. Emerson."

He thrust his hands into his pockets and frowned.

Her eyes on the scene below, she crossed her arms over her chest. "All of this could be yours, Mr. Emerson, if you so desire."

Robert felt as though a stray bolt of lightning had connected with the top of his head. The hair stood up on the back of his neck. He suppressed a shudder as he turned his eyes to meet her piercing gaze. Had she said what he thought, or had he imagined it?

"I need a future guardian for my granddaughter," she continued. "An executor with full power of attorney."

"Surely Mr. Boston would be a better choice. He's had a deal more experience than I."

Mrs. Sanderson turned away from the window and strolled across the oriental carpet to the chair recently occupied by Robert. She lowered herself into the chair and gestured for him to sit beside her. "William Boston is too near my age. There's no guarantee he'll outlive me. No, I need someone like you, Mr. Emerson. I need someone of sound mind. Someone goal oriented, with strong principles." She leveled her gaze at him. "I hope you'll think about it. Take your time. Talk it over with William and your father. Just don't take too long. There's a lot at stake here."

After leaving Amelia's office, Robert walked for nearly an hour. When he finally arrived back at Boston Emerson, he met William Boston and his father on their way out to lunch.

His father invited him to join them. "I believe you have something you need to discuss with us?"

Robert nodded. "I could use your guidance, yes."

Over lunch, he gave them his interpretation of the meeting with Mrs. Sanderson.

Daniel Emerson glanced at William Boston then thumped his forefinger against the table. "We can't tell you what to do, son. This would be a huge undertaking. If anything were to happen to Amelia, you'd step into her position as head of the conglomerate until her granddaughter reaches maturity. You'd have to keep that monster viable.

"Now, I would hope you'd have time to prepare for such an important role. But there's no guarantee, as you well know. None of us knows what tomorrow may bring. That's a chance you'd take, if you accept this offer."

Robert moved his gaze to William Boston, who'd been quietly enjoying his lunch. William nodded in agreement with Daniel. "You'd retain your position at Boston Emerson, of course, on retainer to Woods-Sanderson. You'd sit in on their board meetings and be available for any necessary litigation, etc."

Robert sipped his water and touched his lips with his napkin. "So I'd be replacing you?"

William stirred sugar into his coffee. "No, I'm a member of the board. I'll still be at the board meetings and any official functions. So you'll have backup if you're concerned about that."

"I didn't know you were a member of the board," Robert said.

William nodded. "Voted in last year. One more reason Amelia's been looking to bring in another lawyer. She didn't want anyone to cry 'conflict of interest.'"

Robert glanced at his watch then returned it to its pocket in his vest. "I've got a two o'clock, so I'd better go. I appreciate your input. As you have suggested, I'll take my time thinking this over."

Daniel patted his son's shoulder. "I'm confident you'll give it prayerful thought as well. Your mother and I will also."

"You may depend on mine as well," William said, lifting his water glass as though to toast.

Sunday, June 1, 1924

Robert combed his hair into place then made a final adjustment to his tie. He stepped back and took inventory of his appearance. Gray summer-weight suit, white shirt, navy silk tie with red diagonal stripes (a gift from his mother). He stuffed a handkerchief into his breast pocket, chose the soft gray Homburg hat from his collection and strode from the room.

Today was his first day on the job as retainer for Woods-Sanderson. But it wasn't a typical day. He'd been invited to attend a graduation party for Nancy. Of course, he would have gone regardless of his decision to take the job.

In his usual methodical fashion, he'd resolved to work for Mrs. Sanderson because it would fast-track his original goal of corporate attorney for a large, multifaceted company. Mrs. Sanderson was in her late fifties and the picture of health, so he expected to have many years to learn the business. But that wasn't his only reason for taking the job.

"Will you have any problem answering to a woman?" Mrs. Sanderson had asked.

"None at all," he'd assured her. And he didn't anticipate any problems. A brilliant businesswoman with a stellar reputation, she'd paved new roads into a formerly male-dominated world. He could learn a lot from her.

He arrived at the Woods-Sanderson estate half an hour ahead of the other guests. Plenty of time to meet with Mrs. Sanderson and obtain his orders for the day.

Robert stood some distance from Mrs. Sanderson, hands in his pockets, stealing occasional glances at Nancy. He had long held an interest in the young chestnut-haired beauty. She captivated him with an elusive wild streak he felt certain would disappear with time. The disparity in their ages could pose a problem. He'd been eight years old when she was born.

He grabbed a cup of lemonade from a passing servant and took a sip.

He'd always figured by age thirty, he'd be ready to settle down. By his calculation, she'd be twenty-two. If she was still single, perhaps then … He swallowed the rest of the lemonade and set the glass on a nearby table. A little maturity was all she needed. He watched her interacting with her friends. She laughed often, tossed her head back carelessly, unconscious of her effect on every male within sight of her.

He strolled past a privet hedge as an old Ford jalopy rattled into the drive. Robert detected a change in Nancy's expression. He followed her line of vision to see Nate Conners walking toward her.

He had known Nate for years. They ran in different circles, but it would have been difficult to ignore such a colorful character. When he saw them set off toward Nancy's grandmother, he spun on his heel to join them. Mrs. Sanderson was not going to be happy.

He came upon them as Nancy introduced Nate to her grandmother.

Mrs. Sanderson greeted Nate with a chilly glance and the barest civility. "How do you do?"

Robert had seen that look before. He moved in behind Mrs. Sanderson, hoping to draw Nancy's attention.

She would not meet his gaze.

Nate gave Mrs. Sanderson a slow nod. "Very well, thank you, and you?"

Robert caught his cool smile and elevated brow and almost chuckled aloud at Nate's arrogance. Did the boy realize whom he was dealing with? Amelia Sanderson could be a formidable foe.

Nancy tugged at Nate's sleeve to draw him away from Grandmother and her sidekick. A backward glance assured her they'd left a stunned silence in their wake. She giggled and squeezed Nate's arm.

He leaned close to her ear and whispered, "Careful, little kitten. Grandma's claws are showing."

She lifted her chin. "For once, I don't care. I feel positively free." At the first opportunity, Nate ducked out of sight with her and drew her into the arbor. She tried to pull away. "The party is given in my honor. I really should—"

He silenced her with a kiss full on the lips.

Though she had wished for it and dreamed of nothing else since their first meeting, she could not enjoy it. The timing was less than perfect.

Her hands shook. Her knees quivered. *What on earth?* Before she could recover, he drew back. He grinned and traced the outline of a spit curl on her cheek. "I'm afraid that'll have to do for a graduation gift. I'm broke, but then I usually am."

Heat rose up Nancy's neck and flushed her face. She attempted to turn away from him, but he caught her arm and forced her back. Strong arms held her captive as he leaned close and gazed into her eyes. "You may as well get used to it, young lady, because I mean to do it often."

She pushed him away, tossed her hair, and thrust out her chin. "I'm leaving next week you know, for most of the summer."

"Yes, and then you'll be off to Jennings. I'll be a junior at Madison and very busy winning football games." He chuckled. "But you should expect to see me at every opportunity."

She huffed. *How sure of himself he is*. She drew in a deep breath and tried very hard to turn her eyes from his. What was happening to her? Instead of being offended by his attitude, she felt more drawn to him than ever. Odd. He was a very bad boy, and she was falling for him.

She turned away and walked back toward the party. When he didn't follow her, she turned to him. "I have to get back before I'm missed. I hope you'll be staying?"

He raised his brows and spared her a dazzling smile. "'Til Mrs. Grundy and her sidekick toss me out."

She glanced toward the party then back at him again. "Please wait until I'm gone before you return."

"Don't worry about your precious reputation, sweetheart." He held his hands up, palms out. "It's safe in my big, empty hands." He glanced over his shoulder. "I'll take a pass through the gardens and come back around from the front of the house."

Nancy smiled. "Thank you." After a quick inventory of her appearance, she bit her lips and pinched her cheeks. She couldn't seem to shake the feeling that everyone would know she'd been kissed.

Mrs. Sanderson gripped Robert's arm. "Look there." She nodded toward Nancy and Nate as they made their way through a throng of partygoers. Then she turned back to Robert. "Who is this Nate Conners?"

His eyes never left the subject of their conversation as he answered, "He's a football player from Madison College." *Busy wasting a valuable scholarship.*

"A meathead?" She smiled into Robert's eyes. "Yes, I do know a few words of slang. I try to keep up, somewhat."

He grinned. "I believe the term you're thinking of is leatherhead, though meathead probably fits well, too."

She sniffed. "Whoever or whatever he is, we'd best keep an eye on him."

Robert's eyes narrowed. "My thoughts exactly."

She released her grip on his arm. "She is, after all, a young woman of fortune."

He nodded, still gazing at Nate and Nancy. What, if anything, could he do to discourage her friendship with Nate Conners?

He'd turned away for only a moment to greet an old friend. When he turned back, they had disappeared. That could not be good. He took a tentative step forward then halted. What Nancy did was really none of his business, other than helping out his client. He wasn't Nancy's chaperone. Still, if anything happened … drat! He'd never agreed to play nursemaid to Mrs. Sanderson's wayward granddaughter.

He strolled to a spot near the punchbowl as a slightly flustered Nancy crept back across the lawn from the far corner of the house. A moment later, he noticed Nate slipping back into the crowd.

Robert shook his head and squared his shoulders. Picking up a second cup of punch, he strode out to meet Nancy halfway.

"I thought you might be thirsty by now." He kept his voice calm as he handed her the cup.

Her hand shook as she took it from him. She gave him a quick smile, no doubt to win him over with her charm. Her voice dripped honey. "You are so thoughtful, Mr. Emerson. Thank you."

He gave her a sideways glance.

She didn't fool him. This charming little attitude was so foreign to her former demeanor, he almost laughed out loud. Instead, he watched her sip the punch. He enjoyed seeing her squirm. "So, we'll be losing you to Jennings soon, I hear." He gestured toward the tables beneath the tent and stepped forward.

"Yes, in September." She fell into step beside him. "It's a grand old place—a very proper finishing school for young ladies—which is all Grandmother would stand for." She gazed up at him. "What about you, Mr. Emerson? Was law your idea, or were you pressured to follow in your father's footsteps?"

Robert smiled, pleased at her interest in him, though he suspected she was only being polite. "Please call me Robert, Miss Nancy. You make me feel old addressing me so formally."

They had managed to progress as far as the dining tent by this time, so he pulled out a chair for her. Once she was seated, he sat down beside her. "My mother always told me I was a natural-born lawyer. I questioned everything, even before I could talk properly." He took a sip of his drink and smiled. "I actually enjoy it."

"That's a good thing, I suppose." She fingered the crisply starched linen tablecloth. "To be happy at your chosen profession is certainly desirable." Their eyes met briefly. She cleared her throat and set down her cup.

He admired the smooth turn of her cheek against the rich color of her hair. "What about you, Miss Nancy? What are your interests?"

Her eyes flashed. Or was it only the afternoon sunlight?

She took her lower lip between her teeth. For a brief second, her composure seemed to falter. "I ... hardly know. I haven't given it much thought, Mr—" She flashed a smile. "*Robert.*"

"No? Well, you have plenty of time for that, I suppose." He caught her gaze and held it.

Her lips parted as if she was about to say something else. Instead, she took another sip of punch then set the cup next to his. Her lips curved into a small smile. "You're right. I do, and I intend to take my time, Robert. One of the advantages of having money is, you get to take your time."

She smoothed her skirt as she rose from her chair. "I'd better see to my other guests." She cast a sideways glance at him. "Good afternoon, Robert."

He stood and attempted to assist her, but she was already several steps away. After she'd gone, he sat back down. As she made her way across the lawn, greeting the guests, he watched her. He took a sip of punch, set the cup down, and eased back in his chair.

"My, my," Mrs. Sanderson said as she took the seat vacated by her granddaughter. "Don't you look like the cat that ate the canary?"

He shot her a smile.

She cocked her head at him. A light frown played across her brow. "I do hope you're making progress, Mr. Emerson. I am concerned about this Mr. Conners. I don't want him to get too strong a hold on her. I know how quickly these things can develop."

"I am quite satisfied with my progress for now." Robert held her steady gaze until her expression changed.

A smile crept into her hazel eyes, though it didn't spread as far as her lips. She shook her head at him.

"You may be a very successful lawyer, my dear Mr. Emerson, but don't get too complacent where my granddaughter is concerned. She has just enough of her mother in her to be troublesome."

Chapter Four

Summer, 1924

Nancy stood at the rail of the *Mauretania* watching the sun set over the water. She'd loved everything about the voyage to Europe. The weather had been fine. They attended dinner parties every night. She smiled at the memories of music and dancing.

Grandmother had actually encouraged her to mingle with the other guests. "It's good to acquaint yourself with people of other cultures, Nancy, become comfortable among them. One day, you'll understand you've an obligation to fulfill."

Nancy sighed and let her head fall back in the embrace of an invigorating breeze. The sounds of soft jazz filtered out from the dining room. Grandmother despised it. She insisted it was, "Barbaric! Immoral!" She preferred classical music, which Nancy also liked, but you couldn't do the Charleston to Chopin or Beethoven, and she dearly loved dancing.

On the way back to the room, she tucked a wisp of hair into her hat, a tight-fitting Cloche that hid the fact her hair was long and not bobbed. It seemed everyone these days wore a bob, and she hated that Grandmother was so old-fashioned.

Nancy let herself into their stateroom as the maid put the final touches on Grandmother's appearance. Grandmother eyed her in the mirror. "Getting a breath of air?"

"The sunset is beautiful tonight." She crossed to her bed and sat down. "Dinner smells wonderful."

"I'm famished." Grandmother darted a look at the maid. "Are you finished?"

The maid, a young French woman named Lisette, dropped her hands and took a backward step. She barely ever spoke a word.

Grandmother rose, took up her shawl and crossed to the door. Nancy followed her into the corridor, now filled with people. "The best ocean liners are British," she overheard one of the passengers say. "I have no confidence in American workmanship. I don't believe they'll be any serious competition." His companion gave a rather vulgar snort followed by, "May I remind you of the *Titanic*? Was it not British?"

She didn't like to be reminded of the *Titanic*. She tried to close her ears. Tried to center her mind on the music that grew louder with each step. Her heart beat in time with the music, and she imagined herself dancing, swirling around a ballroom, in Nate's strong arms. If only he'd learn to waltz.

The maître d' led them to the table they shared with six other people. Her eyes swept over the room, taking in the crisp white linens, sparkling china, gold-plated flatware—everything always impeccably clean. Tuxedoed waiters dashed about, pouring wine and spreading napkins on laps.

"Excuse me. May I sit beside you?"

Nancy continued to dance in her mind, swirling around the dining room, quick-stepping between the tables. She turned to look at the young woman whose voice had broken into her fantasy. Large, cornflower blue eyes stared back at Nancy. Eyes sparkling with amusement.

Nancy blinked and nodded. The seat had been vacant until now, its occupant too ill to attend meals. The two of them sat down together, almost in unison.

The girl giggled.

Nancy gave her a quick once-over. She had auburn hair in the latest style, banded with a wide pink ribbon. She seemed quite a fashionable young woman.

Behind them, the waiter shook out a linen napkin and laid it across Nancy's lap. She slid closer to the table and reached for her water glass.

The girl leaned forward to peer into Nancy's eyes. "I'm Rebecca Lewis."

Nancy smiled. "Nancy Sanderson."

Grandmother sat down on the opposite side of Nancy and eyed Rebecca. "Of the Newport Lewises?"

Rebecca sent her a brilliant smile. "Absolutely."

Grandmother made a great show of scanning the room. "I haven't seen your parents."

Rebecca's gaze shifted from Nancy back to Grandmother's face. "They are in a very important conference at the moment. I'm certain you'll see them later."

Grandmother nodded and took a sip of sparkling white wine.

Rebecca leaned close to Nancy's ear. "Actually, they're at the gaming tables. That wine is not the only perk to sailing on a European vessel."

As the evening progressed, she learned Rebecca was also due to begin at Jennings in September. They talked throughout dinner, and by the end of the evening, they knew almost everything about each other. Nancy had never met anyone quite like Rebecca.

Nancy and her grandmother took a train from London to Paris and then to the coast where they again met Rebecca Lewis and her family. Together, they travelled to Nice on the Riviera where the girls discovered the Promenade, though Nancy had little hope of spending much time there. Grandmother would never approve.

"I envy you," she told Rebecca one afternoon.

Rebecca sniffed and examined a new bauble on her fingers, a large topaz ring, exactly the same color of the shift she wore that day. "You complain of your grandmother watching over you like a mother hen, and my parents couldn't care less where I am and what I'm doing, so long as I'm not in their way."

Nancy sighed. "You have an endless amount of funds and total freedom." She glanced at Rebecca. "Well, as free as any young woman ever is. I, on the other hand, seem to be destined to live someone else's life. Grandmother is determined I shouldn't be myself, by any means. She has a plan for every spare second of my life."

Rebecca touched the back of her hand to her forehead in dramatic fashion. "Oh my dear." She glanced at Nancy. "I will admit she is a funny old bird."

She'd spent most of the morning with Rebecca on a terrace overlooking the Riviera. After exhausting every possible topic of conversation, Rebecca jumped up. "Let's go for a stroll."

Nancy shifted in her chair. "I'd love to, but Grandmother will never give me permission for an unchaperoned saunter through a strange village."

"Then we'll throw up a smoke screen," Rebecca said. She pulled Nancy inside the room, crossed to a side table and picked up a candlestick phone. With a smug smile, she lifted the receiver and held it to her ear. "Mrs. Woods-Sanderson's room, please."

Nancy sat openmouthed as Rebecca launched into a very good impersonation of Mrs. Alton Lewis and asked that Nancy be allowed to accompany her and her daughter on a shopping trip into town. She bit her lip and beckoned to Nancy. They pressed their heads together against the receiver.

"Of course she may. Thank you so much for including her," Grandmother said.

They rushed off before Grandmother had time to change her mind.

Rebecca bought colorful ostrich feathers and silk ribbons to fashion new hats for herself and Nancy. Afterwards, they dawdled away an hour at a street-side cafe, sipping espresso. Rebecca nudged Nancy. "See those rogues over there? The dark-eyed one's been ogling you for the last half hour."

Nancy scoffed. "He's nothing but a drugstore cowboy. They'll send him out to deliver groceries in a minute." She brushed imaginary crumbs from the table. "He doesn't have the where-with-all to keep me happy."

Rebecca cackled. "Listen to you. I knew I'd drag you down to my level." She emptied her cup. "Let's get a wiggle-on before Gram sends the troops out."

They set off down the narrow street toward their hotel. They hadn't gone far when Nancy noticed the two young men from the cafe. She leaned close to Rebecca. "I think we're being followed."

Rebecca glanced over her shoulder. "You're exactly right, doll face, and I think I know why."

One of the young men, a swarthy blond, lifted Rebecca's shopping bag into the air. "*Mam'selle?*"

Rebecca took the bag and cast a flirtatious glance at the bearer. "*Merci, Monsieur—mille fois merci.*"

The young man grinned. "*Parlez-vous français?*"

Nancy wished she'd paid more attention in French class. She could barely keep up with the conversation that flowed so easily between her new friend and the young man.

Rebecca laid her hand on Nancy's arm. "His name is Arnaud, and he thinks I am very beautiful." She grinned. "His friend's name is Paul-Henri, and they would like to accompany us on our walk."

Nancy opened her mouth. Walk? With two strangers? Was she crazy? Rebecca's tinkling laughter echoed off the cobblestones. "I can read your expression quite well, my friend. Just think. What would Gram say?" She tilted her head, tempting Nancy.

Nancy acquiesced. "All right, but we mustn't be seen near the hotel."

Rebecca turned to Arnaud. Whatever she said to him, he seemed to like her answer. He offered her his arm and nodded to Paul-Henri, the dark-eyed young man who'd been ogling Nancy back at the cafe.

He gave Nancy the creeps. She made a mental note to remind Rebecca of her involvement with Nate.

The alley opened onto a wide boulevard garnished by an ancient fountain. The creepy guy did not stop ogling her. When they paused to admire the fountain, he tightened his fingers on her arm and pressed his lips against her cheek. She reclaimed her arm and ran ahead on the pretense of dropping a coin into the fountain.

Paul-Henri followed close behind her. She ducked into a gift shop and hid behind a display of … she did a double-take. Porkpie hats?

Paul-Henri crept past the window. He hadn't seen her. She released a pent-up breath and frowned at the hat display. Then she picked one up and used it to fan her flushed cheeks.

A moment later, Rebecca stuck her head in the door. "Really, Nancy?"

"He gave me the heebie-jeebies."

Rebecca rolled her eyes. "You're going to have to toughen up, little girl. The world is full of Paul-Henris." She patted Nancy's cheek. "You flirt a little bit. You let him think the bank is open. He spends a few coins on you. Then you give him the cold shoulder. We're only going to be in town another couple of days. Loosen up, lady. Have some fun." She grabbed

Nancy's hands and pulled her out into the street. "We're in France!"

"Oh heavenly days," Nancy said, stretching her long legs on the blanket. She and Rebecca were lying on the beach, reading novels. "I'm so glad Grandmother is preoccupied with business."

Rebecca grinned back at her. "And left you in Mother's very capable hands." Both girls sighed simultaneously then lapsed into giggles. Rebecca pushed a stray curl back under her hat. "I'd be bored stiff by now. It's so much nicer to have someone with whom to while away the hours."

"If Grandmother only knew," Nancy began to say and then stared openmouthed as a young woman paraded past wearing one of the briefest bathing suits she'd ever seen. It was cut low, revealing a bit of cleavage, had no sleeves and no legs. Nancy had underthings that covered more skin. "How on earth can they walk around in public like that?"

"Oh, I think it would be fun," Rebecca said, shading her eyes with her novel. "Perhaps we should go and buy one?"

Nancy stared slack-jawed at Rebecca. "Oh my, no. Surely you must be joking? Her thighs are completely exposed." She gave a soft chuckle. "Grandmother would be certain to hear of it."

"Oh well, I suppose she would." Rebecca leaned her head close to Nancy's. "But wouldn't the fun of the doing be worth the punishment?"

Nancy tried in vain to picture herself wearing something like what she'd just seen. The color rose in her cheeks at the thought. She gave her head a toss that sent her curls flying. "No, no, I couldn't do it."

Rebecca laughed. "You're such a prude, Nancy Sanderson." She waved her book in the air. "I predict that'll change in the next few months." She fingered Nancy's hair. "Among other things."

Nancy wrinkled her nose. "I read in the school manual that short hair is strictly discouraged."

"Discouraged is not forbidden."

Nancy pursed her lips and gave her head a shake. "Grandmother can be formidable."

Rebecca grinned. "But she needn't know." She touched her own hair. "There are ways to hide it."

Nancy drew in a breath and sat up. She lifted the bulk of Rebecca's hair and found a lot less there than she expected. "You didn't."

Rebecca giggled. "In Paris."

"I could never do that. I couldn't defy Grandmother. She'd skin
me alive and hang me out to dry." She ran her fingers through her hair. "She'd disinherit me. She's always threatening to."

"Now what did you tell me your grandmother did to your father? She threatened to disinherit him, but did she? No, she didn't. And she won't disinherit you. You mustn't think of it. We're only young once, you know."

"Oh, listen to you," Nancy said. "You sound so old and experienced. What are you—two whole months older than I?"

"Two months and three days to be exact, and oh, so much more experienced."

Rebecca avoided the cheap novel Nancy threw at her head. "Here now. I'm bored to tears. Let's do something fun."

Apprehension tickled Nancy's belly, but she squelched it. Still she shivered at the memory of yesterday's jaunt when she was accosted by that Bohemian Paul Henri. European boys seemed to have little regard for respectable young ladies.

The English Channel seemed dull and gray without
Rebecca. Nancy hugged herself against the chill. Her teeth
chattered relentlessly, and she longed for the warmth of the
Mediterranean Sea. But Grandmother had business in London
before they boarded the ship to head home. Something to do
with Parliament and labor laws.

"It'll do you good to see how things are done in other
countries. Perhaps you'll appreciate your own life better."

"Yes, ma'am," she'd said. *Spineless.* She gazed through
coal smudged glass at the choppy waters of the Channel. The
day had started out sunny, but as they drew nearer to Britain's
shore, clouds rolled in and rain threatened. Her expectations
hung about as low as those clouds.

Though she tried, Nancy could not dismiss the sadness
that permeated the atmosphere of London. Something stirred
deep within her at the sight of the long queues outside soup
kitchens. "Lost sheep," Grandmother whispered as they drove
past.

Nancy turned to gaze at her then back to the lines of
hungry people. "What do you mean by 'lost sheep?'"

Grandmother seemed startled. Perhaps she hadn't meant to
speak aloud. "They've followed along behind the wrong
shepherd and lost their way. There's been such a fuss about
wages and unions. But I suppose change is inevitable." She
turned to stare out the window again, her forehead creased with
worry.

Nancy tried to concentrate on what lay ahead but could
not seem to do so. Did Grandmother worry that this would
happen to Woods-Sanderson employees? Was this one of her
reasons for coming to Europe? To assess the situation
firsthand?

She shifted in her seat as a slow tide of awareness rolled over her. Face to face with a harsh reality of hunger and despair, Nancy could understand her grandmother's attitudes regarding her responsibilities. By the time they reached their hotel and relaxed in the luxury to which they were accustomed, Nancy's mind had already moved on. The plight of distressed Londoners was soon displaced by concern over Nate. She tried to picture him pining away for her company. But in her heart of hearts, the picture was quite different.

The next few days passed in a whirlwind of activity that included a visit to Parliament, High Tea with the prime minister, and dinner at a castle. But all of London's high society held no interest for Nancy. She longed to return home to Nate and Jennings, where she'd be rooming with Rebecca. Since meeting Rebecca, her future seemed very bright, and she was so ready for it.

Nancy had written and mailed numerous cards to Nate throughout the summer in hopes he would somehow find a way to meet them when they arrived. She longed for a glimpse of him. But she didn't see Nate's face in the crowd waiting for them to disembark.

She saw Robert Emerson's.

"Your grandmother ordered me to clear my calendar so I'd be available to escort you home," he said when Nancy stood at his side.

She felt too disappointed for words, but held her head high. She hadn't missed the look in Grandmother's eyes, however. Nancy had a strange sense of foreboding, which both puzzled and alarmed her.

She stared out the window as Robert and Grandmother droned on and on all the way home. How could they possibly be so interested in business matters? The unrest in Europe. Delays and changes because of rioting in Italy. How they did go on. She suppressed a yawn. When they launched into a spirited debate over English politics, she leaned back and closed her eyes.

"I'm afraid we're boring poor Nancy," Robert said.

She kept her eyes closed but answered, "Oh no, I think the English way of debating issues is so much more efficient than our system, as well as being more entertaining." Peering out through lowered eyelids, she observed two open mouths.

Robert's quickly changed into a grin. She kind of liked the way his lips curled up on one side, revealing the dimple. She closed her eyes again. He was almost handsome ... when he smiled.

The car rolled to a halt in front of the house. Finally. She made herself wait until Kip opened her door before vaulting forth and darting up the steps. She intended to put as much space between herself and her grandmother as possible.

Robert stood aside as Mrs. Sanderson got out of the car. He could tell she was upset by Nancy's curt departure.

She pushed past Robert. "Young lady, you come back here!"

He closed the car door and touched her arm. "We have a great deal of business to discuss if you're not too tired."

She squared her shoulders and lifted her chin. Her eyes sparked with energy. "Of course I'm not too tired." As they entered the foyer, she barked orders at Sissy and led Robert to her office.

He followed at a more leisurely rate, searching the upper landing where a door closed softly. He smiled. Looking out for Nancy's interests was not going to be an easy task, but he loved a challenge.

Chapter Five

Winter, 1925

The train whistle broke into Nancy's slumber as she
shifted in her seat. With every turn of the wheels she was closer
to home, and she did not look forward to it. The Christmas
holidays loomed before her, a great dark chasm to be crossed
and endured. After a difficult round of finals, she'd hoped to
spend Christmas break as she had the year before—with the
Lewises.

Nancy sighed and her breath fogged the window. She
backed away and raised her eyes to peer over the heads of the
passengers seated in front of her. Why had Grandmother
insisted she return home? She'd even threatened to send
someone for her. Nancy cringed at the thought. It would
probably be Robert Emerson, her grandmother's lackey these
days. He wasn't a bad sort, and she liked him well enough, but
he was too close to Grandmother for her comfort. He'd been a
fixture in their home over summer break, but she'd seen very
little of him in the last few months.

The whistle blew again as the train chugged into another
tiny village. Nancy straightened her sleeves and folded her
hands in her lap.

What was so important that she must return home now?

She pouted and glared out the window at the gray dawn.
The past couple of weeks had been a whirlwind of activity,
with cramming and finals, so she'd really looked forward to the
break. And she would miss Nate, a frequent visitor on
weekends and holidays. He usually stayed in the Lewis's

guesthouse. Rebecca was always occupied with her latest beaux, and her parents were almost never home. So Nancy had spent many hours in Nate's company.

She'd come to know him well, not necessarily a good thing. He tended to drink too much, and lately he'd fallen into the habit of borrowing money. Not a big deal, really. She had plenty since she rarely spent all of her allowance. But he never attempted to pay it back.

She scoffed. What would Grandmother think if she knew how much time the Lewises spent at various casinos worldwide? Nancy guarded that secret well.

A sudden thought occurred to her. She frowned as the train lurched forward again. Perhaps Grandmother had learned the truth. Could this be why she'd been summoned home? Her face warmed as she contemplated the possibilities.

The train pulled into the station at exactly one minute after noon, according to the conductor. Nancy's searching gaze found Kip waiting on the platform. Thank goodness. She wouldn't have to put up with her grandmother all the way home.

Kip gave her a welcoming smile as he held the door open for her. "Mrs. Sanderson sends her regrets."

"Thank you, Kip," Nancy said as she took her seat. She'd have several miles of solitude in which to come up with proper answers for her grandmother.

The long driveway of the Sanderson country estate afforded panoramic views of the surrounding countryside. Nancy had always loved it. She gazed at the house as the dark sedan made its slow and steady way up the lane. Snow lay over the landscape—a mere dusting—but enough to paint everything a shimmering white. Gray clouds hung low in the afternoon sky, promising more precipitation, possibly by evening. She'd be trapped here if it turned into a blizzard.

Sissy opened the front door as Nancy climbed the steps. "Your grandmother is waiting for you. She's in her room."

Nancy searched Sissy's face. "In her room?" *This late in the day?*

"Yes, miss. Where she's been these two weeks." Sissy frowned. "Don't tell me you didn't know?"

"What's happened?"

Sissy took her coat and hung it up. "Oh la, Miss Nancy. She's had a heart attack, the doctor said."

Nancy lost her breath. Why had no one told her? She'd actually argued on the phone with Grandmother over coming home.

Sissy touched her arm. "But don't you worry. It wasn't such a bad one. Doctor said she needed a good rest is all."

Nancy rushed upstairs, coming to a halt outside her grandmother's room. After a deep breath to steady her emotions, she knocked.

"Yes?" Grandmother called.

Nancy opened the door and slipped inside.

Grandmother's pale countenance, as she lay huddled in bed, was such a contrast to all Nancy had ever known. She crossed the room and sat down in a chair facing the bed. "Grandmother, are you all right?"

Grandmother gave a wan smile. "I'm on the mend." She leveled her steely gaze on Nancy. "You're looking well. I regret I've interrupted your holiday plans."

"Grandmother ... if I had only known I would have—"

Her grandmother waved her hand in dismissal. "I gave orders no one should alert you. I knew you had midterms. Anyway, you are here now, and that's all that matters." She paused to take a breath. "When you've had a chance to settle in, dear, please come to me. We'll have a talk."

"Yes, Grandmother." Nancy turned to go, hesitated a moment at the door, started to say more, but thought better of it. She let herself out.

Grandmother had called her "dear." That tiny word had thrown Nancy completely off balance. Had the brush with death changed her?

Nancy sat at the small table in Grandmother's parlor. Sissy set a bowl of tomato bisque in front of each of them then quietly left the room.

Grandmother took a sip of the bisque and raised her gaze to Nancy's face. "I find I'm going to need your help, dear."

Nancy gazed into her soup. *Oh good gracious.* It sounded really bad.

Grandmother dabbed her lips with a linen napkin. "You know how many social engagements I usually attend during the holidays, and of course the company festivities." After a moment, she drew in a breath and exhaled. "I would like for you to put in an appearance at a few of the most important of those."

Nancy looked up from her bowl, speechless.

"There are the charity functions, which are among the most important, and the company dinner." She peered over the top of her spectacles. "You would be going as my representative."

"Alone—" Nancy swallowed. "By myself?"

"No ..." Grandmother paused to take a sip of tea. "Robert Emerson will accompany you. I've already spoken to him about it. He's been a great help to me. You'll be safe with him. He can help you through any awkwardness."

Nancy laid down her soupspoon. Not what she'd expected, but how could she refuse? After only a moment's hesitation, she answered. "Of course, Grandmother, I'll be more than happy to assist you in any way. I—just—are you sure Mr. Emerson couldn't go in our place? I could stay with you—"

Her grandmother's expression changed to one of amusement. "My dear, I appreciate that, but I'd really prefer you do this. You're a Sanderson. We must always strive to please our clients and our employees alike. It's our greatest strength. It's part of what has made our firm successful." She pressed her lips together but couldn't mask the spark of pride in her eyes. "Along with some rather brilliant business moves."

Nancy hid a smile behind her napkin. Grandmother could never pass up the opportunity to gloat. Perhaps she really was going to make a full recovery. They spent the remainder of the meal laying out plans for the next couple of weeks.

As Grandmother spoke, a ripple of excitement tickled Nancy's tummy. Like a newsreel, Nancy's fertile imagination rolled. *Miss Nancy Sanderson arrives at the Woods-Sanderson Gala in the absence of Mrs. Amelia Woods-Sanderson who has suffered a devastating heart attack ...*

"Well, what do you think?" Grandmother set down her teacup and stared at Nancy, who realized with a start, her mind had been wandering again. She'd missed something important. Probably best to own up to it.

"I'm sorry, Grandmother. I'm afraid I wasn't listening to that last."

"I've arranged a shopping trip for you in the morning." Humility seemed to make its desired effect on her grandmother. She spoke with a surprising degree of patience. "You may choose whatever you wish to wear to each of these events." She retrieved a sheet of paper from the bedside table and held it out to Nancy. "I have your itinerary here. So what do you think?"

Nancy had to admit she relished the idea of shopping. She glanced at the paper. There were twelve different events, but several occurred on the same day or night, so she could wear the same outfit for those. Her head whirled with thoughts of all the things she would need.

"You may of course, use any of my jewelry or furs you wish. I can help you choose what to wear with each outfit. I do have one stipulation—I would like to see what you buy and"— her voice drifted off as a frown tugged at her brow—"Listen to me, rattling on as if you were a child or one of my employees. I am sorry, dear."

Nancy stared back at her. Something had definitely changed. "It's all right, Grandmother. You've every right to make sure I'm dressed appropriately. I'll be glad to come in and show you what I find."

Grandmother sipped her tea. Nancy watched her through narrowed eyes, still suspicious. This could all be a ruse to draw her home away from Rebecca and Nate. She still wondered if Grandmother had heard something. Perhaps someone told her what the Lewises were actually like. Then she noticed her grandmother's pallor, and she felt ashamed. Grandmother really was very ill.

Nancy visited all her favorite shops, chose only the best, which she knew her grandmother would approve. The sales ladies catered to her every whim. She couldn't remember when she'd had so much fun. She returned home thoroughly exhausted but excessively happy.

As she ascended the stairs to her room, she came face-to-face with Robert Emerson, just leaving her grandmother's room.

He seemed different, more self-assured, in command. Strength oozed from his presence as he smiled down at her. A dark gray pinstriped suit added to the aura.

"Nancy, I'd heard you were home. How are you?" His words sounded pleasant enough.

She relaxed. "Quite well, thank you, though a little tired."

"Well, you'd better get plenty of rest before the rush begins. You've seen the itinerary, I presume?"

"Yes, I have. I've returned from a mad dash about town, outfitting myself for my debut."

The crooked smile made its appearance. "Ah, the bane of a woman's existence, having to look ravishing no matter how she feels."

"Actually, I'm quite looking forward to it."

He gazed at her for several seconds. What was he thinking?

"Well, Miss Nancy," he said. "I'll see you on Tuesday. I'll pick you up at eleven for the luncheon."

She nodded her assent and watched as he descended the stairs where Sissy waited with his overcoat. After the door closed behind him, Nancy gripped the ornately carved finial. Wouldn't it be wonderful if Nate could escort her, instead of stuffy old Robert Emerson? But when she gave it further thought, she knew Nate would never do. He wasn't the type to be at ease with the country club crowd. She turned and strolled toward her room. Robert Emerson was a much better choice in this instance, and if she could manage to befriend him, he'd make a good ally in the days to come. A smile tugged at her lips. Rebecca would be green with envy.

Chapter Six

Nancy wrote a long letter to Rebecca regarding all that had occurred since her return home. "I hope you won't be too bored without me."

She leaned an elbow on her writing desk and examined her pen. Right now, she was the one who was bored. She missed Nate. He always stayed in the Lewises' guest house during the holidays and hadn't wanted to change his plans. She couldn't blame him.

She cleaned the tip of the pen and dipped it in the ink. Then she laid it aside, too distracted to continue. She wished Nate could be as welcome a guest in the Sanderson home as at the Lewis's. Grandmother may have lightened up a little but not enough for that. Nate seemed to take it all in stride.

"It's best for both of us if the old lady doesn't know how much time we spend together," he'd said, caressing Nancy's cheek with his fingers. He'd told her she must do whatever needed to be done to keep the lines of communication open between Grandmother and herself. "There's too much at stake. The old bat isn't going to live forever." He'd given her a rakish grin and kissed her soundly on the mouth.

Nancy frowned at the memory of his words and the kiss that followed. She hadn't liked it then, but it really rubbed her wrong now.

Since her return home, she had come to respect her grandmother. A sort of loyalty had risen up within her when she'd discovered her grandmother's illness. There were certain family obligations that must be met and—a tremor of shock ran through her—she was defending herself, in her mind at least, against Nate.

She stared out the window at the frozen landscape. She loved Nate. Her first love, and she had no doubt she would always love him. She signed the letter, folded it, and tucked it into an envelope. She would just have to make her grandmother understand.

"I'm truly impressed with your sense of style," Grandmother told Nancy as she examined the last of her purchases. "You'll make quite an impression, I don't doubt. I can't wait to see what the society column will say after your debut."

The society column. The only thing Nancy cared about was the obvious pride on her grandmother's face. After all these years, she'd finally done something to please the woman. She took a step forward. "I thought I'd start with the royal blue tomorrow. What do you think?"

"Excellent choice. Run and get my jewelry case from the safe. You do remember the combination?"

Nancy went at once to her grandmother's study where the safe was hidden in the bookcase. She opened the door and pulled out a black box ornamented with intricate carvings. After closing the safe, she carried the box to her grandmother.

"Remember my sapphires?" Grandmother asked, raising her beautifully arched eyebrows. "I think they'll do marvelously with the royal blue." She pointed to a drawer in the wooden chest. "I'll set the ones we choose in this chamber. You can get them whenever you need them. I trust you, dear, to keep everything locked up safely. Some of these are quite old, you know."

"I know. I'll take care of it."

Grandmother laid her hand on Nancy's arm. "You've grown up these last couple of years. I'm quite impressed by the depth of your maturity and the fact that you've done so well at school. My … illness has caused me to redirect some of my energy. I realize I've been quite … difficult."

Nancy's eyes lingered on her grandmother's hand. For the first time, she noticed how age had changed it. Though the nails were still well manicured and polished, her skin was pale. Blue veins stood out, garish and ugly. She raised her eyes to her grandmother's face, noticing the wrinkles and the sagging skin. A lump formed in Nancy's throat. She found herself unable to respond.

Grandmother seemed not to notice. She laid out several more pieces. "Here. You choose what you'd like to wear with the other things."

Nancy chose several, including a set her grandmother told her had belonged to Nancy's great-great grandmother. Rubies and diamonds sparkled in floral shapes, knit together with gold. Nancy planned to wear it with a black and white dress she'd chosen for New Year's Eve. Grandmother laid the pieces carefully in the specified section of the velvet-lined box and closed it. She held the key out to Nancy.

"Put this back in my drawer there, if you will please. Then put the jewelry back in the safe. I think I'd like to rest now." She leaned back into her pillow with a sigh.

"Can I do anything for you before I go?"

Grandmother patted Nancy's hand. "You've done so much already. Quite enough really. You go rest up for tomorrow. We'll talk more at dinner."

At dinner, Grandmother outlined the next few days' activities. She familiarized Nancy with people and causes and companies until Nancy's head whirled with the information. She took it all in, sometimes repeating names and asking her grandmother for further clarification.

"Mr. Ardmore of Ardmore Insurance gives a significant donation each year to the children's fund. You must find out if he intends to do so again this year. I'm the chairperson, and I usually try to make as many connections as possible at these holiday functions." Grandmother picked at the fruit compote on her plate, a substitution for the apple pie Nancy enjoyed. "I'll be so glad to be able to eat real food again."

Nancy was mildly surprised. This was the closest thing to a complaint she'd heard from her grandmother since coming home.

Nancy finished off the last bite of pie then covered her plate with her napkin. "Dr. Farber thinks it was your rich diet that encouraged the heart attack, Grandmother."

"Dr. Farber blames everything on diet. He's much too young. I liked his father better," Grandmother said, sliding out of her chair.

Nancy jumped up to assist her. "Here. Don't be in such a hurry. Where are you going?"

"To my comfy chair beside the fire. I think I'd like to read for a while. Do you feel confident about tomorrow? Any more questions?"

Nancy helped her settle into her chair. "I think I'm okay with it. I'm sure I can depend on Mr. Emerson to help me if I forget anything."

"Oh, yes, indeed. He's quite capable. That's why I chose him. He'll do very nicely." Grandmother sat back in her chair and allowed Nancy to cover her with the afghan. Then she reached for her book and reading glasses. "Just bring me my water. I'll be fine, dear. I'll ring for Sissy when I'm ready for bed."

Nancy twirled in front of the full-length mirror, admiring the royal blue silk of her dress. The low waistline was accented with a large silk flower near her hip. Rows of organza and tulle fell away to mid-calf. Her short hair was done up in finger waves and ornamented with white feathers. Sapphires and diamonds sparkled at her neck. She was ready.

Robert Emerson had already arrived. He'd come early to spend several minutes in conference with her grandmother. So when she entered the room, Nancy met with two pair of wide eyes.

Grandmother was the first to speak. "Oh, my dear, you do look lovely."

Robert stood. "You look splendid. I hardly feel suited to escort such finery."

Nancy glanced from one to the other as warmth flooded her face. She'd been so used to taking second place in this household. She settled her gaze on Robert and intertwined her fingers. "I'm ready to go if you are."

As he helped her into the borrowed coat, Nancy cast a glance at Grandmother. She looked so tired. Or was it something else? Could it be envy? Nancy suspected she would miss the round of holiday parties and all the attention. "Good-bye, Grandmother."

Grandmother gave a wan smile and leaned her head back against the cushions. "Thank you, dear. Have a good time." Her gaze lingered on Robert. "Both of you."

Robert watched Nancy for several moments as they drove through town. At times she seemed so self-assured and at other times, young and naïve. Not at all like her grandmother. He had never really known her parents, only seen them from a distance. He had heard from Mrs. Sanderson that Nancy's mother had been "unsuitable," but he wasn't sure what had rendered her so in Amelia's mind. Was it by reason of her birth?

Nancy glanced over at him and smiled into his eyes. His hand moved toward her. He stopped it just in time. Too soon for that. "Are you all right? Not regretting this, I hope?"

She shook her head. "No, not regretting—a little nervous perhaps—or excited." She twisted her gloved hands in her lap. It was a habit of hers he'd noticed when she was nervous.

She pulled them apart, spread her fingers, and smoothed the fur of the thick black coat.

Nancy felt butterflies the size of Delaware fluttering in her stomach. It wasn't just the thought of this first engagement. Her eyes flitted to Robert's. There was something about this man that made her nervous.

She pushed her hands into Grandmother's coat. If she'd been alone, she would have removed her gloves and buried her bare fingers in its softness. Instead, she gazed out the window, taking in the sights and sounds of the town in which she'd grown up.

Having been away for a while in the smaller college town of Rutherford, she was surprised at the increase in traffic. It seemed everyone had a car these days. When she was a young child, there were few cars on the road, usually owned by the very wealthy. Now she saw only a few horse-drawn conveyances. The situation had reversed. "They're going to need to widen the streets, I think," she said, almost to herself.

Robert chuckled. "The time is coming, I believe, when they'll do exactly that. Traffic will only increase. Everyone will have a car of their own someday."

She faced him. Something had changed about him. His hair? Had he always parted it down the middle? Perhaps it was shorter.

He grinned at her. "Am I dressed to your satisfaction, Miss Sanderson?"

She bit back a smile. "You know how well you look. I thought perhaps you'd changed your hair."

"I have actually. It's shorter. My barber persuaded me to go with a more modern style."

Heat rushed up Nancy's neck and into her face. Had she been too forward? What must he think of her? Could she be any more paranoid? She gave her attention to her gloves, smoothing out invisible wrinkles until the car rolled to a stop at their first destination. Kip held the door open as Robert exited. He then turned to help Nancy. Her hand trembled as Robert drew it into the crook of his arm. Her heart pounded against her chest as they stepped into the doorway of the *Antilles Room*.

"Miss Nancy Sanderson and Mr. Robert Emerson," the butler called out as they made their entrance. The room grew quiet. Everyone's gaze seemed to rest upon them. Almost immediately, tongues began to wag.

She looked up to see Kate Branson of the *Exhibitor* make her way discreetly out of the room, no doubt to the nearest phone to tell of her latest discovery. Suddenly Nancy didn't care. She smiled at her partner as they were caught up in the glow of warmth that quickly surrounded them.

Everyone wanted to know how her grandmother was faring. With all the patience she could muster, she repeated the phrase over and over, "Grandmother is gaining strength daily."

Robert's constant presence at her side gave her a feeling of stability. She looked to him several times to explain something she didn't quite understand or to add his opinion when she was uncertain. Her grandmother had been right about him. He was quite capable.

"You were marvelous," he whispered in her ear as they descended the steps after the luncheon. "Your grandmother has very good reason to be proud of you."

Excitement flowed through Nancy as she allowed Robert to help her into the car. When the car began to move, she finally let go and began to laugh.

At first, Robert watched her, his eyebrows raised. Then he joined in.

Nancy was so relieved to have this first hurdle over. Now she could look forward to the next one.

Chapter Seven

With two more successes under her belt, Nancy's self-doubt eased into confidence as she joined her grandmother for breakfast.

"The highlight of the evening," Grandmother read aloud to Nancy, "was the arrival of Miss Nancy Sanderson, granddaughter of Amelia Woods-Sanderson, with her devoted escort, Mr. Robert Emerson. Miss Sanderson's attire was of the latest style in a most delicious shade of emerald green. We hope to see more of this lovely young couple during the holiday social season."

Nancy winced when her grandmother read the "devoted escort" part and the "lovely young couple" phrase. She hoped no one from college would see that. These society columns were utter nonsense. What if Nate were to see them? Then again, he might become jealous and realize he could no longer put off—

Suddenly Nancy realized it was quiet. Too quiet. Grandmother had finished reading and sat watching her. After a pause, Grandmother spoke. "My dear, you really must strive to control your daydreaming." She refolded the paper she'd been reading. "I told you they would love you."

"I'm sorry, Grandmother. I think I'm still a little tired."

"Of course you are," she said, dismissing it with a wave of her hand. "Get plenty of rest today. The ball tonight will, no doubt, be the high point of this whole round of events."

Nancy sincerely hoped so. She was beginning to have serious concerns. Nate was bound to find out. He'd been so moody lately. And when he was moody, he tended to drink more than he should.

She shifted in her chair. What would the society columns say about her after the ball? More than likely, she'd be dancing with Robert the entire evening. Her face grew hot. She turned away so her grandmother would not see her blush.

Robert was so tall. Though slimmer than Nate, he exuded strength. What kind of dancer was Nate?

She stood, almost too quickly, made a lame excuse to her grandmother, and left the room.

Back in her own bedroom, she closed the door and drew a deep breath. For a moment, she'd felt as if she was in over her head.

"The Belle of the Ball"—she heard the phrase spoken repeatedly that night, even as she was whirled around the room in the arms of not only Robert, but a score of other men, young and old alike. She had never felt this way before. She was absolutely giddy. It took great control to keep her wits about her, but she managed, even when Mr. Ardmore told her she was her grandmother all over again.

"She must be very proud of you," he said as they floated around the room.

Swallowing back her true feelings about that comparison, Nancy smiled her most gracious smile. "She speaks very well of you."

"Speaks very well of my annual gift to the Children's Fund, I imagine," he said. "You tell her that the opportunity to dance with such a lovely young lady as yourself is well worth my continued support."

Nancy graced him with a smile. "I'm sure anything you can do will be greatly appreciated."

"Young Emerson is a mighty lucky young man," he whispered in her ear as the dance ended.

It was all she could do to keep her cool as Robert came to claim her.

Greeting Robert's parents was unexpected and a little awkward. Of course, she'd known them all her life, but never in these particular circumstances—as a grownup, out on the town with their only son. Nancy knew they'd read the society section. Apparently, everyone had.

It took great effort on her part to keep the pink out of her cheeks as Juliana Emerson squeezed her hand. "My dear, how grown up you are."

Daniel Emerson smiled and said, "You've become quite a beautiful young lady."

Nancy did not miss the glance that passed between the two of them.

The ever-vigilant Robert steered her back to the dance floor where she relaxed in his strong embrace. After the dancing, they entered the dining room where tuxedoed waiters served heaping plates to the guests. Robert held out a chair for her.

Nancy smiled across the table at William and Devina Boston.

Devina leaned forward to make herself heard above the noise. "Will you be finished with school in the spring, Miss Sanderson?"

"Yes, ma'am. Grandmother wants me home. She feels I've had quite enough education."

Devina nodded. "I tend to agree. My generation was taught to be a good wife and mother—our highest calling."

Nancy gazed at her. "There are few things quite so rewarding, I imagine, as being the wife of a successful man, and the mother of four very responsible young people."

Devina's eyes sparkled. William gave her an approving nod. "How do you like your sudden introduction into society, Miss Nancy?"

"It's an adventure for me, I must confess. But Grandmother prepared me well. And she provided me with a very capable escort." She glanced at Robert, who was conversing with his neighbor on the other side.

William cut into a thick steak. "Yes, yes indeed. Well, is she satisfied with your performance so far?"

Devina glared at her husband. "William."

Nancy laughed and after another quick glance at Robert said, "She seems quite pleased, thank you." To Devina she said, "Are all of your children in for the holidays?" Out of the corner of her eye, Nancy saw William smile. Score one for Nancy. Devina was more than happy to supply her with all the latest news pertaining to her children.

When Nancy entered her grandmother's room the next morning, the older lady peered at her over the top of her spectacles. "I hear William and Devina Boston were really impressed with you."

Nancy, unable to suppress a smile, sat down across from her. "News travels fast around here."

Grandmother's lips eased into a complacent smile. "I spoke with Robert this morning. He had nothing but praise for you."

Nancy tried not to think about that. "Mr. Ardmore has pledged another year."

"Wonderful, how did you manage that?" Grandmother eased back in her chair.

"I danced with him."

Grandmother gazed at her for a long moment. "Hah! Well, what do you know about that? He's a dirty old man."

Nancy grinned as Sissy entered with the tea tray. Sissy filled the cups and set one beside Grandmother and the other beside Nancy. "May I get you anything else, Mrs. Sanderson?"

"No thank you, Sissy. You may go." Grandmother reached her hand out to Nancy. "How are you holding up? Tired yet?"

Nancy took a breath. "A little, but I'll make it. Tonight's the prep school alumni banquet. Many of my friends will be there."

"That's right. Won't they be surprised to see you? You'll be the envy of everyone there, you know."

Nancy glanced over the rim of her cup. "What do you mean?"

"Well, you've changed since you went away, grown up a little, and ..."

Nancy arched a brow. She could guess where this was going.

Grandmother nodded. "Well, you are with Robert Emerson. Only the most eligible bachelor in town."

Nancy wanted to object and say they needn't be envious over her relationship with Robert Emerson. She had no intention of taking away anyone's chances there. Robert was a friend. That was all. She wanted to say all these things but didn't. Instead she watched her grandmother's expression and held her tongue.

Grandmother covered her mouth with her napkin and cleared her throat. "Well, they have no way of knowing it's just ... a business arrangement."

Nancy's stomach roiled with an unfamiliar sensation. *A business arrangement?* Robert? Could it be true?

After leaving her grandmother's room, she stood on the landing, looking out the window. So what? She loved Nate anyway, so why should it matter to her? She closed her eyes and leaned her forehead against the cold windowpane.

Who was she kidding? It did matter.

Chapter Eight

Nancy fingered the beautiful white evening gown, threaded with gold and tugged at the white fur stole over her shoulders. She kept her eyes on Robert as she descended the stairs. He turned, straightened, and took a deep breath. If he was being paid, he covered it well.

He led her to the car, allowing her to enter first. Then he followed. As Kip drove away, she gazed out the window, watched the familiar scenery as they passed—a whisper in the night. White puffy clouds layered the dark sky, threatening snow. Her nervous fingers tugged at the stole again. Perhaps she should have worn the full-length coat.

She didn't have to look to know Robert's gaze remained on her. She hoped he wouldn't talk. She had no heart for conversation.

"You're very quiet. Nervous about tonight?"

She shook her head. What was this heavy feeling? Was it Nate? She hadn't heard from him in over a week. *Wretch.*

"Cold?" Robert asked. "Kip, can you turn up the heat a little?"

"I'm all right," Nancy said, her voice barely above a whisper.

"Are you sure? You're not ill?"

His voice held concern.

She swallowed. "No. I was just wondering something, Robert."

"Yes?"

Dare she go on? How did one go about asking such a thing? She couldn't even look at him but continued to gaze out the window. "Are you being paid to escort me?"

His quick intake of breath filled the void in her heart, which waited to hear what he had to say.

"What on earth would make you think that? Did someone say I was being paid?" He kept his voice so low, she knew he didn't wish to be overheard.

Still, she refused to look at him. The soft glow of the golden threads in the fabric of her dress kept her attention as she answered him. "Grandmother said … she said it was a business arrangement."

Robert stayed quiet for so long she finally turned to look at him. But in the semidarkness, she had trouble making out his expression.

"I don't know why she'd say such a thing to you, Nancy. I honestly don't. She asked for my assistance, yes. But it's strictly voluntary. As your participation is … voluntary." He pivoted toward her and reached over to take her hand.

Her first inclination was to draw back, but she couldn't seem to do so.

"It's been a pleasure for me, Nancy. If that's not been apparent to you, then I apologize. I've enjoyed every moment. I hoped … well, I *thought* you and I were … friends."

Nancy bit her lip. Had she misunderstood her grandmother? No, she didn't think so. Why would Grandmother say such a thing, unless …? She recalled the conversation and realized her attitude may have alarmed her grandmother.

She forced a smile as she peered at Robert. "Perhaps Grandmother was covering her tracks." At his perplexed look, she explained. "She didn't want me to think she was playing the matchmaker."

Robert laughed, and she joined him. Only when they pulled to a stop at their destination, did she realize Robert still held her hand.

Draped in pine boughs, the high school gymnasium glittered with ribbon and tinsel as Nancy and Robert joined the crowd of well-dressed alumni. Nancy's former headmistress received her graciously. "I was delighted to read of your recent successes about town, Nancy. I can't tell you how proud I felt when I saw your picture in the paper. I knew if you applied yourself, you'd make a great success someday."

Nancy thanked her and tried to move forward in the press, wishing they'd arrived a few minutes later, after the crowd had time to clear. When she heard her name called, she turned and caught sight of Emily Crenshaw, her closest friend during the years she'd spent in this place.

Emily pushed through the crowd to reach Nancy's side. "Oh, I hoped I'd see you here. Mother told me you were home and taking Mrs. Sanderson's place in society for the holidays." Emily leaned close to whisper in her ear. "I was never more shocked."

Noticing Emily's preoccupation with Robert, Nancy turned to introduce them then whispered to Emily, "Why were you so shocked?"

Emily arched an elegant brow and glanced pointedly at Robert. "Well, it's so unlike you, Nancy. You used to kick and scream every time she made you attend her fetes."

Robert laid a comforting hand on Nancy's shoulder and leaned forward to add, "She's grown up a lot in the last couple of years." He spoke to Emily, but his eyes were on Nancy, who could barely suppress a smile. A thrill danced down her spine.

What must Emily be thinking now? How would the society section read tomorrow?

She graced Emily with a brilliant smile. "I'm enjoying myself. Really, Emily, how often does a girl get to dress up in beautiful new clothes and go to parties every night? Even in my high school days, I dreamed of such things."

Emily tore her eyes away from Robert long enough to compliment Nancy's outfit. "Those shoes are the Ritz. You've always had style. Will you be returning to school after this?"

"Yes, I graduate in the spring."

Emily's escort came for her; a lanky young man with freckles and a thin red mustache.

Nancy recognized him. He and Emily had dated since the second year of high school. "Call me," Emily mouthed as she trailed her date to their designated table.

Nancy turned to look up at Robert. "Thank you."

He smiled as he tucked her hand in the crook of his arm.

Overall, Nancy considered it another successful evening, if you didn't count the glass she'd turned over at the beginning. At least it held only water. Now they were free until after Christmas. The New Year's Eve Ball was the last event on Grandmother's agenda.

When Robert wished her good night, she thought she detected a note of sadness in his voice. "Well, you won't be seeing me again until after Christmas. I leave in the morning to spend the holidays with my family in the country."

Nancy gazed up at him, searching for the proper words to say. "Then let me wish you a Merry Christmas. Please give my best to your parents."

His lips quirked into a half-smile as though amused by her stilted response. He cleared his throat. "I'll be back in town on the thirtieth. You probably won't see me until I come to pick you up on New Year's Eve." His gaze drifted to the landing then back to Nancy. She suspected her grandmother listened, but she didn't turn to see.

Robert took her hand in his. "If you or Mrs. Sanderson need anything, you can reach me by phone. Your grandmother knows how to contact me." He squeezed her hand then let it go. "I hope you have a wonderful holiday, Nancy."

A lump rose in her throat as she nodded. They'd been so often together in the past few days she would miss him. She watched through the stained glass of the door until his car pulled away then climbed the stairs to her room.

As she crossed the landing, her grandmother called out. Nancy found her propped up in bed with a favorite book lying face down on her lap.

"You're still awake?"

"I couldn't sleep, so I thought we could have our little chat now instead of in the morning. How did you find the old school?"

Nancy pulled up a chair and sat. "So changed—the new gymnasium is wonderful—and so many new teachers, I hear. What's happened to cause such a turnover?"

"The parents are making demands. They want updated teaching techniques and new subjects. Those things could only be accomplished by bringing in new blood. Some of the older teachers objected and left on their own, quite a scandal at the time." She settled her blankets around her and folded her hands on her lap. "Did you see anyone you knew?"

"Mrs. Stowe, of course, and Emily Crenshaw, soon to be Mrs. Jackson Stuart."

Grandmother's brow wrinkled. "Jackson Stuart, is that Patsy's son?" At Nancy's affirmative nod, she continued. "I

hadn't heard he was to marry. And to Emily? I never would
have thought ..."

"You don't think they're suited?" Nancy smiled. *Still
trying to plan everyone's future.*

"Well ..." Grandmother dismissed the subject with a wave
of her hand. "It's really none of my business."

Nancy gave a soft chuckle. "Grandmother, I know how
you are. You needn't spare me your opinions. Haven't I grown
up in their shadow?"

Grandmother gazed at her through tired, red-rimmed eyes.
"My opinions have often alienated me from those I care about,
Nancy."

"But they are your opinions, Grandmother. I'm not sure I
can respect you if you choose to withhold them at this late
date." Nancy slipped out of her shoes. "I can only assume you
think Jackson Stuart is not quite worthy of a Crenshaw."

Grandmother huffed. "Well, for one thing, will he be able
to keep her in the manner to which she is accustomed? This
defines suitability, my dear. You must admit, Emily is a bit
spoiled, being an only child and fussed over from birth." She
stopped suddenly. Nancy watched her. Had she remembered
she was speaking to an only child?

Nancy barely suppressed a guffaw. "Therein lies the
difference, I assume. Yes, you are right. Emily is spoiled and
no doubt in for a rude awakening. Unless, of course, her
parents step in and remedy the situation. I heard they've
already offered to help them buy a house."

Grandmother's face registered surprise. After a moment,
she smiled at Nancy. "Is that what you've heard, then?"

"From Emily herself. You know I don't approve of gossip,
Grandmother."

Grandmother gave a hearty laugh. "Oh dear, I don't know
when I've laughed so hard. If you could only hear yourself.
Sometimes, you remind me so much of my dear Henry." She

laid her head back on the pillows. "I wish you could have known him. I do believe you would have liked him, and I know for certain he would have liked you."

Nancy smiled and reached over to lay her hand on her grandmother's. "You should try to get some rest now, Grandmother. I'm going to put the jewelry away and then I think I'll turn in. Suddenly, I feel tired." When she moved forward to kiss Grandmother's cheek, a tear rolled down the older woman's wrinkled face. Nancy wiped it away with her thumb.

"Good night, Grandmother."

Nancy crept into the next room, closed the door, and turned on the lamp, then drew back. What was that sound, and why were the curtains opened? She crossed to the unlatched window. *Strange. Perhaps Grandmother came in here earlier?* Peering out into the darkness, she closed the latch and drew the draperies. After a moment's hesitation, she stepped to the safe, rolled the dial back and forth in the proper combination, and pulled the door open. She removed the box, set it down on the desk, and unlocked it with the key from her grandmother's key ring.

Nancy hummed as she removed the earrings from her ears, reliving the best moments of the night. She laid the earrings inside the box and reached to unhook the necklace, but paused, her fingers still on the clasp.

There came the sound she thought she'd heard. The creak of a floorboard.

She shook her head and worked to undo the clasp. The sound came again, and she spun toward the door, her arms still raised.

The shadowy figure of a man stood near the window.

Nancy jumped. The necklace fell loose, and she nearly dropped it.

The figure stepped toward her.

Nate.

Nancy cradled the necklace in the palm of her hand. "What are you doing in here?"

"Waiting for you." He spoke in a husky tone as he stepped nearer. "I've missed you."

She scoffed. "Missed me? You never even called me."

His lips curled into the barest smile. "You were obviously busy."

Her hands shook as she placed the necklace in the compartment then closed and locked it. "You could have called."

He closed the distance between them and brushed his lips against her hair. "I thought you might have lost interest in little ole Nate after spending a week in grand society with the esteemed Mr. Robert Emerson."

His words seemed tinged with anger, or jealousy. He'd no right to either. If anyone should be angry—she drew in a breath. He'd been drinking again.

She placed the jewelry box inside the open safe then closed the door and spun the dial. Nate stood right behind her, definitely a little too interested in the safe. Nancy raised her chin and watched him through narrowed eyes. "How did you get in here?"

He nodded toward the window. "Found an open window." He grinned. "Imagine that. I'm not exactly welcome in this house, remember?" He moved closer to her then angled over to the bookcase where he eyed the books she had set aside. "I saw you leave." He tossed a glance at her over his shoulder. "With that Mr. Emerson, so I spent some time down at the old hangout and stopped back by here just in time to see you safely delivered back to your door."

Nancy looked down at her hands, realized they were trembling, and intertwined her fingers. Her stomach contracted painfully. Nate closed the distance between them and lifted her chin with his fingertips. She cringed inwardly as he bent forward and kissed her lightly on the mouth. He smelled of cigarettes and stale beer.

She'd never minded before, but now—since she'd been escorted by a man who neither smoked nor drank—the stench repulsed her.

Robert's face drifted into her mind.

When Nate pulled back, his eyes were dark, piercing hers. "What—I'm not good enough for you now?"

She stepped past him to replace the books that hid the safe. "It's just—this isn't the place. Let's go down to the parlor."

He'd obviously had too much to drink. She hoped and prayed he wouldn't cause a scene and wake Grandmother. She crept through the outer door into the hall and blew out a relieved breath when he followed her.

In the parlor, she crossed to the lamp and switched it on then pushed the door closed behind him. When she turned, he stood with his hands in his pockets watching her. His coal-black hair glistened with pomade. He sucked at his teeth, as though nervous.

She must try to reassure him, not upset him. "It's good to see you again, Nate. I've missed you."

It wasn't really a lie. She had missed him, though she wasn't sure why.

He took a step nearer. "Rebecca kept me apprised of all the latest from the society section. You've been the toast of the town. You and Mr. Emerson, that is."

She clasped her hands together. "I've been filling in at these functions for my grandmother. She's very ill, which is why I was so concerned when I discovered you in her room."

He watched her through narrowed eyes. "I didn't realize it was her room. It didn't look like anyone's room." He shrugged his shoulders and reached for her hand. "Look, it's late. I need to get on out of here. I don't want to argue with you. I only wanted to see you and make sure you haven't forgotten me." He knew her well. Maybe too well.

The clock in the hall struck twice. Nancy jumped and withdrew her hand. "I had no idea it was so late."

Nate reclaimed her hand and pulled her close. The kiss that followed seemed a little too passionate, but it happened so suddenly, she had no time to pull away. He stepped past her, through the door, and into the foyer. Her breath caught in her throat. Without even so much as a glance over his shoulder, he was gone.

The odd feeling in her middle wouldn't go away. She checked every window in the house, save those in the servants' quarters and in Grandmother's bedroom. She secured the outer doors. Satisfied the house was locked up tight, she went into the parlor to turn out the light. Her eyes felt drawn to the portrait above the fireplace, and she hesitated, her hand still on the lamp. Grandmother and Grandfather seemed to be looking down on her, their eyes condemning. She closed her eyes. *I really am trying to be good.*

Weariness overwhelmed her along with the stress of the evening. She put out the lamp and climbed the stairs.

Though she was so tired, she slept fitfully and woke frequently. Nightmares, freakish visions in the night, left her frightened and wearier than ever. What was happening to her? She tried to close her mind to thought, tried to free herself of all the anxieties that seemed to press in on her at once. Finally, she drifted into a deep sleep and didn't waken until well after noon.

A light lunch of clam chowder and buttered toast greeted Nancy in her grandmother's parlor. For the first few minutes, the two ate in silence.

"Well, young lady, you had quite a night last night."

Nancy's soup spoon halted in midair. *Had Grandmother heard of Nate's visit?* She glanced up into a complacent smile on her grandmother's lips.

"I'm sorry I kept you up so late talking. You must have been desperately tired."

A cool stream of relief rushed through Nancy. She sucked in a breath and blinked. "No, it's all right. I had … difficulty going to sleep … all the excitement, I guess."

"You must take it easy and rest today."

Nancy swallowed a spoonful of chowder. "Good idea."

"Christmas is only two days away. You should be fully recovered by then. I suppose we'll have the usual influx of distant relatives coming by to visit." She pursed her lips. "I plan to receive them in the parlor."

Nancy frowned. The cousins were such a bore. "Are you sure you're up to that?"

"Oh, yes. I can sit down there just as well as I can sit up here. It'll feel good to be up and dressed. I'm not one to enjoy lying about."

"Yes, I know."

Alone in her room, Nancy sat down to write a letter to Rebecca. Last night's encounter with Nate had left her shaken, more so than she cared to think. She tapped her pen on the paper. How she wished she could talk to Rebecca in person.

She'd tried calling several times, but Rebecca was never at home.

Nancy huffed out an impatient breath. The words wouldn't come. Probably better to wait until she could talk to Rebecca face-to-face. She wadded up the sheet of paper and threw it in the trash.

She moved to the window seat and sank into the cushions. More snow had fallen overnight. Occasional puffs of wind blew shimmering ice crystals from the roof. Long, jagged icicles dripped in the afternoon sun. Once, when she was a little girl, she had opened this window and reached out to touch one of the icicles. She pressed her fingertips against the glass, remembering the cold, the sudden fear she would slip and fall. It was not unlike what she experienced now.

For nearly five years, she had known and loved Nate. She curled up against the pillows of the window seat and pulled an afghan over her. Why then had she been so badly affected by him last night? Because he had let himself into her home? She stared at the icicles and shivered. She knew why.

Grandmother's sitting room—the very room that housed the safe. Grandmother's jewels. Entrusted to Nancy's safekeeping. A warm glow began in the area of her heart and spread right down to her toes. She felt older, more mature. *What happens when life returns to normal?* Could she go back to the way things were?

Chapter Nine

Nancy couldn't remember a better Christmas holiday. Even with enduring the long, boring visits of the elderly relatives who felt duty-bound to come all the way out to the Sanderson house in what they referred to as "such treacherous weather."

"You're welcome to stay," Grandmother told her two sisters-in-law, the last of the visitors.

"Oh, how nice of you to offer," Lettie Arnold said, patting her sister Mary Lou's hand. "But I'm afraid we must venture back out into the elements."

Mary Lou agreed with a nod that set her dangly ear-bobs dancing. "Our families may come by. They would worry so."

Nancy called for their driver. After they bid Grandmother good-bye, she followed them into the foyer. Lettie caressed Nancy's cheek. "I can't get over how much you favor Amelia."

"The way Amelia used to look, you mean," Mary Lou whispered. "Have you ever seen anyone so changed?"

A light knock at the door sent them out to where their driver stood waiting to assist them.

Nancy gathered her sweater close as she stood waving. Back in the parlor, she began to clear away the tea things since Sissy had gone to be with her family.

Grandmother waved a weary hand. "Let that be for now, dear." She sighed. "Help me back up to my room."

Nancy rushed to help her. "I'm sorry, Grandmother. You must be exhausted."

Grandmother caught her breath as Nancy helped her up. "Yes, I'm afraid so." Once on her feet, she seemed better, but they made slow progress up the stairs, stopping often to rest.

"I think you overdid your first excursion," Nancy told her as she helped her get ready for bed. "Is there anything else you need?"

Grandmother closed her eyes briefly. "No, dear, just a little rest. It has been a long day." She drew in a deep breath and exhaled with a sigh. "But a nice day, don't you think?"

"Yes, Grandmother. A very nice day. Thank you again for the beautiful sweater. I certainly didn't expect anything after the wardrobe ..." She tucked the covers under her grandmother.

Grandmother laid a cold hand on Nancy's wrist. "I feel I must make up for the years I've missed. I should have had you out doing those things earlier."

Nancy shook her head. "I doubt if I'd have been ready. I was much too caught up in ... childish things."

Grandmother chuckled. "Well, dear, I'm glad you think the time is right." She suppressed a yawn. "Now if you'll excuse me, I think I'll have a nap."

Returning to the parlor alone, Nancy finished clearing up the dishes and carried the tray to the kitchen. With everyone gone home and Grandmother sleeping, she felt free to do as she pleased. So she fixed a cup of hot chocolate and carried it back to the parlor where a bright fire still burned. The earthy evergreen scent of the Christmas tree filled the room. She sipped the cocoa as she thumbed through the book her great-aunts had brought. *Pride and Prejudice*, by Jane Austen. They told her it had been in the family for years. Judging by its condition, it had seldom been read.

Two paragraphs into the second chapter, she heard a soft sound at the window. She raised her eyes to see Nate peering at her. *Not now.*

With a huff, she crossed to the door to let him in. He bent to kiss her as he pushed open the door. He wore a leather jacket. A knitted scarf draped his neck, but he still looked cold.

"How long have you been out there?"

"Not long. I left the car out of sight." He crossed over to the fireplace to warm himself. "Since your grandmother's been sick, I thought maybe you could use some company."

"I thought you'd be with your mother or back at Rebecca's."

"'Becca's in the mountains, skiing with some fool named Georgio." He screwed up his face at the name. "And Ma's busy with the sisters and their families. Too many kids."

She arched a brow at him. "I see." At least she'd learned why she couldn't reach Rebecca on the phone.

"So I thought I'd like to spend at least part of Christmas with the girl I love." He gazed at her, probably expecting a reaction.

She offered a tight smile.

He reached into his jacket pocket and pulled out a small package. "Here. I brought your Christmas present."

Warmth crept up her neck into her cheeks. In all the commotion, she had forgotten him. "Oh, I don't have anything for you."

He gazed down at her for a moment, irritation flickering in his dark eyes. He hunched his shoulders as he pushed the package forward. "You're always giving me things."

She smiled as she unwrapped a velvet box. Inside, she found a gold, heart-shaped locket. She pulled it out of the box and held it up. It was actually quite nice.

He took it from her to fasten around her neck. "It opens, so you can put pictures in it."

Nancy looked down at the locket, touched it with her fingers, and gazed into his eyes. "Thank you, Nate. It's beautiful."

He scoffed. "It's not nearly so spiffy as something Mr. Robert Emerson would buy for you."

A strange sensation fluttered in her breast. What should she say to that?

"Mr. Robert Emerson has a lot more at his disposal. Poor old Nate Conners—" He tilted his head back and gazed into the fire. "He's got nothing."

Nancy frowned at him. The fault was Nate's, but she could never say it, especially not when he was in such a dark mood. She swallowed. "The fact that you have so little makes this worth much more to me."

He shook his head as he uttered a low chuckle. Did he not believe her? His fingers caressed her cheek then moved under her chin. He raised her face to his and kissed her. When he pulled back, his eyes shone dark, sending a chill through Nancy. "Has he ever done that for you?"

She took a backward step. "Nate, why are you doing this? You've never—we've never—" She cast about desperately for the right words. They weren't engaged or even going steady.

Nate gripped her shoulders. "Well, has he?"

"No." Tears stung her eyes. She fingered the locket and forced herself to meet his gaze. "As far as I know, you and I have no understanding. So you have no right to question me."

"Hah! No right? We've been seeing each other for … a … long time and … that should give me some right." His voice rose steadily.

Nancy lifted a shaky hand to silence him. "Please, Nate, do be quiet. Grandmother's resting." She sighed and gestured toward the sofa. "Here, sit down. Let's discuss this rationally."

He did sit down, but on the edge of the chair across from the sofa. She sat down opposite him. He seemed uneasy. Nervous.

"You can't know how it is to hear your girl being talked about as if it was a settled matter between her and some other guy. A regular Dapper Dan who could take care of her proper. Give her everything." He dropped his head in his hands. "It's all those dang females in my family can talk about." He drew a deep breath as he raised his eyes to hers. "It's not like there's any chance of us ever really ending up together."

She kept her voice steady and low. "Nate, we've talked about this before."

"Yeah, you talked about it. Nancy, you know there's no way that old lady up there will ever let you marry a loser like me." He looked down at his hands, examined them in the firelight.

Nancy closed her eyes. It had all been such a wonderful fantasy. She'd never considered Nate's feelings. Well, she had, but she'd ignored them. She risked a glance at him. He still sulked.

"You could make something of yourself," she said. "You could get a good job ..."

He glared at her. "Doing what? I barely made it through my classes, Nancy. You know that. I'm not fit for anything that'd make Amelia Woods-Sanderson—or anyone else for that matter—smile on me."

The vehemence of his reply shocked Nancy. She bit her lip.

Nate cast a glance at her. "I did hear of something."

Nancy recognized the look. She'd seen it many times before. She held her breath for what she knew would come next.

He reached up and rubbed the back of his neck. "I'd need a small investment though, and I don't ... uh ... have it."

She closed her eyes and counted to ten. How many times had he borrowed money from her, never paying it back? Of course she hadn't really minded, since it was never very much. She swallowed and opened her eyes to find him looking at her.

He stood and approached the fire, picked up the poker, and pushed at a wayward log. Sparks flew up the chimney.

Nancy stared into the flames. "How much?"

He cleared his throat. "A thousand."

Her heart skipped. Had she heard him right? "What?"

His face brightened. He returned to sit beside her. "It's a cherry deal. I could get in on the ground floor of a great new product." He smiled as he took her hands in his. "I could have it back to you with interest in six months—a year at most."

His words were all too familiar. How many times had she heard those promises? Too many. "And where would I get a thousand dollars?"

He pointed to the ceiling.

She shook her head. "That is Grandmother's money."

"Well, five hundred would get me halfway. I know you have that much. I could maybe come up with the rest." He gave her a sideways glance.

She pulled her hands from his and turned her face away. Her stomach contracted into a tight ball as tears stung her eyes. Why did he always put her in this position? Five hundred dollars was a lot of money. For a few moments, the only sound in the room was the ticking of the clock and an occasional crackling noise from the fireplace. Finally, she turned back to face him. "What is this new *product?*"

He got up again and crossed to the fireplace, lifted a log, and placed it carefully on the fire. Then he stood and brushed his hands over the hearth. She knew he didn't want to look at her. Probably making it all up.

"It's a formula for some new kinda rubber in automobile tires, supposed to hold up longer." He shot a glance over his shoulder.

She fingered the crocheted doily on the table beside her as she swallowed the lump in her throat. It seemed all he cared about was the money. "I don't have it now. You'll have to come back."

He dropped to his knees beside her as he had so often in the past. "Nancy, you're the greatest."

She gritted her teeth. Forced her eyes to his. Why did she continue to put up with him? "I'll have it on the thirtieth."

He kissed her with a loud smack on the cheek. "This money will do it for me, sweetheart, I know it. And if everything works out as planned, the next time I get on my knees in front of you, it'll be to propose."

She couldn't look at him. She'd heard it all before. He stood and pulled her into his arms. She felt helpless as he kissed her again, a long, lingering kiss. Passionless.

He broke away. "I'll call you soon, sweetheart."

Nancy sat for a long time staring into the fire, feeling miserable. What could she do? Nate was like a bad habit she couldn't seem to break. At this moment, she couldn't say whether she even loved him at all.

Chapter Ten

On the morning of the thirtieth, Nancy awoke with panic fluttering in her breast. Robert hadn't called. Would he return in time to escort her to the New Year's Eve Ball?

The day crept by. She wrote another letter to Rebecca, who hadn't answered either of her former ones. Grandmother kept her busy for nearly an hour writing thank you notes. Then she had to file the holiday cards, so Grandmother would know who to send them to next year. In between her duties, Nancy stared out the window and wondered if the weather would strand Robert in the country. Would this day never end?

When the phone finally rang at six thirty, she stood with her hand on the receiver and whispered, "Please be Robert." But when she lifted it and answered, the voice she heard was not Robert's. "Hey, Nance."

Nate. She squeezed her eyes shut. The telephone lines crackled and popped from the freezing temperatures outside, but she could still make out most of his words. "I have to be in New York first thing in the morning … need that money … manage to get it?"

Nancy swallowed her ire, along with a healthy dose of pride. "I have it. Were you able to get the rest?"

"Uh, yeah, I got it … gonna hit it big this time … promise … be over in about an hour. Okay?"

"Later would be better, if you can swing it. Grandmother and I have dinner at about that time." He remained silent for a few moments. Had he heard her? Perhaps he was angry? He'd better not sound off. She was in no mood.

"Eight thirty then. See you." With a loud click, the line went dead.

She watched from the window when headlights announced his arrival, prompt for once. Nancy dashed to the door, hoping to encourage a short visit. She needn't have worried. He stayed only long enough to get the promised money. "Got a train to catch," he said with a smack to her cheek. "I'll keep in touch."

With mixed emotions, she bid him good-bye.

Robert phoned on New Year's Eve to ask after Grandmother's health and to confirm their schedule for the evening. "Sorry I haven't called sooner," he told her. "The telephone was out of service at my grandmother's. On my way back in, I noticed the lines were down. It happens a lot this time of year."

If only they'd been down in the other direction. Nate's call still rankled.

She spent a good part of the afternoon trying on her dress for the evening, a full-length black silk gown. She gazed at her reflection in the mirror, pivoting to reveal a white sash that wound over her left shoulder to drop down behind in a lovely, relaxed bow just below the waist. The dress fit as though it had been made for her. She loved the long, slender appearance. Her cheeks flushed a soft pink at the thought of Robert's possible reaction.

Whenever she thought of him, something akin to an electrical current shot through her, stimulating her nerves. After hanging the dress on its hanger, she returned it to the closet. She dashed cold water on her face and patted it dry. "Keep your head, Nancy," she said to herself in the mirror.

After all, Robert had never given her any reason to believe he felt anything for her other than friendship. She was well aware he could have any woman he wanted. The difference in their ages made it highly unlikely he would ever look at her in a romantic way. She smiled at her reflection. He certainly didn't need her money.

She still ruminated on Robert's marital status an hour later when she heard his arrival. He always came early to spend time with her grandmother. She paced and fidgeted a few more minutes to give them time alone. Then she drew in a deep breath, smoothed her dress for the hundredth time, and grabbed her beaded clutch.

Robert rose from his chair as Nancy entered the room. He should say something, but he was so busy admiring, his brain needed time to catch up. She looked amazing.

Mrs. Sanderson cleared her throat. "You look lovely, dear."

Robert kept his eyes fastened on Nancy as he answered. "That's not nearly good enough, Mrs. Sanderson. I'd say elegant … or even enchanting."

She laughed. "Don't get too carried away, Robert. You have the whole evening yet. Nancy, Sissy has brought down the black coat. Is that acceptable to you?"

Nancy looked as though she hadn't heard her grandmother. Her gaze was caught in Robert's and neither one of them seemed able to turn away.

Until Mrs. Sanderson uttered a polite cough. "It's frigid out. The black coat is very warm. Robert, will you get it for her?"

With a nod, he picked up the black coat and draped it over his arm. He turned to Nancy. "Ready?"

When Nancy started toward the door, Robert followed but suddenly remembered his manners. He glanced over his shoulder at Mrs. Sanderson, who gave him a wry smile and shook her head.

"Really, Nancy? Leaving without so much as a bye your leave?" She raised her hand in a halfhearted wave. "Well, go on, then. Don't give it a thought. You two have a good time."

Nancy seemed to recover a bit of sense. She stepped lightly across the room to plant a kiss on her grandmother's cheek. "I'm sorry. Good night, Grandmother."

Nancy closed Grandmother's door so the older woman wouldn't catch a draft from the outer door when Robert opened it.

"You do look wonderful," Robert said as he helped her into the coat.

She allowed her gaze to sweep over him, taking in his solid black tuxedo, diamond-studded cufflinks, and a shiny top hat. Rebecca would call him a sheik. "You look very smart yourself."

As they stepped outside, great fluffy flakes swirled around them and landed softly. Nancy could almost hear them falling in the stillness of the night. A magical evening, though a bittersweet one for her. Their last night together.

Robert smiled as Nancy gazed wide-eyed at the falling snow. Her unaffected beauty sent an arrow deep into his heart. He would miss her. These last two weeks he'd come to know her as an intelligent young woman, surprisingly gentle. He saw no trace of the wild streak of earlier years.

He helped her into the car then walked around to take his seat on the other side. Kip closed the door for him. A moment later, they were underway.

She sat still as a statue on her side of the car, gloved hands neatly folded in her lap. If he didn't know her better, he'd think she was at peace. But he could feel a glow of energy emanating from her. She was a bundle of nerves. With a smile, he laid his hand over hers.

Her gaze met his. How he wished he could read her mind. "Nervous?"

She gave a quick nod and squared her shoulders. "Part excitement, part terror."

He chuckled. "I'll be right beside you."

"I depend upon it. I can't thank you enough for all you've done."

He squeezed her hands. "It's been a pleasure." *A pleasure.* He sat back and concentrated on breathing. He dared not contemplate the emotions churning in his midsection. So much for remaining aloof. She'd stolen his heart when he wasn't looking.

The great ballroom of the old hotel fairly shone with all the gold and silver tinsel. It sparkled like jewels in the lamplight. Music filled the air. Already, couples sailed around the dance floor to the tune of *I'm Sitting on Top of the World.* Nancy trembled with excitement as Robert escorted her through the lines of official greeters. She met the mayor and his lady, several other well-known politicians and, of course, Mr. and Mrs. Ardmore, the Bostons, and the Emersons.

She danced with so many different partners, she lost track of them all. She worried about becoming separated from Robert, because she wished to be with him when the midnight hour came. Would he follow tradition? Would he kiss her?

At exactly two minutes before midnight, the master of ceremonies stood at the microphone. "It's about that time, folks! If everyone would please return to your original partner—your honey, your sugarplum."

Robert stood by her side as the midnight waltz began to play. For Nancy, time stood still. The noise abated until only the two of them existed in the world, drifting around the dance floor, connected to one another. Then the bells began to toll. Everyone stood still, poised to raise a cheer. The noise seemed deafening.

Nancy laughed aloud as confetti fell from the rafters. Then Robert kissed her. Not a long, lingering kiss that demanded more than she cared to give, but a nice kiss. A first kiss between friends.

Her heartbeat slowed. Tears darted to her eyes. It ended much too soon.

Robert spoke in her ear. "We'd better go now, while we can."

Nancy turned her head to look at him. Surely she'd misunderstood. Why must they leave before everyone else? "Is it over?"

His hand at the small of her back guided her through the crush. "Not really, but it gets worse as it gets later. No place for a young lady."

She scowled at him.

He grinned. "Now don't take that the wrong way. I only meant it's no place for an honorable young lady like you."

When they reached the coatroom, he bent his head and spoke more softly as they waited for their coats. "My mother will be among the first to leave if she's not already gone." He tipped the attendant and held Nancy's coat for her. The band began to play "You Forgot to Remember."

Nancy loved Irving Berlin, but she couldn't pay attention. Her curiosity piqued. "What do they do?"

Robert leveled his gaze at her. "They drink too much, which in itself is bad enough, since it's illegal. They say things they shouldn't, and … well, they do a lot of things they regret the next day. That is, if they remember it the next day."

Nancy knew that feeling all too well. She tried hard not to think any more about it, but when they were seated in the car, she turned to him. "Did Grandmother order you to bring me home early?"

Robert looked for a moment as if he would laugh at her. "No, Nancy. She didn't. I doubt if she has any knowledge of what goes on after midnight."

"But … she always goes to the New Year's Eve Ball. She *must* know."

Robert shook his head slowly. "She never stays above an hour." His eyes pierced hers as he spoke softly. "It's how she was able to do so much, Nancy. She put in appearances everywhere." He sent her a quick smile. "Kind of like a queen."

Nancy laughed. How well she could imagine Grandmother going about making appearances to keep her public happy. "I'm sorry for being so peevish, Robert."

He shook his head. "It's quite all right. I had fun tonight. I hope you did, too."

She folded her hands in her lap. "Oh, yes." It had been all she'd hoped, truly the high point of the holidays for her. She laid her head back against the seat cushion and sighed.

"So how many men did you dance with, anyway?"

She could hear the smile in his voice. He was teasing her. "I lost count somewhere around thirty-five."

He chuckled.

Her heart warmed to that sound. Though it was dark in the backseat, she knew his eyes were shining.

Almost before she knew it, they were pulling into the drive. Their wonderful, almost ethereal adventure had ended. Her heart ached with that realization. In a couple of days, she would return to school. This would all fade away into a beautiful memory.

Robert saw her to the door. He stepped inside for a moment but refused her offer of refreshment.

"I really must be going, but I wanted to tell you how much I've enjoyed being with you." He gazed at her, his back to the door, hat in hand.

She set her gloves and purse on the table. "I enjoyed it, too."

"When do you leave?"

"Day after tomorrow."

He arched a brow. "Do I hear regret? I thought you'd be eager to get back."

"Oh, in some ways, I am. But I have enjoyed the holidays."

"You sound surprised. I hope I had something to do with that."

She smiled, suddenly shy. When she lifted her eyes, he bent forward and kissed her. He set his hat on his head and touched the brim with his fingertips. "May I call you sometime?"

She did her best to rein in the smile. "I'd like that."

In another moment, he was gone. Nancy pressed her fingertips against her lips.

What would Nate think about that?

Ready to go, Nancy checked her room to be sure she had everything. Only one thing left to do: a last minute conference called by her grandmother. She entered the parlor to find the older woman sitting at her desk, holding a sheaf of papers in her hand.

At her grandmother's prompting, Nancy closed the parlor door. "It's good to see you at your desk again, Grandmother."

"Doc says I may do a few things, taking it very slowly of course. Please sit down, dear."

Nancy sat down, remembering all the other times she'd waited like this for the axe to fall. But not today. She relaxed in the chair. Grandmother was different now.

Grandmother started slowly, her eyes on Nancy. "I thought it only fair to apprise you of certain changes in our situation."

Nancy raised her eyebrows. Before she could respond, however, her grandmother continued, "My declining health," she waved her hand at Nancy's attempt to interrupt. "No dear, it's true. The doctor says I will never fully recover. Which is why I've made some changes to my will." She shuffled the papers in her hands, settled them again, and gazed at Nancy. "I wanted to tell you myself."

Nancy's spine tingled as a strange sense of foreboding tightened icy fingers around her. Meanwhile, Grandmother's voice droned on. "I must insure the stability of the company, my dear, above all things. Many lives, not just our own, depend upon its continued success. Of that much you are aware, I am sure. I hope to remain in position for some time longer but feel I must prepare for … well, whatever comes." She took a deep breath and exhaled slowly before she continued.

To Nancy, those few moments seemed an eternity.

"I have chosen someone to take my place in the business. Someone well qualified, who will be able to learn from me, who will not deviate from my prime directives." She smiled into Nancy's eyes. "That someone is well known to you. And I hope well respected and liked by you, as well."

Nancy could feel her lips forming the question—*Who?* But she couldn't find the strength to voice it. She had suddenly gone weak all over. *It's not me, so ... who? Uncle William, perhaps?*

Grandmother licked her lips and smiled. "Robert Emerson."

Her words echoed in Nancy's mind. *Robert Emerson.* Of course. She shook her head. "But what of his father's law firm?"

"He'll stay there for now, practicing law until it becomes necessary for him to give more time to the company. I must say I was quite happy with his acceptance of my offer."

He had already accepted the offer? Then he knew ... "But—" Nancy struggled for words. Words that wouldn't come. He had never mentioned any of this to her. Never even hinted at it. He could've at least warned her.

She glared at Grandmother, who seemed oblivious to Nancy's seething emotions.

"One day, I hope you'll be able to move into a position on the board, my dear. You'll own the company when you come of age." She folded her hands in front of her on the desk and kept her eyes averted. "There will be stipulations, of course."

Nancy pursed her lips as blood rushed into her face. The old clamps tightened. She tried to keep her voice steady. "Stipulations?"

Grandmother stood and with the help of her cane, walked slowly around her desk to sit in the chair facing Nancy. Once settled, she continued. "Provided, of course that you marry suitably."

The bomb had dropped. Nancy looked at her grandmother, who lowered her gaze and began fingering her cane. "I confess. It is my greatest wish, my dearest hope—that you marry Robert."

Nancy sucked in a quick breath, blinked her eyes and bit her lip. Her grandmother had no idea—no idea of the turmoil inside her at this moment. Nancy's hand went to her throat. *One ... two ... three ...*

Grandmother tapped her cane. "You needn't say anything yet, my dear. Only give it some thought. I was so impressed with your successes over the holidays. I'm convinced as well, that Robert is quite taken with you. Yes, quite taken."

Nancy glared at her. How could she be so smug? "Grandmother, I ... could never, I mean—"

"There's no rush, Nancy." Grandmother spoke slowly, as if to a child. "None at all. I only meant to voice my approval of such a union. Robert is a fine man. The two of you are so well suited."

"What if ..." Nancy swallowed hard, forcing out the words. "What if I don't marry him?"

Grandmother's gaze bore into Nancy. "Have you someone else in mind?"

Nancy examined her hands, struggling for control. The grandmother of her childhood had returned. "No, not really."

Grandmother sat back in her chair.

Sissy entered with the tea tray. Her eyes darted back and forth between the two women. After setting the tray on the table, she backed out the door and closed it slowly, no doubt to linger on the other side of it, eavesdropping.

Nancy sat forward to pour the tea, holding out a cup to her grandmother. Then she poured herself a cup. With trembling hands, she held it to her lips.

Grandmother's brow furrowed. "What is it, child? I thought we had gotten past these charades."

Nancy gazed at her grandmother. She hated the tears that stood in her eyes. They revealed more than she cared to show. But she would not wipe them away and acknowledge their presence.

"My dear," Grandmother said, as she set her teacup down and reached for Nancy's hand. "I never meant to upset you. What is it?"

"You make it sound so cut and dry, Grandmother, as if I were a ... a ..."

"A prized mare being bred to a champion racehorse?" Grandmother's eyes held a faraway look. "Those were my words dear—to my father, so many years ago."

Dared she hope? "But you married—"

Grandmother nodded. "I married Henry Sanderson, yes." She offered Nancy a wry smile. "The champion racehorse. And I never regretted it, though there were some rather difficult times."

Hope ebbed away. Nancy wanted to argue with her grandmother. She wanted to scream. *Times are different. I am different.* But it would be in vain. Grandmother would never relent. As long as she had her way, she was tender, even loving. But she'd made it plain. She still ruled the roost.

"There was a time, before the holidays, before my health took a turn for the worse, when I considered—" She glanced at Nancy. "I had decided to deliver an ultimatum. I felt compelled to do so. I'd heard of your continued fraternizing with certain unsuitable ..."

Nancy sat forward in her chair. "You mean Nate Conners?"

Grandmother nodded, her gaze boring into Nancy's eyes.

Nancy felt the heat rising in her neck, flushing her cheeks. She rose from the chair. "And the ultimatum? I think I would like to hear it."

Grandmother sighed and tightened her grip on the cane. "I had hoped you had—oh, devil take it." She struck the floor with the cane and leaned forward, meeting Nancy's challenge. "If you persist in this relationship with so unsuitable a young man, I fear I must withdraw your income, permanently. You will have nothing, Nancy."

Nancy closed her eyes. *Breathe. Hold steady. Don't let your emotions rule.* She opened her eyes and took a breath. "So let me get this straight. If I marry Robert Emerson, I'm in your good graces. I inherit the kingdom. And if I marry Nate Conners, I die a pauper."

Grandmother's eyes darkened. "How quaint." She closed her eyes and touched her fingertips to her temples. Her hands shook.

Nancy frowned. Yes, she felt anger, but she didn't want to cause Grandmother to suffer a second attack. "I'll give it some thought." She turned and started out of the room. At the door, she paused. Without turning, she said, "Good-bye, Grandmother."

Outside the door, she nearly doubled over. She barely made it to her room before the tears began to flow. Curled up on her bed in a fetal position, she sobbed out her pain.

Two hours later, Sissy knocked at the door. "Miss Nancy, Kip is ready with the car."

Nancy stood, straightened her hair and smoothed her skirt. She descended the stairs, donned her coat and hat, and stepped through the door.

Chapter Eleven

Nancy got up and strolled around her dorm room. She paused in front of the window and pressed her fingertips against the cold pane. When the wind whistled outside, it sounded almost like a nor'easter. Chilled, she rubbed her arms and returned to lie down on her bed.

Rebecca glanced up from the floor where she sat cross-legged, arranging newspaper clippings. "What's with you? You're acting like the hamster in science lab. Look, what do you think?" She'd cut out all the society page pictures and articles featuring Nancy and Robert.

Nancy tried to show an interest, but her heart just wasn't there. Rebecca had no idea, and Nancy couldn't fault her since she hadn't confided in her. She couldn't bring herself to talk about it. Not yet.

Rebecca leaned back against the side of the bed. "You did far better than I, Nancy. I'm positively green with envy."

Nancy lay on her stomach, chin propped on the heel of one hand. "What about Georgio?"

Rebecca frowned. "How did you hear about Georgio?"

"Nate—he came by after visiting his mother."

"Oh, he's worse than a woman. I wanted to tell you all about Georgio. You'll never believe half of it."

Nancy smiled into her friend's twinkling eyes. Rebecca was always ready with a good story. First, she glanced over her shoulder, toward the door, then back at Nancy. "You are looking at a *married* woman," she whispered.

Nancy turned over onto her side. "*Married?*"

Rebecca shushed her.

Nancy lowered her voice. "You married him?"

Tinkling laughter filled the room. Nancy thought she'd been had, until Rebecca sobered, took a deep breath and said, "Only for a few days." She rolled her eyes. "It was a *disastrous* mistake. Mother and Daddy came and got me." She threw her hands up in the air. "Would you believe it? I finally got their attention."

Nancy relaxed. "Is that why you did it?"

"Oh, you know me too well."

Nancy pressed her lips together. She fingered the fabric of the bedspread. "But, what about …?" Her eyes darted to Rebecca's.

Rebecca leaned in close and whispered, "Yes, there was a wedding night, but my parents were still able to get the whole thing annulled. By the time Daddy finished with Georgio, he was only too happy to sign the papers."

Nancy blinked. She had nothing to say to that.

Rebecca giggled behind her hand. "Oh, I know I've shocked you to the very core of your being. You're such a good little girl. I guess that's why you ended up with someone like Robert Emerson."

Nancy dropped her head into the crook of one arm. "I haven't ended up with him." If Rebecca only knew.

Rebecca pushed at her playfully. "Oh, yes you have. You haven't heard the last from him."

Nancy took a deep breath. "But you don't know the circumstances, the … difficulties." She sat up on the side of the bed and massaged her temples with her fingertips.

"Oh dear, if you're referring to Nate, I can't help you there. He is a problem—a very exciting, devilishly good-looking problem. But you know you can never marry someone like Nate, Nancy." She examined her fingernails. "None of us can marry a Nate."

Nancy reached down to rearrange the newspaper clippings. "He is trying to better himself."

"Listen to you defending him. 'Trying to better himself.'" She tossed her head and peered at Nancy through narrowed eyelids. "No doubt he's lying in some hole right now, recovering from a long binge. If he's found money to pay for one, that is."

Nancy blushed and hid her face in her hands.

"Oh, don't tell me. You've loaned him money again, haven't you? Oh, Nancy you're such a pushover." Rebecca reached over and smoothed Nancy's hair away from her face. "You have to think of your future now. You're going to be Mrs. Robert Emerson."

Nancy couldn't hold the tears any longer. Rebecca sat beside her on the bed. She encircled Nancy's shoulders with her arms. "Nancy, what is it? What's happened?"

Nancy sobbed out all the pent-up tears she'd been holding in for days.

Rebecca rubbed her back. "Is it Gran? Has she taken a turn for the worse?"

"No." Another bout of weeping gripped her.

Rebecca left her to get a cool rag to press against Nancy's forehead and wiped her tears. "You'll feel much better now. You'll see. I'll help you. We'll get through this together."

Nancy blew her nose. If only Rebecca could help. If it were only that easy.

The next few days came and went in a haze of activity as Nancy and Rebecca settled back into their routine. Nancy tried hard not to dwell on her troubles. Her sleep was interrupted by worry.

The weird nightmares continued, similar to the one she'd had at home, dark, foreboding. She sat up in bed, after one such occurrence, afraid she'd disturbed Rebecca. The only sound in the room was her roommate's even breathing. Good. She had not wakened her. She leaned against the headboard and drew her knees up to rest her chin.

She could not believe her grandmother would do such a horrible thing. The worst part, Nancy had actually been drawn to Robert. She'd entertained thoughts of him, had feelings for him, and all the time, he was only after her fortune. Though he'd denied it, she now believed he'd been acting on orders from her grandmother. The woman had to control everything.

Nancy got up and crept to the window. Outside, snow sparkled on the sloping lawn. The bare branches of an elm tree cast weird shadows. She shook with cold. The register below the window gave off little heat. Back in her bed, she snuggled under the covers. What if she could talk Nate into elopement? She was so tempted at this moment just to spite her grandmother. Who cared if she lost her fortune? She scowled into the darkness. Probably a good thing Nate was in New York.

Chapter Twelve

On their first free weekend, Nancy and Rebecca prepared to take the train to the mountains for a weekend of skiing. As they boarded, Nate dashed up to join them on the platform. "I thought I'd missed you."

"No chance of that," Rebecca said, dodging his hand as he swatted at her.

"Smart mouth." He gave an exaggerated shrug. "I didn't have time to grab my skis. I guess I can rent something up there."

Rebecca and Nancy exchanged glances. Both knew he had no skis and both knew he'd be bumming money off them to rent equipment.

A powdering of fresh snow lay on the ground by the time they reached the mountain resort. Nate and Rebecca joined a group of midnight skiers, but Nancy felt tired and cold. She wanted to sit in front of a warm fire and drink hot chocolate.

Less than an hour later, Rebecca joined her, massaging a sore foot. "I took a spill on the very first run."

Nate came in a few minutes later. He strode to the fire and rubbed his hands together near the flames. "You should've seen Becca flying down that slope."

Rebecca rubbed her arm. "I very nearly broke my arm 'flying down that slope.'" She beckoned to Nancy. "I'm all in. Let's go to bed."

They headed upstairs to their room.

Nancy cast a glance over her shoulder at Nate as he disappeared around the corner. She knew where he'd headed.

The ski lodge had a piano lounge that played live music far into the night on the weekends.

Saturday morning, the sun garnished a clear blue sky and promised a beautiful day. The slopes were full. Rebecca joined up with a group of Italian tourists, some of whom she'd had an acquaintance in Italy.

Nancy and Nate spent the day together. Almost like old times. Nancy confided a little in him, telling him part, but not all of her conversation with her grandmother. They stood at the top of a slope, waiting for some of the crowd to clear before starting down.

Nate struck at the snow with his pole. "I think you should go along with the old broad, Nance." He squinted into the bright light. "She's an old lady and not a healthy one at that. How long can she live?"

Nancy adjusted her goggles. "She could *live* a long time." She might be angry with her grandmother, but she didn't wish her to die.

Nate laughed at her. "I wish you could see your face. Look, sweetheart, I know it sounds callous, but think about what you're losing. What will you live on? Can you marry a guy like me and live in some run-down bungalow on the wrong end of town, raise a houseful of dirty little kids? How would you take care of them?" He tucked the ski pole under his left arm then reached to take her hand. "Honey, it sounds to me like she's planning to turn over all her assets to this Emerson guy either way. She could be blowing smoke, or she could be for real. If she's got it in her will, it's law, sweetheart."

Nancy concentrated on keeping the tears from tumbling down her cheeks. First, her grandmother had hurt her. Now Nate had caved in on her. It made her so angry she didn't even want to look at him. "What are you suggesting I do?"

Nate bent down to pull the goggles away from her face. He searched her eyes. "I'm telling you what to do—cooperate.

Let me tell you something about rich people, Nancy." He straightened, took the ski pole out from under his arm and waved it over the valley below. "I've been around them all my life, men and women alike. They don't marry for love. They marry for money and power. You mark my words, within a month of marrying you, Mr. Emerson will have himself a mistress. And when he does, I'll know about it. I have ways of finding out these things."

He pointed at Nancy. "You can divorce him easy for that kind of thing. With proof of adultery, you can get half of everything—*everything*—Nancy. Free and clear. 'Til then, our relationship doesn't need to change." His lips curved in a wry smile. "We can still see each other. We can be whatever you want, sweetheart, as long as we're discreet."

Nancy wanted to slap that smile right off his face. She felt sick, as if the breath had been knocked right out of her. She knew exactly what he suggested. With those words, he'd revealed his true character. In one fell swoop, her world crumbled around her. She struck the ground with her poles and flew down the slope in a cloud of snow, with Nate right behind her.

She wouldn't listen to anything else he had to say. She threw down her equipment, stripped off her boots, and marched straight up the stairs.

Later in the evening, the lodge hosted a party. Nancy, tired from the day outdoors and still very upset with Nate, did not plan to attend. She ordered a hot chocolate, intending to carry it to her room where she could relax.

Nate slid into place beside her. "What? All partied out? Here, I've got just the thing." He offered her a sip of a hot toddy, which she refused. She knew he'd probably laced it with hooch.

"Ah, come on. Don't be such a bluenose. You need to relax. This'll help you sleep."

Nancy had little hope of falling asleep on her own, with her head and heart so troubled. Nightmarish memories would crowd into her brain the moment she lay down. She closed her eyes and drew a deep breath. Nate took hold of her hand and set the steaming cup against it. She closed her fingers around the handle and took a sip. It tasted warm and sweet. She took another sip.

Nancy awoke the next morning with a brutal headache, dragged herself out of bed as if pushing through a thick fog, only to realize she was not in her own room. Panicky, she swung around to find Nate asleep on the other side of the bed.

She had to get out of there.

She found her clothes draped over a chair, grabbed them, and shut herself in the frigid bathroom. Her hands shook so badly she had difficulty dressing. The door creaked when she opened it, but Nate did not wake. Carrying her shoes, she slipped out.

Back in the room she shared with Rebecca, she collapsed onto the unoccupied bed. Rebecca must have gone down for an early breakfast.

After a hot bath, she curled up on top of her bed and wept. She had no memory of the night's passing but felt certain of two things: she'd been intimate with Nate, and her life would never be the same.

Chapter Thirteen

On Monday, Nancy sat in her American History class, her mind wandering.

The door opened. A student entered that Nancy recognized as a teacher's aide. The girl handed a note to the teacher, who, after reading the note, lifted her eyes to Nancy.

"Miss Sanderson, you are wanted in the front office. Mrs. Hornbill says to bring your things."

Nancy gathered her belongings and calmly ignored the smirks of her classmates. A few minutes later, she entered the front office expecting to see Mrs. Hornbill. Instead she found Robert Emerson. She drew up short. What did he want? "Robert, what are you doing here?"

Her heart thrum-thrummed in her chest. Had they somehow gotten wind of her weekend with Nate?

Robert extended his hand toward a divan. "Please sit down, Nancy."

She didn't like the look on his face. "Robert, what's happened?" A new thought pierced her heart. "Has Grandmother taken a turn for the worse?"

He sat next to her on the divan and clasped her hand in his. "In a manner of speaking, Nancy. Your grandmother was murdered last night."

All the air left her lungs in a whoosh. She raised both hands to her face. Robert slid his arm over her shoulders. She turned into his embrace as her former rage against him dissolved in a rush of tears. With trembling fingers, she extracted a handkerchief from her pocket and dabbed at her eyes and nose.

Robert's quiet voice soothed her. "Someone broke into the house late last night. It looks like a robbery. They broke into the safe and emptied it." He exhaled. "Whoever it was, crept into her room, covered her face with a pillow and—"

Nancy squeezed her eyes tight as a fresh wave of sorrow rolled over her.

"There didn't seem to be much of a struggle." He touched her arm. "They don't think she suffered, Nancy."

She lifted her eyes to his. "Who would do such a thing?" She hiccupped. Her hands shook violently. Robert took them in his.

"I don't know. The police are conducting an investigation." He gave her hands a light squeeze. "I've come to take you home. We need to leave right away."

Nancy nodded and rose from her seat. When she wavered, Robert put his arm around her waist to steady her.

As they exited the office, Mrs. Hornbill came rushing to meet them. She gripped Nancy's hand. "I've sent Rebecca to pack your things." She glanced at Robert. "I asked her to be quick about it, Mr. Emerson. I know you're in a rush to be away. Are you sure you won't stay overnight? It's so dangerous on the road at night in this weather."

"No, thank you, Mrs. Hornbill, though I do appreciate your offer. I must get Nancy home at once." Turning to Nancy he spoke as though to a child. "I'm going out to warm up the car. I'll be right back."

Mrs. Hornbill's presence did little to comfort Nancy. She bit her trembling lips as tears threatened again. Rebecca rushed into the room, set an overnight bag on the floor, and embraced Nancy. "I can't believe it." Her breath caught in her throat. "Please let me know if I can do anything."

Nancy gave a stiff nod, unable to speak. She allowed Mrs. Hornbill to help her on with her coat.

Rebecca wrapped a scarf around Nancy's neck and held out her mittens.

A moment later, Robert returned and grabbed the overnight bag. His other arm circled Nancy's waist. He led her outside where a two-toned *Pierce-Arrow* sat at the curb, its engine purring.

Rebecca stood with her, as he put the suitcase in the backseat. She brushed the tears from Nancy's cheek and gazed into her eyes. "If you need me, I'll be right there. Do you hear me?"

Robert helped Nancy into the passenger seat and tucked a blanket around her legs. After he closed the door, he spoke to Rebecca before he ran around to the driver's side and got in.

Nancy sat in stunned silence as he maneuvered the car through the streets of town. A five-hour drive lay ahead of them.

As they left Rutherford, Nancy turned her head to look at Robert. There were so many questions running through her mind, but she couldn't seem to put them into words.

He glanced at her. "You should relax. Try to get some rest. I know it won't be easy, but you're going to need it."

She watched his handsome profile as he gave all his attention to threading through afternoon traffic in the small metropolis. She leaned her head back and tried to rest.

She didn't sleep. Foremost in her mind was her behavior those last few minutes with her grandmother. Shame filled her breast. To think her last words had been flung out in anger. When she left, she hadn't even spoken to Grandmother.

A lump rose in Nancy's throat. She swallowed and forced back tears. Since that day, she'd not written a single letter to her.

Even worse, in Nancy's mind—she'd spent a weekend partying—the last weekend of her grandmother's life. Tears rolled down her cheeks. She searched her pockets for another handkerchief but couldn't find one. Robert offered his. She accepted it with a quick glance at his face.

Without turning his eyes from the road, he spoke. "I thought you were asleep."

"I can't." She dabbed at the tears as they continued to flow down her cheeks. She closed her eyes again.

Robert glanced at Nancy from time to time, as he drove. If only he could do more to help her, but he must drive. He needed to get her home tonight.

He gripped the wheel, sat forward enough to draw in a deep breath and exhaled as he cast a glance at the mirror. Traffic was light. If the weather held, he'd have her home by nine o'clock. At least, he'd been available to come after her. Otherwise, she'd be making this trip on the train, with a detective.

He clenched his jaw. Somehow, on the long trip back, he'd have to break the news to her. She was a prime suspect in her grandmother's death. He glanced at her childlike face. She'd finally drifted off to sleep. He turned his attention to the road, but his mind didn't stay there long.

The *Pierce-Arrow* hugged the road, so the numerous curves and rough spots weren't too threatening. Robert had plenty of time to think about what lay ahead. As executor of Amelia's estate, Nancy had become his ward. He'd been privy to Amelia's will, but that didn't mean he agreed with all of her provisions. There'd be loopholes—there always were—and he would find them.

Nancy woke suddenly. They had stopped. There was a strong scent of gasoline, but she didn't see Robert. He must have gone inside. A strange yellowish light flickered through the windshield. She peered up to see a flashing neon sign.

She opened the door, threw off the blanket, then shivered violently. Robert stood at the counter as she hurried through the door of the small café. He was paying for coffee and sandwiches. When he looked up, she motioned she was going to the restroom. A few minutes later, she joined him at a small table near the window.

"I was going to eat in the car, but since you're awake, let's sit in here. It's nice to have a break from driving."

Still shivering, she picked up the coffee mug and cupped her hands around it to warm them.

Robert laid his hand on her wrist. "That hot coffee will warm you up. I hope you like chicken sandwiches?"

Nancy nodded, reluctant to speak.

He urged her to eat. "You'll need your strength." He bit into his sandwich and chewed in silence. After taking a sip of steaming coffee, he spoke again. "We're lucky this place stays open late for the ironworks plant."

Nancy took a bite of her sandwich. "This is good." She finished most of it then drank another cup of coffee. Somewhere in the distance, a whistle blew.

"We'd better get going before the next shift comes in," Robert whispered.

The screen door screeched when he opened it for her. The sound echoed in the darkness. Neither spoke as they walked to the car.

Robert reached in front of Nancy to open the door. She caught hold of his hand. Her eyes searched his. So many questions troubled her mind, but she found only one that could be put into words. "Why did *you* come?"

He straightened. "I wanted to." His eyes held hers for several seconds. Then he opened the car door. "Please get in, Nancy. It's too cold out here. We can talk on the way."

The *Pierce-Arrow's* engine hummed as Robert kept a steady foot on the accelerator. Nancy's question still troubled him. *Why did you come?* He stopped at an intersection, checked both directions, then continued straight across. When he could let his eyes leave the road for a moment, he darted a glance at Nancy. Her silence troubled him. Should he encourage her to vocalize her feelings? Or was it something else? He recalled the last time they'd spoken she'd consented to his calling her. Weeks had passed, and he had never taken the time. Would she understand that he'd been busy?

"Nancy, I'm sorry I didn't call you earlier. I wanted to, but I was busy …"

She gazed at him, her expression impossible to read. After several long, silent moments, she spoke. "Grandmother told me before I left home."

He glanced at her, trying not to let his eyes stray from the road too long.

She stared straight ahead, so he couldn't discern her meaning.

He cleared his throat. "Told you what?"

"About you."

He felt her gaze before he looked at her.

The air inside the car seemed heavy with emotion.

No other cars were on the road, so he let the car slow to a crawl. Moonlight reflecting off snow, made it bright enough to see her face. "What about me?

"She told me you had agreed to run the company for her."

Still puzzled, he nodded. "Yes, that's true." The look in her eyes pierced his soul as she spoke in measured phrases.

"She told me … if I didn't marry you, I would be disinherited."

Robert stopped the car in the middle of the road. Then thinking better of it, he pulled over to the side and turned to face her.

"She said *what*?"

"She'd changed her will. She said if I persisted in—" She glanced out of the window.

"So that's what you two argued about before you left."

Her eyes snapped back to his. "Who told you we argued?"

"Sissy mentioned it. The police jumped on it. They want to question you."

Nancy stared back at him, openmouthed. "The police?"

"That's the reason I came for you, Nancy. I wanted to be with you when they question you."

"Question me? Why?" She swallowed. "Do I need a lawyer?"

Robert stared back at her. After all they'd been through? He'd worked so hard to gain her trust. He shook his head. "No. As your *friend*." He reached over and lifted her chin to look into her eyes, "As someone who cares for you."

She returned his gaze. Even in the semidarkness, he recognized that look. He'd seen it once before on the night she'd asked him if her grandmother had paid him to escort her. He dropped his hands and leaned back in the seat. "How can I persuade you to believe in me?"

He gripped the wheel so tightly his knuckles paled. He should start driving again. But he could sense her pain.

She seemed like an injured bird, a fragile thing. Over the next couple of days, she'd need strong support. Whether she wanted it or not, he meant to provide it. He spoke into the stillness. "I know your grandmother had plans for us, but they were her plans, not mine. I had plans of my own." He sucked in a deep draught of air and released it. Then he turned to her.

Her eyes were on him.

He thumped the steering wheel with the palm of one hand. "I thought if I could help your grandmother, if I could get close to her, I could persuade her to trust you. Drop her demands on your life."

Nancy's eyes widened, but he could tell she still didn't trust him. She raised her chin in that proud way of hers. "Why would you do that for me, Robert?"

Because I love you. The thought surprised him. He'd never acknowledged it before, even to himself. Incredible, but clearly not the right time. He put the car in gear and released the clutch. "I thought we were friends."

Nancy folded her hands in her lap. She closed her eyes and leaned her head back. He stared straight ahead. She'd drawn back into her shell, and there was nothing to be done about it. He felt at a loss. How could he gain her trust, convince her he had her best interests at heart?

He would have to find a way to prove it.

Nancy's eyes were closed, but her brain worked feverishly. *Friends.* He thought they were friends. What did she know about friendship? Or love, for that matter. Look where her idea of love had taken her. She swallowed the panic that rose in her throat.

She must be strong. She must show everyone she could stand on her own. She didn't need anyone. As she had learned very recently, no one could be trusted, not even her closest friends. She pressed her palms against her cheeks, hoping to wake up from this terrible nightmare.

Chapter Fourteen

Nancy woke to silence again. They had arrived.

Robert escorted her to the front door where Sissy met them, dressed in her robe and slippers. She enveloped Nancy in a warm embrace. "Miss Nancy, I'm so glad you're here."

Nancy barely returned the attention.

Sissy seemed not to notice. "I've been on pins and needles all evening." She blew her nose and stood aside for them to pass. "I've got your room ready. We were to come back to town today, you know." Her voice broke. She turned away to hang Nancy's coat and scarf on the rack.

Nancy frowned into Robert's gaze. "They weren't here when … it happened?"

He shook his head. "No, they were still in the country."

A memory of the open window in Grandmother's study coursed through Nancy's mind. Of Nate standing there, looking at the bookshelf where the safe was housed. The sensation almost overwhelmed her. Her knees went weak. She sat down on the nearest chair.

Robert moved quickly to her side. "Nancy, are you all right?"

"What?" She looked up at him, distracted. "Oh, yes. I … I hadn't known they were not in town."

Robert hesitated. Then he strode to the door. "I'd best be going, but I'll be back early." He stood with his hand on the doorknob, watching her.

Panic rose in her throat. She wanted to cry out. Instead, she stood up, wringing her hands. "You're leaving?"

Robert took a step nearer. He seemed uncertain. "Why don't you go up and go to bed—get some rest?"

Nancy fought a new rush of tears as Robert closed his eyes. Was he angry with her? A resigned look settled over his face as he removed his coat.

He gestured toward the parlor. "Here, let's sit down for a few minutes."

Though relieved that he would stay a while, she felt as stiff as a marble statue when he put his arm around her and pulled her closer. Perhaps she should've allowed him to leave. She rested her head against his shoulder.

Guilt crept into her mind, but she had no one else right now. He'd said he was her friend. Then let him act as one.

She drew in a deep breath and relaxed as the flames in the fireplace died into a soft glow.

Nancy woke to the sound of Sissy's loud gasp as she realized there was someone in the room. "Oh, I'm sorry, Miss Nancy, I—"

Robert's eyes flew open. He raised his head to peer around the room. "It's all right, Sissy. I guess we fell asleep."

Nancy made a face at Robert.

He stood up, rubbing the back of his neck.

She watched his movements with renewed feelings of guilt. So much for her self-proclamation. She was going to be so strong, show everyone she could stand on her own. Great start. Robert had lost a good night's rest because of her.

He grabbed his coat and draped it over one arm. "I need to get home and change. I'll be back here before eight o'clock. Sissy, if the police show up before then, put them in here and serve them coffee or something." His gaze slid to Nancy's. "I don't want them talking to Nancy without me. Is that understood?"

Sissy gave a quick nod. "Yes, sir."

Nancy chewed her lip as panic rose in her throat.

Robert's eyes softened as he gazed at her. "They're going to ask a lot of questions, Nancy." He slipped into his coat and tugged at the end of his sleeve. "Mrs. Hornbill told me you were away all weekend."

She cocked her head. What was he implying? "On a ski trip. We go often this time of year."

His face darkened. "We?"

Nancy's mouth went dry. Suddenly, she felt like a child again. "Rebecca and I. And ... Nate, among others."

A frown crinkled his brow as he turned to the door.

She followed him. "Robert, I—"

He stopped but didn't look at her. "Don't worry, Nancy. We'll get through this."

"Thank you for staying."

He paused with his hand on the doorknob. Finally, he looked at her again. With a wry smile he replied, "Anytime." He left.

Sissy cleared her throat. "I really am sorry, Miss Nancy."

Nancy jumped. She'd forgotten about Sissy. "No. It's all right, really. I should go upstairs and get changed." She started for the door then turned back to Sissy who was already plumping cushions. "Please have plenty of coffee ready. I imagine we're going to need it."

"Yes, Miss Nancy. Should I bring you some breakfast?"

Nancy bit her lip. She was hungry. "Maybe a boiled egg and toast—in my room." She needed to bathe and change, and she had only an hour.

Robert's guess had been correct; the police did come early. Nancy watched as they climbed the outside steps to the front door. Her heart pounded in her chest. Why did they want to question her? She could hear their muffled voices as Sissy greeted them. After the parlor door was closed, Nancy stepped out onto the landing to wait for Robert.

He arrived promptly at eight o'clock. When Nancy started down the steps, he held up his hand to stay her. "Wait five minutes," he mouthed. He opened the parlor door and stepped aside as Sissy arrived with a pot of steaming coffee.

Nancy glanced at the clock in the hall. Three minutes to go. Sissy came back out of the parlor with Robert's coat, which she hung up in the closet beneath the staircase. After she'd gone, Nancy descended the stairs.

All three men stood as she entered. Her eyes were drawn instinctively to her grandmother's chair, which stood empty. A lump rose in her throat. She diverted her eyes.

Robert introduced the men. "Nancy Sanderson, this is Sheriff Lawton and Deputy Pressman."

Nancy gave them what she hoped was a polite nod as she poured a cup of coffee then took a seat across from the two men. They sat on the sofa where she and Robert had so recently spent the night.

Pressman, the younger of the two, spoke first. "Miss Sanderson, please accept our condolences. Your grandmother will be greatly missed."

"Thank you," she whispered.

Sheriff Lawton cleared his throat and spoke in a gravelly voice. "I apologize, Miss Sanderson, but we're going to need to ask you a few questions."

Nancy nodded with a glance at Robert, who observed in silence.

Sheriff Lawton drew out a small notebook and a stubby pencil from his pocket. He touched the pencil point to his tongue then scribbled on the notepaper. "Where were you this past Sunday evening, Miss Sanderson?" He sat forward in his chair, his pencil poised, ready to jot down her answers.

"At Jennings, in my room, after about 7:00."

His brow arched, sending ripples into his hairline. "Is there anyone who can vouch for that?"

Nancy nodded. "We have to sign out when we leave and sign in again when we return. Miss Pincet, the housemother, is very strict. If any one of the girls is missing, she could be dismissed." Nancy swallowed another sip of coffee as Sheriff Lawton scribbled. "I also have a roommate who was with me Sunday evening."

"Miss Pin-cet," he repeated writing the name down. His eyes bored into hers. "Who would be dismissed? The missing girl or the housemother?"

"The housemother."

"And the name of the roommate?"

She set her cup on the side table. "Rebecca Lewis."

"Now, Miss Sanderson, I understand that you argued with your grandmother before you went back to school."

Robert came to attention. Nancy glanced at him then at her hands in her lap. "We often argued, Sheriff Lawton." She drew in a breath and slowly exhaled before giving her answer. "We seldom agreed on … anything."

He scribbled on the notepad. The pencil stopped. He tapped the point of the pencil against the pad several times. Then he wrote something else. Without looking up, he asked, "What exactly did you argue about that day?"

Robert interrupted, "You don't have to answer that, Nancy." Looking at the sheriff, he explained, "It was a personal matter, sir."

Sheriff Lawton raised his eyes to Robert. He pressed his lips together then made a quick note. "Miss Sanderson, your …

uh … housekeeper said there was quite a ruckus. You must've been terribly upset over something."

Nancy turned her full gaze on him. "A *ruckus*?"

He nodded, "Loud voices—that's how she described it, wasn't it, Pressman?" Deputy Pressman's Adam's apple bobbed up and down as he answered, "Yes, sir."

"Sir, I—" Nancy's gaze drifted to Robert then back to the sheriff as Grandmother's admonition replayed in her mind. *A lady never raises her voice.* "Neither my grandmother nor I ever raised our voices." After a moment's hesitation, she continued, "She taught me never to raise my voice, no matter how upset I became. What's more—I don't remember Grandmother ever raising her voice. She was in a very delicate state of health."

The sheriff sat back. "Well then, Miss Sanderson, who did the housekeeper hear?"

Nancy's jaw went slack. He didn't believe her. Before she could respond, Robert interrupted.

"Sheriff Lawton, have you any further questions for my client?"

The sheriff cleared his throat again, glancing from Robert to Nancy. "Hmm. I do not." He faced Nancy. "Again, my apologies, Miss Sanderson. You have our deepest sympathy." He pocketed his pad and pencil and rose from the sofa. "Come, Pressman, let's get out of these folks' way. I'm sure they have plenty to do." He looked at Robert. "We'll be in touch, Mr. Emerson."

Deputy Pressman offered Nancy an apologetic smile. "Thank you for the coffee, Miss Sanderson."

After the officers had gone, Nancy went to gather the coffee cups, placing them on the tray. She was arrested again by the sight of her grandmother's chair. Her fingertips caressed the brocade fabric. After a moment, she turned and sat down on the edge of it and cried.

In two long strides, Robert drew next to her. She pulled a handkerchief from her sleeve and dabbed at her eyes.

"I'm sorry, Robert. I thought I'd finished with all that."

"You've lost someone very close to you. It's normal to grieve."

"I wish I had more control."

He gave her a sad smile. "It's only me."

Only me. His words echoed in her head. It had been only him since yesterday. Why did he remain with her? She had to admit his presence comforted her, but she felt so confused. So much had happened, in one weekend. Her life—her entire existence—had forever changed. She didn't trust herself anymore. Dare she trust him?

He cleared his throat. "I do need to go out for a short while. I have to ... see to all the arrangements ... for the memorial service." He started for the door.

Nancy stood and faced him. "She had everything written down."

He nodded. "Yes, she did. William turned it over to me. She didn't want anyone to be burdened with ... all that. You know how she was." He opened the door. "Call me should you need anything. And Nancy, don't talk to anyone. I'll do my best to keep the reporters away."

"Reporters?"

The door closed.

Nancy gazed into the fire. "Reporters?"

At noon, the doorbell rang. Nancy stayed in her room, obeying Robert's orders not to see anyone. After a few minutes, she heard Sissy on the stairs and opened her door. Sissy held two packages. "These came for you, Miss Nancy."

Nancy stepped aside. "Here, set them down on the bed." She looked at Sissy. "Who are they from?"

"Davenor's."

Nancy frowned. She loosed the string on the top box then lifted the cover. Inside, she found a small black hat with a sheer veil. In the second box, she pulled aside white tissue paper to reveal a black crepe dress. A card lay on top, with a note that the things had been ordered for her by Mr. Robert Emerson.

Sissy smiled. "That man thinks of everything."

Nancy lifted the dress from the box. Its simple style seemed perfect for a funeral. She handed it to Sissy, who went to press out the wrinkles. The hat looked well on her.

Guilt stabbed at her heart. How could she be so vain when Grandmother—she removed the hat and returned it to the hatbox. In the old days, they would've covered every mirror in the house with black crepe. And stopped all the clocks.

Nancy strolled to the window to gaze at the back lawn though the bare, gray branches of the maple tree. She thought of all the times she'd climbed down those branches to join Nate on some nocturnal jaunt. It seemed like another lifetime.

Sitting cross-legged on the window seat, she forced herself to focus on Grandmother's last moments. Her heart throbbed so hard in her chest, she could barely breathe.

Had Nate anything to do with it? He certainly knew the location of the safe and her grandmother's bedroom. He'd stood right there, in Grandmother's study, his eyes on the safe. He'd picked up books and looked them over, as if memorizing their location.

No, it could not be true.

She closed her eyes trying to block the memory. But he had obviously taken advantage of her when she was … when she'd had too much to drink. A groan escaped her lips. She leaned back against the cold wall. She would not think of it today.

Chapter Fifteen

As soon as she stepped inside the door of the funeral home, scenes from Nancy's childhood haunted her. Two shiny black coffins, tightly closed, sitting on pedestals, surrounded by banks of flowers. She squeezed her eyes shut hoping to dispel the memory.

When muted voices echoed through the long corridor, she strolled toward an especially beautiful arrangement of white roses and baby's breath. A placard identified the Boston Emerson Law Firm as the giver.

Robert stayed close as they walked into the shadowy room where her grandmother lay, looking quite regal in her favorite dark blue suit. Nancy reached out to touch the fine white skin but drew up short of touching it. Something was missing from her grandmother's form. No jewelry lay about her neck. No earrings hung from her earlobes. No rings adorned her fingers. Nancy's breath caught in her throat.

She glanced at Robert and found him watching her. "All of her beautiful jewels. She would have wanted to wear them now, when she would be seen by everyone."

He agreed, his eyes never leaving Nancy's face. "You're right. She would have. Give me two minutes. I'll be right back."

Beside her grandmother's casket, she gazed at the lifeless form. "I'm so sorry, Grandmother. I … hate that we argued at the last." With trembling fingers, she smoothed her grandmother's sleeve. "I do love you. I always have. I don't know why we quarreled so much." She dabbed at her eyes with

a black lace handkerchief. "If only we'd listened to each
other."

There was no doubt in Nancy's mind. Her grandmother
had been very wise. She'd always tried to do right by everyone.
She cared as much for those who labored in her factories, as
she did for those of her own household.

Robert reappeared at her side with no explanation of his
absence. He took her arm. "Come sit in the parlor for a few
moments. The crowds will be coming in soon to pay their
respects, and you'll be on your feet for hours." In the quiet
recessed parlor, he faced her. "She had her wake and funeral
planned to the smallest detail. She didn't want you to have to
worry about any of it."

Nancy managed a smile. "Still in charge, even in death."

Robert smiled back. He sat forward with his elbows on his
knees, his long fingers intertwined. His smile soon faded
behind a remoteness she could not understand. Did he have
haunting memories, too?

She knew his grandfather had died within the last few
years. She'd forgotten when. Perhaps he thought of that, or did
he also mourn Grandmother?

She allowed her gaze to linger on his face as she searched
for clues. He'd worked with her grandmother for over two
years, time enough to develop a friendship.

A clock chimed twice.

Robert stood, holding out his arm for her.

By the time people began streaming in to pay their last
respects, Nancy noticed a pearl necklace around her
grandmother's neck, pearl drop earrings, and a garnet ring,
similar to the one Grandmother had always worn. She glanced
around the room for Robert, to thank him. But he was involved
in conversation with the mayor and his wife. A moment later,
the Bostons and Robert's parents joined her. They stayed by

her side throughout the afternoon. Their presence comforted her more than she could say.

Though kind, others seemed leery of her. Could they really think she had killed her own grandmother? The woman who had raised her?

Tears slid down her cheek. She swiped them away, drew in a breath, and forced her lips into a small smile.

The day of the funeral was cold and overcast. Nancy almost wept when she heard Rebecca's voice in the foyer. She'd arrived early, set to stay with Nancy for a few days. The girls embraced and, again, Nancy fought tears.

Rebecca drew back. "You look tired. Let's go upstairs, and I'll fix your hair." Only too happy to let Rebecca order her about, Nancy led the way to her room.

Rebecca chatted as she brushed Nancy's hair. "The folks will be at the funeral. I had them drop me off. So you won't have to make that long train ride by yourself." She gazed at Nancy's reflection in the mirror. "I hope you intend to finish school?"

Nancy peered up at her. "I haven't given it much thought. I suppose I must."

"You're right you must." She took up the hat that lay where Nancy had left it on the dressing table. "Great hat. She checked the inside. "Davenor's. Nice." She placed the hat on Nancy's head then took a backward step. "'*Sei bellissima*,' as Georgio would say." She kissed her fingertips and grinned.

Neither of the girls spoke as Kip drove the newly polished sedan down Main Street to the church. Nancy gazed up at the steeple, topped by an ornate cross. Grandmother had attended church twice a year for as long as Nancy could remember, on Christmas and Easter.

Kip pulled the car up to the steps where Robert waited for them. He stepped forward to open the door. He offered Nancy his hand and then turned back to help Rebecca.

Nancy watched as her friend's admiring gaze swept over Robert's form. Nancy could well imagine what she thought.

It seemed as though the whole town had turned out for the service. Woods-Sanderson Associates had closed for the day, its flag at half-mast, the portals draped with black crepe. Crowds huddled outside the packed church.

The service was formal, presided over by the elder pastor, a man Nancy barely knew. The mayor praised Amelia Woods-Sanderson, saying, "Her grit and determination kept our city thriving during very difficult times." Nancy tried not to squirm when he made eye contact with her. "Sometimes such determination requires sacrifices."

Sacrifices. She knew all about that. Beside her, Rebecca dabbed her eyes and blew her nose.

Nancy's eyes were dry. She wondered whether the townsfolk would feel more sympathy toward her if she cried, too. Or would they say she was faking or only felt sorry for what she'd done? Her gaze, hidden behind the hat's veil, shifted to Robert, who sat on the pew opposite her. He stared straight ahead. She dropped her gaze as guilt stabbed her heart. He'd been so vigilant and kind. Still she wondered if she could trust him.

The mayor sat down and the pastor came to lead one more prayer. Then silence reigned as everyone's eyes were drawn to Nancy.

Robert crossed the aisle to escort her from the church.

William stepped close on her other side.

She kept her head down as the two men supported her.

She and Rebecca rode to the cemetery with the Bostons. Rebecca held Nancy's hand as the car threaded its way through crowds of onlookers held at bay by uniformed policemen.

More policemen stood guard at the gravesite, against the mass of people who wanted to press in. As Amelia had requested, the graveside service was a private ceremony by invitation only. But that didn't stop the townsfolk. Many had worked for Amelia over the years. If they wanted to witness her interment, Nancy would not turn them away.

Family and closest friends stood at the gravesite to witness the last rites. Nancy stood between Robert and William Boston. She folded her gloved hands together as the pastor's voice faded into the distance.

She was a child again, standing between her grandmother and William Boston. Rain threatened. Someone behind them complained the pastor was too long-winded. Finally, Grandmother stepped forward to lay a single white rose on her son's coffin. William Boston led Nancy to the other coffin, and lifted her so she could place a red rose there. After depositing the rose, Nancy laid her pudgy six-year-old hand on the cold surface of the wood and began to sob. Mr. Boston comforted her as he would have his own child. When they returned to the line of people waiting, Grandmother had already gone.

Nancy closed her eyes and willed the memory to leave. She wouldn't think of it today.

The pastor cleared his throat and nodded to her. She stepped forward to lay a white rose on Grandmother's coffin. When she returned, Robert took her arm in his and led her to the car.

Woods-Sanderson hosted a lavish gourmet luncheon in their cafeteria. Literally hundreds of people streamed by offering their deepest sympathy. Nancy felt as if she stood outside the group, observing. In a weird way, she felt detached from the scenes playing out all around her.

Robert, his head bowed as he spoke with a small gray-haired woman, seemed unruffled by the overwhelming circumstances. He patted the woman on the back and smiled at her as if she was family.

Nancy could only admire him. He treated everyone the same. She began to see why her grandmother had chosen him to lead the company.

After what seemed an eternity, the crowds thinned out. Robert escorted Nancy and Rebecca to the car where Kip waited to drive them home. Robert turned to Nancy. His dark eyes seemed warm, but beneath the surface something lingered. She couldn't quite make it out.

"I'll come for you tomorrow for the reading of the will. It will be at Boston Emerson, and your presence is required, of course." After a nod to Rebecca, he stepped away.

"I wish I didn't even have to go," she said to Rebecca, while removing her hat. "I already know what's in it." She set the hat on her lap and folded the veil across the top.

Rebecca laid her head back on the seat. "You may be surprised. She may have changed it, or it may not read exactly as she discussed with you. Now," she raised her head and leveled her gaze at Nancy, "tell me again why you're objecting so heartily to marriage with that darling man?"

Nancy glowered at her. "Would you want to be told who to marry? It's so … archaic."

Rebecca grinned. "I wouldn't mind, if he looked like Robert, had plenty of money, and a beautiful home. What else could you possibly want?"

Nancy lowered her voice. "He told me it wasn't his idea, and he had meant to get me out of it."

Rebecca's eyes widened. "He *told* you that?"

"Yes, he did, so obviously he doesn't *want* to marry me." Nancy realized with a start this was what bothered her most.

It's one thing to reject someone but quite another to be rejected.

The next morning, when Nancy went down to breakfast, Sissy handed her a handkerchief. "I found it 'neath your grandmother's bed, the morning I ... when I found her."

Nancy turned the handkerchief over, wondering why she felt the need to give it to her. "Why are you giving it to me, Sissy?"

The woman's brown eyes slid past Nancy to the linen tablecloth where she brushed at an imaginary wrinkle.

Nancy watched her movements.

She'd never seen Sissy in such a nervous state.

"I went in Miss Amelia's room because she wasn't up yet, and it was getting late. When I stepped over nearer to the bed, I put my foot on something soft. I looked and there was this handkerchief. I picked it up, thinking it must be hers. That was when I saw her hand, hanging down so limp and all, and I knew she had ... gone. I put the 'kerchief in my pocket, still thinking it was hers. I was so upset, you know. I ran right in to the study and called the police and then is when I saw the mess in there. In her study."

Nancy examined the handkerchief. There seemed nothing unusual about it. "Please sit down and tell me what's troubling you so about this."

Sissy poked a finger at the embroidered monogram in the corner. "It ain't hers." Nancy looked more closely at it. The initials "EAE" were embroidered in white silk thread in one corner. The E's were larger than the A, fashioned in a fancy curlicue. She fingered the monogram. Something stirred in her memory but quickly disappeared.

"Do you have any idea whose it could be?"

She hesitated a moment. "Well, you know … your mother … she was an Elliott."

Nancy looked back down at the monogram. Her mother's name was Georgia, so it could not have been hers, possibly left here from long ago. Perhaps Grandmother had kept it? "What should we do with it?"

"Well, I thought we must turn it over to those detectives, but I'm afraid, 'cause they told me not to touch anything."

After a moment's thought, Nancy folded the handkerchief and placed it in her pocket. "When Mr. Emerson comes for me, I'll ask him what to do."

Sissy released a pent-up breath as she poured Nancy a cup of coffee.

"Do you think Miss Lewis will be wanting breakfast soon?"

Nancy smiled. "Don't hold anything for her. She'll more than likely sleep quite late. Then all she'll want is coffee."

"Yes, ma'am."

"We'll only be staying through the weekend. We need to get back to school. I'm so close to finishing—" She noticed the crestfallen look on Sissy's face. "Mr. Emerson will be close by if you should need anything. He'll be taking over all of Grandmother's obligations."

Sissy's eyes brimmed with tears. "It won't ever be the same, will it, Miss Nancy?"

Nancy laid her hand on the woman's shoulder. "No, it won't. I know you miss her and so do I, very much."

Sissy dabbed at the corners of her eyes with her apron then patted Nancy's hand. She turned and left the room mumbling something about eggs.

When Robert arrived, Nancy showed him the handkerchief and related Sissy's explanation.

Robert's brows knit as he examined the monogram. Nancy did not miss the tiny spark of recognition in his eyes. He tucked it into his pocket and held his hand out to her. "Let's go. We don't want to be late."

The reading of the will took place at the Boston Emerson Law Firm. William Boston sat at the head of the table, where a very thick blue folder lay in front of him. Nancy sat next to Robert. The door opened again as the Sandersons' servants entered and took their places on the other side of the table. Nancy let her gaze sweep over them, giving each one a small welcoming smile.

A long, extremely dull process followed. Nancy had all she could do to sit through it without falling asleep. Her grandmother had thought of everything. Finally, all the servants were dealt with. Each one would be well compensated for their years of "exemplary service." At that point, they were ushered from the room.

Nancy folded her hands on the table and drew a deep breath, acutely aware of Robert's presence beside her. As William began to read, she swallowed and forced herself to pay close attention. She must remain aloof, with no visible emotions to give her away, as if she was very much aware of the contents of the will.

"The bulk of the estate," William read, "including various properties, the controlling stock in Woods-Sanderson Associates, and related business ventures, etc., and etc.—"

Nancy held her breath and leveled her gaze at William. Had she been wrong?

"Nancy Mae Sanderson, as my only living heir, with Robert Daniel Emerson as executor until her thirtieth year."

Nancy closed her eyes and tightened her fingers until they hurt. She opened both when William cleared his throat.

His gaze was on her as he turned the page. Then he read, "*If* during this passage of time, Nancy Mae Sanderson should marry, any and all monies, properties, etc., will be forfeit"— William glanced at Nancy—"to the executor."

She sat in complete silence. She had not been wrong. Grandmother had gotten the last word.

Chapter Sixteen

Robert and his father sat in William Boston's office, discussing the Woods-Sanderson holdings when William's phone rang. "Put him through," William spoke into the phone. He nodded at Robert and whispered, "Detective Lawson."

Robert sat forward, barely breathing.

"Yes, Detective, I'm here," William said. "I understand. Are there any other leads? What about that other matter? I see. You can depend upon it." He returned the receiver to its cradle and exhaled. "Nancy's alibi checked out. Both Mrs. Pincet and Mrs. Hornbill vouched for her presence at the school all evening."

Robert closed his eyes as a wave of relief passed over him.

Daniel Emerson leaned forward, his elbows on his knees. "What now? Where do we go from here?"

William drained his coffee cup and set it back in its saucer with a clink. "Detective Lawson has several other leads, one of which seems quite promising."

Robert frowned. "He didn't divulge?"

William shook his head. "No, but I've a pretty good idea. I'm sure you do also."

Daniel stood and straightened his tie. "I'm so glad Nancy is exonerated."

William rose and crossed to the front of his desk. "She was never a serious suspect anyway. No one in their right mind would truly believe that."

Robert thrust his hands in his pants pockets. He strode to the window. "No one who knows her would ever suspect her."

After his father left for an appointment, he turned to face William. "I want to file an amendment to the will."

William stared back at him. "Why?"

"Nancy isn't happy with this, William."

William rested his elbows on his desk and leaned forward. "What about you? Can't you just use the old Emerson charm?"

"Not now," Robert said. "I'd rather things took a more … natural course."

"Is she still seeing Mr. Conners?"

"Is that what all this is about? Amelia objected to him so heartily?"

William didn't answer at first. He dipped his pen in the inkwell and began signing a sheaf of papers. "Nancy's dead set against you, then?"

Robert huffed out a breath. "No not really. I think she's more hurt that her grandmother had so little confidence in her."

"I think you should postpone filing for an amendment, Robert."

"Your reason being?"

"See if you can get Nate Conners out of the picture first."

"You do know there's a large gap in our ages?" He grinned. "She thinks I'm an old man."

William cleaned the point of his pen and set it in the holder. "I think you're wrong about that, Robert. I've seen how she looks at you."

Robert hunched his shoulders, but he knew by the expression on William's face that further pursuit of this subject would prove futile. He'd have to find a way to keep Nancy placated. William may believe she had a crush on him, but Robert knew things that William did not. He'd been hard pressed to keep a friendship alive between them.

Back in his own office, he stood, hands in his pants pockets, looking out the window. He'd been so proud of this office, of its grand view of Main Street, all the way to the courthouse, where his gaze halted. The courthouse. He had fully expected to plead many cases there. Now everything had changed. What an unexpected twist his life had taken.

On the following Monday, Nancy and Rebecca returned to school. As soon as they entered the door to their room, Nancy felt enormous relief. At home, she'd had nothing to do but think, and the more she thought, the more troubled she became.

For the next decade, she would have to answer to Robert. Maybe not such a terrible thing, except she hated the idea of having to ask him for money. Things could be worse, at least he was sympathetic to her, and he had promised to stay in touch.

Weeks passed with no word from him. Then one Wednesday afternoon, she returned from a late class to find a call waiting for her. She dialed the operator and had her put the call through. A few minutes later, the call rang back in. Nancy lifted the receiver.

"Hello?" When she heard Robert's voice, a strange feeling roiled in her middle. Her knees grew weak. She sank into the nearest chair.

He apologized for not calling sooner, but business had taken up much of his time. "May I come by on Saturday? I thought we could go for a ride in the country."

"I'd like that."

"Good. I'll see you then."

She hung up the phone and walked out of the office. Halfway up the stairs, she paused on the landing. Had he just called her for a date? A glance out the window reminded her of the inclement weather. Perhaps she shouldn't let her hopes soar too high.

The weather cleared by the weekend. Robert arrived promptly at eleven o'clock, in the *Pierce-Arrow*. Nancy battled strange emotions at the sight of him. She felt almost giddy, and a little nauseated.

She wore a gray wool suit and sensible shoes, just in case she should need to walk. She put on a warm coat and scarf and pulled on her gloves as she descended the stairs to the parlor where Robert waited. Mrs. Pincet, the live-in teacher who doubled as housemother to the residents, was talking to him.

Nancy could tell by the woman's face that she was very impressed. He looked up with a smile as Nancy entered the room. While she signed out, he said good-bye to Mrs. Pincet.

He led her to the car, parked across the street. She tried not to think of the last time she'd ridden in the *Pierce-Arrow*.

Robert seemed familiar with the area as he drove along the rural roads to a nearby village. He pulled the car into a parking spot in front of a Victorian-style house. A sign in front identified it as the *Garden Court Tea House*. The cafe owner seemed to be an old friend of his. She led them to a table overlooking a lovely garden. Though still clothed in its winter grays, Nancy enjoyed the view.

"You seem right at home here," she said.

He smiled. "Mother's family lives nearby. I'll take you by the old homestead. It's on the way. There's no one home, so we won't be able to stop in, but you can see it very well from the road this time of year."

After lunch, he led her back to the car and opened the door for her. "Are you too cold? I have a blanket in the backseat."

She shook her head. "I'm fine, thank you."

They drove past a lake and then down a narrow, winding road through densely forested hills.

"It's lovely here."

He glanced at her. "I wish you could see it in the spring." He slowed for a covered bridge that spanned a rocky stream. A wide vista opened on the other side. Here, he stopped.

They got out of the car and strolled to the edge of the drive where she could see the name *Perry's Landing,* etched into a small wooden sign. Rock ledges created a natural entrance. A wrought iron gate kept it private. Robert pulled her hand into the crook of his arm and led her across to an outcropping of rock where she could see the house.

A hawk cried overhead, the only sound as Nancy took in the scene before her. A gray stone edifice surrounded on all sides by mature trees. It would be completely hidden in summer. "It's beautiful, though a bit remote."

"Yes, Granddad liked his privacy. He was a senator, and this was his retreat."

She gaped at him. "*Senator* Perry? I'd no idea you were related to him. I've studied about him in state history. He made great strides in agriculture as well as education." She bit her lip. "But of course you'd know all that."

"He was a man of many talents." The sun dipped behind a thick bank of clouds, leaving a chill in the air. Robert laid his hand over hers. "Nancy, you're shivering. Why didn't you say something? Let's get back to the car."

This time she accepted the warm blanket.

As they drove back to school, he talked about his grandfather and the wonderful times he'd had as a boy at Perry's Landing.

From his demeanor, Nancy surmised he'd been very fond of his grandfather. "It must have been very hard to lose him."

"It was."

She smoothed the folds of her skirt. "I never knew my grandfather."

Robert stared straight ahead. "Yes. I guess he died before you were born."

She nodded.

"But your other grandfather—"

She gazed at him. He seemed to think better of whatever he'd meant to say. But he'd ignited a question in her mind. A whole flock of questions. Could there be family from her mother's side? No doubt, her grandmother would have kept Nancy away from them, but there was nothing to keep her away from them now. If they existed.

Robert interrupted her thoughts as they arrived at the town limits.

"I've stated our desire to an amendment. William is considering it. I'll keep you informed of the progress."

Back to business. Nancy couldn't bring herself to look at him. Instead, she watched his hands, strong and capable, as he guided the auto around the courthouse.

"I'd like to see you again soon, if I can work it out. If it's agreeable with you, that is," he added with a quick glance at her.

Her heart sent irregular messages to her brain as she tried to think how to answer him. She wanted to see him, but there were so many reasons why she should not.

"You're having to think about that for too long," he said. The crooked smile returned, and along with it, the dimple she'd grown to love.

She gave a short laugh. "I ... wanted to compose the proper answer. As a young woman of possible substance, I must practice caution."

He chuckled. "Perhaps it would be easier for me to write to you. Do you get much time for letter writing, or are you swamped right now with your studies?"

"Sometimes, yes, sometimes, no," she said. "There will be times when it'll be little more than a note. If you don't mind that, I'd be glad to correspond with you." He pulled up in front of her residence.

He got out and came around to open her door. When she laid her hand in his and he closed his fingers around it, she felt safe and protected. Why is that? Heat rose in her cheeks. She couldn't bring herself to make eye contact.

At the front steps, he relinquished her hand. "I guess that'll have to do then."

She swallowed and dampened her lips. "Thank you, Robert. I had a very nice time. And good luck with your new position. I know you'll do very well."

He smiled down at her. "Thanks. I need a little luck. It's a big responsibility." He gazed at her for several moments, until she reluctantly turned to go.

"Wait, Nancy—"

Her heart skipped with dread that he would turn suddenly serious, forcing her to say what she had no heart to say.

The late afternoon sun lit his face. For the first time, she noticed his dark eyes were deep blue, and not black or dark brown, as she'd always supposed. He reached for her hand.

"Don't worry. I know the rules around this place. I won't try to kiss you. I wanted you to know how much I enjoyed this time together."

She thanked him then stretched up to plant a quick kiss on his cheek. She ran to the door and waved to him from a safe distance.

Robert chuckled as he got into his car. He was starting to like this young woman. She was as unpredictable as an untrained colt. Even if Amelia had never made those stipulations in her will, he'd still have been drawn to Nancy. He remembered the gangly girl of thirteen, running across the lawn as he and his father were leaving a luncheon with Mrs.

Sanderson. She'd stopped suddenly when she saw them. Without a word, she'd lowered her eyes and brushed past them. He remembered feeling sorry for her. How well he understood the uncertainty of that age.

Those beautiful blue-green eyes had haunted him many times over the years with their great depth of sadness. He'd wanted to find out what troubled her so, this girl who had access to everything her heart desired. Now he understood a little more about her.

Amelia's strong character had overshadowed Nancy's for years, even keeping her from her mother's family. Then, during the holiday season, she'd blossomed. He had assumed it was because she'd been given responsibilities that brought her out from under her grandmother's heavy-handed rule. So what would happen in the aftermath of Amelia's death?

And what of her faith? He knew they'd seldom attended church. Would Nancy fit into his family's world? He'd spent nearly every Sunday of his life in a church service of some sort, even in law school. His faith was deeply rooted. Surely, a gifted lawyer with such strong sentiments could make a case for faith and win. If he could win her heart at all. His thoughts returned to the kiss and he smiled. Oh, he could win.

Nancy climbed the stairs to her room where Rebecca met her, grabbed her hands, and pulled her into the room. After closing the door, she squealed and clasped her hands. "I saw you with Robert. Where did you go?"

"He took me for a drive, and we had lunch."

Rebecca leaned in close. "And?"

Nancy shook her head. "And … what?"

"Did he discuss anything important, like ... your future?" She grasped Nancy's hands and gave them a squeeze.

Nancy shook her head again. "No." She pulled away from her and sat down on the side of the bed. After a moment's hesitation, she told her everything they had talked about along the way. Last, she mentioned the side trip to his grandparents' estate.

Rebecca lay across her bed on her stomach and gazed at Nancy. "Oh, he's most certainly thinking marriage if he took you there. You're so lucky. I only hope I can be half as fortunate as you."

"You'll probably do even better." Nancy covered her eyes with her hand. She didn't want to discuss it any more. It felt too personal. If she could only have a moment alone to relive the good parts ... like the surprise on his face when she'd kissed him.

Rebecca droned on. "Not according to my parents. They're convinced I've ruined my life forever. Even with all the cover up, it's sure to come out sometime." She studied her fingernails and sighed. "Mother's talking about sending me away immediately after graduation."

Nancy glanced up. "No! Oh, Rebecca, why?"

"She's convinced I'll be with child."

Nancy's jaw went slack. She closed her mouth and reached for her friend's hand. "Are you?"

Rebecca shook her head. "I don't think so. But it's hard to know for sure, since I'm always late." She glanced at Nancy. "You know. Aunt Ruby's always late for me."

Nancy sniffed. Aunt Ruby was code for their monthly cycle. But instead of the usual grin, Rebecca's face reflected her misery. "All these years, they've paid so little attention to me. Now they can only talk of how I've ruined myself and how humiliated they are."

Nancy moved to sit next to Rebecca and rubbed her back. "It'll come out all right, Rebecca, you'll see. Maybe you're not … with … with child." Shocked at the prospect of her own possible ruination, Nancy could hardly bring herself to say the words. How could she possibly comfort her friend? Worst of all, she could never tell Rebecca the real reason for her own distress.

She'd been a fool. She'd ruined all her chances with Robert. Through one silly, senseless act, she'd ruined herself forever. For she now suspected, though she knew little of such matters, she carried Nate's child. Nancy swallowed hard and forced herself to speak. "You were married to him, at least."

Rebecca tossed her head. "Daddy says that's the only reason Georgio married me, that and money. He thinks I'm rich, but I'm not so sure anymore."

"What? What makes you say such a thing?"

Rebecca turned over and stared up at the ceiling while wiping the tears away with her fingertips. She glanced over at Nancy. "You know how Mother and Daddy are. They're constantly at some casino wasting their fortunes. I have a bad feeling there's not much left to be wasted."

Nancy gave Rebecca a playful push. "Then you'll just have to recover from this and find yourself a rich man to marry."

Rebecca chuckled. "Oh, Nancy, I hope it'll be that simple. I really do."

Nancy went home with Rebecca for the weekend. They planned to spend most of their time studying for the midwinter exams, but their plans were interrupted by an unexpected visitor.

The maid opened the door and stood aside to allow him entry.

Nate.

His gaze swept over them. "Well, aren't you at least going to say hello?" He seemed uncomfortable, which puzzled her. Had he suddenly developed a conscience, or was he involved in her grandmother's murder? Or perhaps both?

Rebecca started forward, "I'm sorry, Nate. Do come in. Here, let me take your coat."

"Hello, Nate." Nancy fought a strange sense of panic in the pit of her stomach. The three sat down, Nancy and Rebecca together on the sofa facing Nate.

"How've you been?" Rebecca asked him.

For a moment, he stared at Nancy. Then he aimed a wicked smirk at Rebecca. "Wonderful. I set off to make my fortune and came back utterly and completely—" He glanced from one to the other then burst out laughing. They watched in silence until he suddenly stopped.

"Not funny, eh? Same ole, Nate. I tried. I failed. End of story."

Nancy forced herself to look at him. "I'm sorry, Nate."

He scoffed. "Are you?

"Of course we are," Rebecca said. "It would be great for you to do well, to be a success, after so many … ventures."

Nancy gazed at her friend. When had Rebecca lost patience with Nate?

He gave another halfhearted laugh. "You two are something else, you know that?" He gazed into Rebecca's eyes. "Would it be possible for me to speak to Nancy alone?"

Rebecca darted a glance at Nancy.

After a moment's hesitation, Nancy nodded.

Rebecca dipped her head and looked harder at Nancy.

"It's all right, Rebecca."

Rebecca rose to leave. Her eyes flashed a warning at Nate. "I'll be right down the hall."

"Why?" He scowled at Nancy. "Say, what's going on here? Can't I get a little time alone with my girl?"

Nancy scoffed. "Am I your girl, Nate?"

"Oh, I see." He got up to cross over to the window. Then he turned to face her. "If I'd come back successful, pockets full-o-cash, what then?"

Nancy met his gaze. "It wouldn't have made any difference."

"Sorry, Mac, the bank's closed." He flashed a wry grin. "Guess I stayed away too long." He turned his back to her again.

She stood and crossed to him. "You never even called me. I didn't know if I'd ever see you again."

He turned to face her. "You know how I am. Sometimes I do things like that."

"Something ... has happened."

He stood still, looking down at her, a slow smile spreading across his face. "Mr. Emerson proposed?"

"No." She wanted to slap his face. Instead she stepped nearer to him. "You heard my grandmother ... was murdered?"

"Yeah, I did ... hear that." His expression changed. She thought she saw a strange flash of something in his eyes. He watched the flames and jingled the coins in his pocket—a rather irritating habit of his. After a short silence, he met her gaze. "What?"

"She left everything in the care of an executor until my thirtieth birthday. If I should marry before I'm thirty, I lose everything." It was the first time she'd spoken the words aloud. Her lips trembled. To her chagrin, tears threatened. She pressed her lips together and breathed in slowly.

Nate stared back at her. Then he stuck his hands deep into his pockets and swung back around to the window, cursing under his breath. He began to pace back and forth, muttering. "I knew it. I knew she'd pull something like this." He looked up at Nancy. "You knew she'd never let you throw away your life on some jerk like me."

The dark face she'd admired for so many years had become ugly to her. She backed away from him. "Nate …"

He threw up his hand. "No, no. I have to think about this. It's too sudden. It happened sooner than I expected. That's all."

She frowned. "What are you talking about?"

He turned suddenly, grabbed her hands, and led her back over to the sofa. He sat down, pulling her down beside him. "Listen, Nance—here's what we'll do." He leaned back and took a deep breath as if composing his thoughts. "You do exactly what ole Grandma wanted."

Nancy started to protest, but Nate quickly moved to cover her mouth with his hand.

"Listen to me. You marry Robert Emerson, just like she wanted."

She threw off his hand. "I can't. The will says that if I marry before I'm thirty, everything is forfeited to the executor."

He grinned. "And who is the executor?"

"Robert … Emerson …" She suddenly realized what Nate was saying. He already knew who was appointed executor.

"Yeah, so if you marry Robert Emerson, he gets everything. But you'll be married to him, so half of all he owns belongs to you."

She bristled. "That's not necessarily true, Nate. The laws are changing daily."

"What do you know of law? Is that what you're studying at that fancy school? I thought you girls were learning how to knit and keep house. You need to leave the thinking to me, sweetheart. I hear things. I know what I'm talking about."

He bent his head to level his eyes at her. "Nancy, don't be a fool. There's a lot at stake here. I know these people, remember?" He rose and surveyed the room. "They marry for money and power, not for love. Remember me telling you that? You give that man two months. He'll have a mistress somewhere." He slapped his knee. "Hah! Probably already has one."

Nancy couldn't bear to think about that. When she tried to rise, he grabbed her hands and squeezed so hard, it hurt. "No, hear me out. Grandma's gone now. After a while, you can get a divorce. He *will* have a mistress, Nancy. You can depend on that. It's what rich guys do. And when he does, I'll know about it. That'll make it easy for you to get the divorce. You could end up with half of everything or maybe even more. Then we could get married and live happily ever after." He sat back again, looking quite satisfied with himself. "Well, what do you think?"

The audacity! Nancy narrowed her eyes at him. "I think you're crazy." Unable to disguise her anger, she continued to stare at him, hating the smirk on his face. How could he believe she could ever do something so underhanded? Did he have so little opinion of her? Did he consider her a cheap little trinket to be passed around? For the second time that evening, she wanted to slap him.

He laughed. "You're really cute when you're mad, you know that?"

Then she did slap him. He grabbed her hand and leaned forward until their noses almost touched. "Don't *ever* do that again."

She pulled away from him.

"What do you expect to do? I don't see where you have any choice."

"I can't marry Robert Emerson."

He turned on his most persuasive tone. "You don't have to love him. You just have to marry him. You can do that."

With a jolt, she realized she'd never said no to this man.

"People do it all the time," he persisted.

Her mind raced ahead, putting facts together. After all, it was in his best interest for Nancy to retain her fortune.

He pulled her hand to his lips and kissed it. "We can still see each other, Nancy. We'll just have to be discreet." He kissed her cheek, moved on to her neck then nuzzled her ear. "Only think how exciting it will be."

She jerked away from him. What would it take to convince him she could never do that? She put her head in her hands, sick to her stomach. After a moment, she looked up at him.

"I can't marry him, because I'm ... going to have a baby."

Nate stared at her—speechless for once. He reached up and rubbed the back of his neck. She could almost see the gears turning in his head. This was definitely something he hadn't expected. She had no doubt he knew he was the father. He probably thought he'd gotten away with it. A big chunk of his bravado drained away with the blood that left his face. He eyed her, cautious. "So what are you thinking to do?"

She glared back at him. "We'll have to get married."

He catapulted from his chair and strode back toward the window.

She halfway expected him to bolt and never show his face again. But he swung back around. His face was difficult to read. Hunching his shoulders, he marched over and sat down next to her. "Sweetheart, I love you—you know I do. But there's no way I could do that to a child, or to you, for that matter. I've got no money and no prospects. You wouldn't have any either." He looked into her eyes. "Nothing, Nancy. Think about it. Do you really want to raise a child like that?"

Her eyes burned with unshed tears. "So what do you suggest?"

"You go back and tell Robert Emerson whatever you need to tell him to get him to marry you right away." He spoke slowly. He'd talked his way out of trouble many times. This was just another test of his skills. "That'll take care of the time thing. Folks'll think the baby came early. It happens all the time." He took her hands again and kissed her forehead. "It'll all work out, you'll see. It'll be best—for the kid."

Unmoved, Nancy watched his face. Smooth, real smooth, Nate. He did know how to talk to women. And then he'd played the trump card. *It'll be best for the kid.*

Misery twisted like a snake in her belly. She wanted to curl up and die. After a few seconds ticked away on the clock, she stood and left the room. She climbed the stairs and closed herself up in Rebecca's guest room.

Chapter Seventeen

Nancy's stomach lurched with the train as they pulled away from Reedsville Depot. She laid her head back on the seat, trying not to think about the nausea. She'd returned to school ahead of Rebecca, packed her belongings, and headed home. Rebecca would be upset with her. Everyone would be disappointed with her once they knew the truth. She contemplated staying on the train, going someplace far away where no one knew her. But she had little money. No place to go.

She glanced out the window. Dark smoke from the engine hung heavy on the air as they began their ascent into the hills. Dread wrapped its cold, hard fingers around her heart. She couldn't pray. She couldn't even escape through one of her fantasies. She'd have to figure something out and soon, before things became apparent.

Unlike Rebecca, Nancy's "visits from Aunt Ruby" were regular. A trip to the school library had yielded an old medical tome that outlined the symptoms well enough for her to be certain. She splayed her fingers. The fingernails were a dead giveaway. She'd never had such long, strong nails.

She tried to watch the scenery outside her window, but the movement of the train nauseated her. She shifted in the seat and kept her eyes on the floor.

The car was only about half full, so she needn't talk to anyone. She closed her eyes and breathed deeply. Should she do what Nate advised? It would mean she'd have to lie to Robert. Could she do that? A tear dropped from the corner of her eye and ran down her cheek. She swiped at it with the back of her hand. She could never lie to Robert.

She'd made a mistake. Now she must pay the price.

The train slowed again as they drew near another small town, the last one. The next stop, Springfield. She felt as if she wore a too-tight corset. She'd never been so afraid. But as executor of Grandmother's estate, Robert was her only course. She should tell him everything, throw herself on his mercy, and let him decide what to do about it. But the thought sickened her even more.

The scene played out in her mind. She'd enter Robert's office through oversized, ornately carved doors. His resembled her grandmother's, only the desk was much larger. Nancy could barely see over it. Robert, a stern look on his face, held a gavel in his hand. "What do you have to say for yourself, Nancy Sanderson?"

She swallowed hard. Her first attempt at speech yielded only a squeak. The gavel banged the desk. Robert's angry voice echoed throughout the room. "What?"

"I made a mistake. I trusted the wrong person."

The gavel hit the desk again. "Guilty! I pronounce you guilty!" His voice pitched higher and higher until it sounded more like a horn blowing. The train lurched and jerked Nancy awake.

Home.

She reached for her bag, and stood, one gloved hand gripping the top of the seat.

"You be careful there, young lady." A uniformed porter had stepped up behind her. He steadied her. Nancy nodded her thanks and made her way carefully down the aisle and onto the steps where another porter assisted her in disembarking.

Her head down, she let her gaze sweep over the platform, hoping no one noticed her. Everyone seemed intent on his or her own pursuits. If not for her luggage, she could walk home, but the heavy bags made that impossible, so she hailed a cab arriving at her door half an hour later and paying the cab driver with the little funds she had left. Sissy stood speechless for about thirty seconds. *That may be a record.*

"La, child, you should've called. Kip gets few opportunities to drive these days. What are you doing home so soon? I thought you said—"

Nancy held up her hand to stop the flow of words. "I'm tired and hungry, Sissy. Have you anything prepared?"

Sissy helped Nancy remove her coat. "I sure do. Cook set a pot of soup on this morning before she left. I'll have Kip take your luggage upstairs. You come on in the parlor and put your feet up. A bowl of soup and a cup of hot tea will be just the thing."

With the fire warming the bottoms of her feet, Nancy snuggled into her chair and waited for Sissy to return. How would her old nursemaid react when she knew the truth? Would she be surprised?

Sissy knew all about Nancy's nocturnal jaunts during her wild years. She clucked her tongue many times over her insensibilities. "Lah, Miss Nancy," she'd say. "You'll give your grandma a heart attack."

A tear escaped Nancy's eye to roll down her cheek. She swiped at it with her fingertips. At least Grandmother would be spared this injury. No doubt, she'd have blamed it all on Nancy's mother.

Nancy raced around, making last minute adjustments to her outfit and her hair. The moment she'd been dreading for several days had arrived. Robert waited for her in the parlor.

She checked the mirror one more time, grimaced at her reflection, then marched downstairs to face the unknown.

When she opened the door, Robert crossed the room to take her hand. His eyes searched her face. His crooked smile brought her immediate relief.

"I was a little surprised by your phone call, but it is good to see you again."

Tears stung her eyes. A lump the size of a baseball rose in her throat. She'd been crazy to think she could do this.

His smile disappeared. He tilted his head to gaze into her eyes. "Nancy, what's wrong? Are you ill?"

She shook her head, pulling away from him to sit on the edge of a chair. She tried desperately to gain control.

"Let's not talk here," he said. "Get your coat. We'll go for a drive."

Nancy did exactly as she was told. She put on her coat and followed him. She admired his patience when he didn't press her for information. They were several miles down the road before she could trust herself to speak.

"I'm sorry, Robert," she said, closing her eyes.

"Don't worry about it." Glancing at her, he said, "I guess you must've heard the news."

She looked up in surprise. "What news?"

"Oh."

"Robert, what is it?"

He glanced over at her again. His eyes back on the road, he said, "I've made no progress on the amendment to the will."

Nancy gazed at him for several moments. She didn't know what to say. "I hadn't given that a thought." She shook her head. Why was he bringing that up? "No progress at all?"

"Never mind, we'll discuss it later." He pulled into a small roadside café. He got out and came around to open her door. She followed him inside, and they sat down at a corner booth, where he ordered coffee. The little café was nearly empty so

Nancy could be open with him. If not for a sudden attack of conscience. He was so thoughtful. So kind. How could she ever go through with what she'd come home to do?

He reached across the table and took her hand in his. "What is it?" After a moment, he changed his question. "What do you want?"

She studied his face. What did he mean by that? Maybe he thought she needed money. "I … want …" She bit her lip and closed her eyes again. She wanted everything to return to normal. She wanted to go back and change her past.

"Nancy? What is it? Talk to me. I can't help you if you won't talk to me." His tender voice penetrated her darkness.

She opened her eyes but couldn't bring herself to look at him. Her mind was as jumbled as a train wreck. All the lies she'd planned were lost. He trusted her. And deep inside, she knew he'd never fall for a lie.

To her great humiliation, she blurted out the truth. Every last critical fact came pouring forth amid a wild rush of tears. She didn't care anymore. He'd never want her now, but at least she could be honest. Throw herself on his mercy, accept whatever decision he made. Perhaps he'd send her away to a place where no one knew her. She'd die in childbirth and no one would ever see her again. She swiped at tears with trembling fingers.

He handed her his handkerchief.

She blew her nose and dabbed at her eyes.

Robert sat in shocked silence as Nancy poured her heart out. It was not at all what he'd expected to hear. Trouble at school or perhaps she'd experienced delayed trauma over her grandmother's death, but not this. He couldn't seem to wrap his mind around it.

He closed his eyes as anger boiled up inside him. He'd never known such wrath. He wanted to jump up, run out, and find that man. Wring his neck like the chicken Nate Conners was.

He sucked in a deep breath to calm his soul. He couldn't react in anger. Nancy would take it personally. He must control his emotions. He'd only heard rumors of such things happening. He'd never actually known anyone involved. He studied her face and her movements. She didn't seem to be lying. Her nervous fingers twisted his handkerchief into a tight knot. Warmth for her filled his heart. In so many ways, she was still so childlike. So like the young girl in her grandmother's yard.

Now he must come up with a solution. How could he make this go away? How could he protect her from ruin? These things happened, especially in this enlightened age, but it was still highly frowned upon by society. Especially a small-town society like theirs. She would be ostracized.

He could hear the tongues wagging already. Years would pass, and they'd still remember. And the child would always be referred to as a bastard. One of the ugliest words in the English language. As his ire cooled, Robert began to process the possibilities.

Nancy's misery grew as she watched the changes in Robert's handsome face. Shock. Anger. Resignation. He was disappointed in her. Probably even repulsed by her.

In a voice so low she could barely make it out he said, "Have you told anyone else besides me … and Nate?"

"No."

They sat in silence for such a long time she grew restless and twisted his handkerchief. Her lips trembled as she forced herself to speak. "I'm so sorry, Robert." She wiped away more tears with the twisted handkerchief.

He glanced up. It seemed as if he'd forgotten her presence. Then he rose from his chair, laid down the money for the coffee, and reached out to her. She allowed him to help her through the café door. When they reached the car, he stopped. Without saying a word, he turned and folded her into his arms.

She'd never known such comfort. He held her for a long time. Not speaking, only stroking her hair. When he spoke, his voice sounded husky. "I'm sorry too, sweetheart."

Nancy began to cry again. She'd lost everything. She could have had so much, had she not so blindly followed a man like Nate.

She fingered the scratchy wool of Robert's overcoat, wanting to cherish this moment, for she was sure this would be the last time he would ever hold her. Her heart was breaking, and still he held her so tightly against him. He kissed the top of her head. His arms relaxed a little as he pulled back and gazed into her eyes.

Is it over? Is this the end?

"Marry me, Nancy."

She caught her breath. "Oh no, Robert. Don't. That's not why I told you. I don't want you to marry me out of pity."

"Be quiet," he said, laying his fingertips over her lips. "Here. You're getting cold. Let's get in the car." He helped her into the car. Then he pulled a blanket from the backseat on his way around to the driver's side. He tucked the cover around her and started the car. Pulling out of the parking lot, he headed down the dark road into the night.

"I know it's late, but I don't think Sissy will worry, knowing you're with me." He glanced at her. She was still wiping away tears and sniffling. His expression relaxed into a shadowy smile. "If you keep that up, you're going to run out of handkerchief."

She released a nervous giggle as she turned to look at him. He concentrated on the road. Her heart constricted. Had he ever looked more handsome?

After several minutes, he pulled into the drive of a house she didn't recognize. He turned off the engine and faced her. He pushed the hair away from her eyes. "I would never marry you out of pity, Nancy. I love you and have loved you for some time now, long before your grandmother approached me. You can believe that—or not."

She sat looking at him in silence, not really knowing how to reply. Her heart had begun to hope again.

"Marry me—tonight. Right now." His eyes held hers in a tangible embrace.

She sniffed. "I … I don't know. I … want to," she said, barely above a whisper.

"Then do it. We'll find a way to explain it. I'll take care of everything, sweetheart. No one need ever know. Only me, and I honestly don't care."

"Nate … he knows," she whispered.

Robert looked at her. "You told me you don't remember what happened. And you said he never mentioned what happened."

She nodded.

"You never mentioned it either, thinking he hadn't remembered."

Again she nodded.

"When you confronted him, did he acknowledge it? Did he claim responsibility?"

She thought for a moment. She remembered everything Nate had said to her that night, but she did not remember ever hearing him acknowledge the act or claim the child as his own.

"He never did." She looked up at Robert. Something fluttered in her chest. Could she do it? Could she marry this man? Part of her wanted to release all of her cares to him. Maybe all of her. Who cared if he ended up with all the money. *If he takes care of me and this child, won't it be worth it in the end?*

He started the engine again and backed the car out of the driveway.

She jerked her eyes back to his. "Where are we going?"

"I know someone—in the next county—a friend, who owes me a favor. Why don't you settle back and get some rest?"

She snuggled down into the blanket. "Thank you, Robert."

"I don't know if you should thank me yet. Let's wait and see how this turns out."

Amelia's Legacy

Chapter Eighteen

When Robert escorted Nancy into the Sanderson house late the next morning, they found Sissy laying a fresh fire in the parlor. Robert caught the searing glance Sissy sent him over her left shoulder, but she did not budge.

"Imagine my surprise, Miss Nancy, when I found you were not in your room and had not been in your room all night. I've been worried sick. After all that has happened to us." She placed the last of the sticks on the pile of wood then struck a match and set the kindling afire. She pushed away from the hearth to face Nancy and Robert with eyes blazing, wiping her hands on her apron. "You didn't come home from your outing."

She scooped up the ash bucket and brush, clattering them with more noise than usual. "First, I find you sleeping together on the parlor sofa, and now you're together all night, who knows where. Land sakes, Miss Nancy, won't Miss Amelia be turning over in her grave?"

The clock on the mantel struck ten. Robert and Nancy exchanged glances, but neither spoke.

Sissy huffed. "Will you be needing anything … sir?"

Robert's mouth twitched as he suppressed a smile. "No, thank you, Sissy. We'll be leaving again, right away."

Sissy stood there holding the bucket and scowling. "Are you taking her back to school, then?"

Robert chuckled. "No. I suppose it's only fair to let you know, Nancy and I … are married. She won't be returning to school."

Sissy's jaw went slack. She plopped down on the sofa. A puff of dust rose from the ashes in the bucket as it hit the floor.

"Go on and get what you'll need." Robert spoke in a low voice to Nancy. "I'll wait here." After she'd gone, he addressed Sissy. "I can see I've shocked you." He crossed to the window and looked out. "I'm taking her with me to Perry's Landing for a short visit with my grandmother."

Sissy stood and took up the bucket again. "I guess I spoke out of turn, sir. But I've cared for her since she was a baby."

Robert faced her. "Your concern for her is understandable. I could never fault that, Sissy."

"It'll all come to rights I expect, in the end." She sniffed and set the bucket back on the hearth. "I should go up and help her pack."

Robert wasn't quite sure what Sissy meant, but they were interrupted by Nancy's reappearance. She gripped an overnight case, which Robert took from her. "This is all you need?"

Nancy bit her lower lip and nodded. "I had not unpacked everything." She glanced at Sissy. "I left instructions for whatever else I'll need."

"I told her where we're going," Robert said.

Her face held a contrite look, one he'd seen a number of times in the last eighteen hours.

With a nod, she moved past him to Sissy, who still stood near the hearth. "Thank you for everything."

Sissy threw her arms around Nancy. "Good-bye, Miss Nancy." Scowling at Robert, she said, "You take good care of my girl."

He grinned. "You know I will. We'll be in touch." He led Nancy to the door and out to the car. "Is this all there is?" he asked again as he set the case in the back.

"Yes, that's it."

"I like a woman who travels light."

"Silly man, the rest will be shipped by train this afternoon." She waited for him to open her door and help her in.

He started the car then leaned over and kissed her soundly on the mouth. He tucked the blanket around her with orders to rest then backed the car around and pulled out of the drive. They had only driven a short distance when Nancy fell asleep.

Robert kept his eyes on the road, but his mind was elsewhere. Too much had happened all at once. Many weeks had passed since Miss Amelia's murder, and the police were no closer to finding a suspect. They'd followed several leads to no avail. Finally, Detective Lawton told Robert, "Until the jewels show up, we've got nothing."

Robert still had that woman's handkerchief. He hadn't turned it over to the police, as he'd promised Nancy. He didn't want to rouse suspicion where none was due. He was almost certain Elizabeth Elliott had nothing to do with Miss Amelia's death. Elizabeth Elliott. He'd not heard that name in a long time.

He glanced at Nancy. She still slept. Should he tell her about Liz?

And then there was Nate. The thought of him made Robert's blood boil. Had Nate hoped to force Nancy into marriage? Robert scoffed. Well, Amelia had taken care of that, hadn't she? Amazing how fast Nate had backpedaled when he realized he wasn't going to get his hands on Nancy's fortune.

Robert silently thanked God for giving Amelia the foresight to take the steps she had taken … just in time.

Nancy stirred, yawned, and stretched. Had she actually slept? Had it all been a dream? Her eyes found his.

Robert smiled. "You're awake. There's a small café down the road about a mile. Are you hungry?"

A sweet dream. She folded her arms over her chest. "Famished."

"Good. So am I."

The atmosphere inside the café felt warm and inviting, smelling of good food and hot coffee. After they had placed their order with the waitress and received cups of steaming coffee, Robert turned to Nancy. "I called my grandmother to let her know we're coming. Once we get there and I've had a chance to talk with her, I'm going to ask her to invite Mother and Dad up for the weekend. I want to talk with them face to face."

She studied his expressions as he spoke. If he dreaded the confrontation, he never showed it, but as a lawyer, he might be used to hiding his emotions. The arrival of the food distracted her.

Robert grinned. "You look hungry."

"I hadn't realized how hungry. This looks wonderful."

They ate in silence until Robert set his fork down and said, "The tenth of January."

She met his gaze. "What's the tenth of January?"

"Our anniversary. At least that's what we'll tell everyone. That way, we can avoid any unpleasantness. We won't have to say the baby came early."

She set her fork down. "Yes, we can substitute one lie for another."

His eyes never left her face as he shrugged. "We'll always know our actual wedding date. We can celebrate privately on March 20."

"You're taking a lot for granted." She picked up her fork and pushed at the crumbs on her plate.

His lips curved into a grin. "What does that mean?"

After a moment's thought, she sobered. "I suppose it's a good thing you're planning to *have* anniversaries."

"Of course I'm planning to have anniversaries, silly." He slid his now empty plate to the side. "Do you feel married yet?"

She shook her head. "I haven't really had time to think about it." Her eyes slid to his. "Do you?"

"I think so. I've been taking care of you now for almost twenty-four hours straight. That's one of the most important requirements, isn't it?"

"And may I say, you are doing wonderfully for your first day on the job? But then when I think about it, I believe you've been taking care of me for a lot longer than that."

He gazed into her eyes for a long moment as a slow smile spread across his face. Then he tapped the table to signal the waitress.

After they enjoyed a wonderful piece of coconut cream pie, he paid the bill. The road stretched out long before them. A three-hour trip by train, it took nearly six to drive. When they pulled up to the wrought-iron gate, Robert got out and unlocked it. Nancy sat in silence as they drove through the narrow, muddy lane that led into and across the valley to the great house. A petite, white-haired woman stepped through the doorway onto the porch. She waved as they drew near.

"That's Grandma," Robert said. "The sweetest lady who ever lived."

"She certainly looks it."

As he brought the car to a halt, Robert glanced at Nancy. "She'll love you."

"I hope so," she said.

A warm fire burned in the fireplace in the front parlor. The decor of the informal room reminded Nancy of a beach cottage. All blue and white and yellow. No stern portraits hung on these walls. Watercolor scenes of lighthouses, misty harbors, and ships at sea shared space with shells, bits of sea glass and nautical paraphernalia. A servant took their coats away and quickly returned with cups of steaming hot chocolate.

"Now tell me all about it," Robert's grandmother said, as she stirred her cocoa. "It all sounds so romantic."

Nancy looked away but felt Robert's eyes on her as he began the narrative of their first meeting. He skipped a few details to tell his grandmother of the elopement. For some strange reason she didn't understand, Nancy's eyes misted over. He was so charming and good, so obviously beloved of his grandmother. And he was lying.

Evelyn Perry's eyes crinkled as she peered at Robert over the rim of her cup. "If you have kept your marriage a secret for so long, why have you decided to bring it out into the open now?"

Nancy saw the twinkle in the older woman's eyes and gave her an answering smile. She suspected the reason. Nancy dropped her eyelids as shame stirred in her breast. If only it were true.

Robert's voice held no trace of guilt. "I think you've already guessed the answer to that, Grandma."

"Oh, how wonderful." She set her cup down and leaned in to plant a kiss on Robert's cheek. Then she took Nancy's hand, squeezed it, gazed into her eyes and said, "I'm going to be a great-grandmother. Oh, how I've longed for this."

"Robert told me you would be pleased," Nancy said.

"It's so like Robert to surprise us this way." She turned to him. "What about your mother and father? What did they say?"

Robert's cheek dimpled. "They don't know yet."

Grandma Perry's eyes lit up. "What? Then I'm the first to know?" At Robert's nod, she hugged him. "Thank you, dear boy. You've made me so happy."

"I wondered if you would mind inviting them up this weekend, Grandma. We want to tell them in person."

"Wonderful. I'll have the perfect opportunity to gloat."

Robert stood with her.

She touched his arm. "No need for you to get up. I'll go at once and make the call."

Only a few minutes had passed when she returned.

Nancy marveled at the light of joy in her eyes. "They'll be here. What fun we'll have. Now you two must be very tired. Especially our little momma, so I'll have Delia show you to your room." Her gaze bounced from Robert to Nancy. "I had two rooms prepared. You can choose between them."

"Thanks for everything, Grandma." Robert bent to kiss Grandma's cheek. He held out his hand to Nancy and led her to the stairs. For some reason beyond her understanding, Nancy's heartbeat sped up as they drew near the base of the stairs.

Robert seemed to sense her discomfort. He tucked her hand in the crook of his arm and laid his hand over hers.

A silly thought crested as she stepped onto the landing. Would he pick her up and carry her through the door of their room? Would he expect …? Her stomach roiled. Nausea.

His intuitive gaze swept over her face. "Are you all right?"

Better own up to it. "Tired, I guess, and a little nauseated."

"Can I get you anything? Perhaps Grandma has something that would help."

"No, I'll be fine once I get to bed." She swallowed.

She needn't have worried. Robert's casual demeanor soon set her at ease.

He led her into a front room. "You'll like this one best. It boasts an expansive view of the valley."

Nancy would have to trust him on that, since darkness hid any view at the moment. The room was painted a soft mint green with sheer lilac curtains and a beautifully crafted double-ring quilt on the four-poster bed. A cocoa colored sofa flanked the foot of the bed and an overstuffed chair sat near the window. A sculpted porcelain lamp sat on a table beside the chair. Nancy decided she could be very comfortable there.

After a warm bath, she put on her nightgown and silk wrapper and curled up on the sofa. While Robert was in the bath, she grew tired and laid down on the bed's soft, downy mattress and promptly fell asleep.

Robert covered Nancy with the quilt then sank into the overstuffed chair near the lamp. What a day they'd had. He'd barely had a moment to think. And that was probably a good thing. He picked up a Bible that lay on the table, opened it to the Psalms, and began to read, hoping to calm his nerves.

The downstairs clock interrupted the silence in the house as it chimed twelve times. He closed the book and set it back on the table. For a moment, he sat listening to Nancy's even breathing. He wanted nothing more than to lie down beside her, pull her into his arms, and hold her. Instead, he reached for an afghan that adorned the arm of the sofa and lay down.

As a lawyer, there were many times he'd had to "fudge" the truth a little. Seldom did his conscience bother him as much as it did now. He was lying to his family. He closed his eyes as the battle continued in the depths of his soul. His only defense, his protective instincts had kicked in.

He opened his eyes to peer into the darkness. How would his mother have reacted to the truth, had he chosen to tell it?

He could well imagine her dismay. So he was also protecting her. She must never find out.

"God, forgive me," he whispered. "I know it's not right to lie. But at this moment, I don't know what else to do. If you'll show me a better way, I'll gladly take it."

Chapter Nineteen

Nancy glanced up as Robert turned from the window.

"They're here." He crossed to the sofa and crouched down in front of her. "Are you sure you don't want to go downstairs with me?"

"If it's all right with you, I think it would be best if I wait here. Just until you've told them." Should she tell him how petrified she was? His gaze seemed to penetrate her soul. Nausea twisted her stomach into a tight knot.

He gave her a quick kiss. "You're probably right. If you were in the room with me, they would know right away."

As he closed the door behind him, she leaned back with a soft sigh. *It is so wonderful to be in love.* Really in love. She smiled at the memory of her first morning in this room, waking up all alone, wondering where Robert had gone. She'd gotten up and crossed to the window where she'd parted the old-fashioned lace curtains and looked out onto a pristine valley. A soft sound behind her had drawn her eyes to him. He lay on the sofa, sound asleep.

She'd crouched on the edge of the chair and watched his face. She had never seen it thus, so relaxed and peaceful. A handsome face, dusky with a day's growth of whiskers.

As she'd watched him, he'd awakened. In that moment, as their eyes met, she knew. He would not sleep on the sofa again.

"I was so surprised to see you already here, my darling," Juliana Emerson told her son when they were settled in the parlor near the fire.

Grandma glanced up as she poured the coffee, a smug smile tugging at her lips.

"I've been here several days," he said. "I asked Grandma to invite you."

His mother's face registered surprise. She glanced from Robert to his father, which prompted him to ask, "What's going on, son?"

Robert leaned forward with his elbows on his knees, and clasped his hands together. "Well, Nancy and I ..."

"You're getting married. Oh, I knew it," his mother said, holding her cup in both hands.

"I'm glad you're so happy about it, Mother," Robert said. "But that's not quite what I was going to say. We're not *going* to get married. We *are* married."

Silence.

His father's left brow arched, an expression he often used when interrogating witnesses. Robert clenched his jaw to keep back a smile as his barrage of questions began.

"When?"

Robert cleared his throat. "A while ago."

His father uncrossed his leg and sat forward. "How long ago?"

Don't hesitate. Dad will notice. "January tenth. We wanted to keep it a secret until after Nancy's graduation, but ... changed our minds."

"January tenth," his mother whispered. "But that was before all the ... you mean to tell me that you were married all the while?"

Robert said nothing, but by his silence, allowed her to believe it was true. He hated lying to his gentle mother, but it seemed better than the alternative.

His father spoke in an even tone. "Well, son, you've always been very well-grounded. I've never known you to make a rash move. I knew when you told me of your decision to leave the firm for Sanderson that it was a well-thought-out decision, so I didn't question it. Neither will I question you now, except to ask what prompted you to let the secret out so much sooner than first planned?"

"I think I know," his mother whispered. She set her cup down.

In that moment's pause, Grandma spoke, "I knew too, right away. I'm going to be a great-grandma."

His mother looked to him for confirmation.

He nodded.

She covered her mouth with her napkin. "Oh dear, a grandchild." She glanced at her husband. "Grandparents."

Robert searched his father's expression as the older man extended his hand. "Congratulations, son." Their gazes locked. Had he passed his father's inspection?

Robert cast a smiling glance at his mother. "If you'll excuse me, I'll go and get my wife."

"Oh my, yes," his mother said. She placed her hand on her husband's knee and gazed into his eyes. "His wife."

Nancy paced the length of the upstairs parlor again. Did they realize she could hear their every word? She stopped near the fireplace. The sound must carry through the chimney flue. At that moment, she heard Mrs. Emerson say, "Why is she not here to greet us? Does she think we would not approve?"

Daniel Emerson's deep voice followed. "She's young, dear. You remember how it was to be young."

The door opened, and Robert's head appeared. Nancy nearly laughed out loud at the sight. He reminded her of a puppet show she'd seen as a child. He stepped inside the door. "Ready?"

His hand at the small of her back, Robert ushered her downstairs. Her hands shook, and she felt unsteady on her feet, though Robert had assured her of their welcome and excitement over the news. She didn't tell him she'd heard the entire conversation.

Grandma Perry clutched Nancy's hand and gave her a warm smile. "I'm just going to the kitchen to check on dinner. I'll be right back."

Daniel and Juliana rose as she entered. Juliana took her hand and kissed her cheek. "Welcome to the family, dear."

Robert settled beside Nancy on the divan, facing his parents. Juliana poured another cup of tea and handed it to Nancy. "Will you be staying long? Spring is so lovely here."

Nancy turned to Robert for help. This was something they had not discussed.

"I wish we could, but I have to get back to work."

Daniel Emerson handed his empty cup to his wife before turning his attention to Nancy. "I can't help thinking of Amelia. She would be so proud."

"She certainly worked hard enough to get us together," Nancy said.

Robert took her hand in his. "I only wish we had been able to tell her before she died."

"Oh yes," Juliana whispered. "It must have been right around the time ..."

Robert nodded.

Nancy gazed out the window and tried not to think of it. How her grandmother would have loved to be here right now, crowing over her success. She bit her lip then swallowed hard. *I miss her.*

"Did they ever find out who—" Daniel glanced up from a close examination of his left shoe. "No, I suppose they did not; we'd surely have heard."

Nancy darted a glance at Robert. Their gazes held as he answered, "All they've been able to prove so far is who did *not* do it."

Juliana's eyes were on Nancy also. "Let's not discuss that right now, dears."

Daniel's brow furrowed. "I'm so sorry, Nancy. That was very insensitive of me."

Nancy turned to him with a quick shake of her head. "It's quite all right, sir."

Juliana reacted. "No, it's not. They have no business talking about such things on this happy occasion. We've just had the most wonderful news of our life."

Grandma padded into the room. "Well, if you are quite finished celebrating, dinner is ready."

Robert and his father went out for a horseback ride after dinner, to enjoy the unseasonably mild weather, warm sunshine tempered by a crisp breeze, and a bright blue sky. They came to the ridge overlooking the valley and dismounted to better admire its beauty.

"I'll never tire of it," Robert said, taking in a deep breath of fresh air. He felt his father's gaze on him and turned to face him. "What is it, Dad?"

"Did you get that girl into trouble?"

Robert hadn't expected that one. He shook his head. "No Dad. I have too much respect for her. I love her Dad, very much."

The senior Emerson hunched his shoulders, as though relieved of a great burden. "That much is obvious, son. I'm sorry. I just … needed to know. It does occasionally happen." He removed his hat and pushed his fingers through his hair.

"Yes, it does." Robert adjusted his horse's bridle. He turned and made eye contact with his father. "Dad, you know how Miss Amelia was. Her illness brought a sense of urgency which prompted her to put undue pressure on Nancy to settle on a husband." He rested his arms on the saddle. "She wanted to make sure her granddaughter chose appropriately."

"Chose you, you mean." His father offered him a wry smile.

Robert's horse jumped at the sudden flight of a bird. He grabbed the reins and spoke in a comforting tone. "Whoa, boy. It's all right. Just a bird."

He turned his attention back to his dad. "Yes, that, too. The pressure got to Nancy. She panicked. I'm glad I was there to catch her. I don't know what she would have done."

His dad brushed at a smudge of dirt on his jeans and replaced his hat. "Life can be confusing at times. I'm proud of you son. Your Mother and I both are."

"I'm sorry to have taken away the prospects of a big wedding. I know how Mother looked forward to it."

"Yes, she did, but she'll get over it. The prospects of a grandchild will keep her well occupied for some time to come, I think. Ready to go?"

Robert mounted his horse in answer, calling a challenge to his father. "Race you back to the barn!"

Chapter Twenty

Nate punched the bell at Rebecca's front gate for the fourth time. What was keeping the footman? He always opened the gate right away. Nate glared through the wrought-iron bars toward the front door. Finally, it opened.

Rebecca stepped out. "Just a minute, Nate."

He scowled as the door closed. An uneasy feeling churned in his middle. "What's up with this? Where are the servants?"

A moment later, Rebecca ambled through the garden gate and down the flagstone path toward the drive. She glanced up as she drew near. The look on her face was not exactly welcoming. "Hello, Nate."

He didn't care what bee was in her bonnet. He had news to share. "She's done it."

Rebecca closed the gate behind him. "Who's done what?"

"Nancy—she married him."

"Come inside. It's still too cool of an evening to stand around outside." She led the way through the arbor to the side door, up the stairs, and into the back parlor where a small fire burned. She turned up the lamp then faced him. "Now, what are you babbling about? Have you been drinking again?"

"No, look. It's right here in the paper." He held the society page in front of her face.

Rebecca read the words aloud. "This reporter has discovered that Miss Nancy Sanderson and Mr. Robert Emerson were married in a private ceremony at an undisclosed location on the tenth of January. The new Mr. and Mrs. Robert Emerson will be returning to town sometime in the spring." Her eyes met his. "This is not news to me."

"Wait a minute. Let me see that." He grabbed the paper from Rebecca and read the words again, silently. "That's not possible. This must be a misprint. They couldn't have married then."

"Why not?"

"She was in the mountains with us that weekend."

Rebecca took the paper back and looked at it again. "That's right. We were." She thought for a moment, her pretty brows knit in concentration. "But that was the day we went home. Nancy left before we did—she took an earlier train, remember? I didn't see her until the next evening, when I arrived back at school."

Nate paced back and forth. When he stopped, he looked at Rebecca and gave a low chuckle. "Well, this is even better."

Rebecca's eyes narrowed to slits. "I would have expected you to be sad, at the very least. I thought you were in love with her."

He grinned. "I still am, as much as I have ever been."

She crossed her arms over her chest. "All that time, they were secretly married. So that's why ..."

"Why, what?"

Rebecca looked up. "That's why she was so sad and preoccupied after Christmas break, and why she was so quiet after he came to visit her."

Nate closed the gap between them. "I can't believe she didn't tell you. I thought you two told each other everything."

"Not everything." She turned away, stirring the fire.

He watched her through narrowed eyes. She avoided his gaze as she replaced the poker. She brushed her hands together then adjusted the screen before she faced him again. "They would have kicked her out of school immediately had they known."

"Uh-huh. Yeah, that was my thought, too." He started for the door. As his fingers encircled the doorknob, he remembered something. "Where are all your servants, Becca? You've always had a regular platoon around here."

Rebecca fingered the hem of her sweater. "They've gone to the lake house to get it ready for summer." She wouldn't meet his gaze.

"Right. Well, I've got to run. I thought you'd like to hear the news."

"Thanks for thinking of me."

She seemed more than happy to have him leave. Almost relieved. As he strode away from the gate, he glanced over his shoulder at the darkened edifice. They'd always kept the place well lit and practically had a servant for every room. Something was definitely up.

He climbed into the front seat of his car, slamming the door. No doubt those high-rollin' parents of hers had lost a bundle. Gravel flew as he skidded out of the drive.

The Lewises' demise was no concern of his. He had bigger thoughts to think. He guided the car with his knee while he rolled a cigarette, licked the paper to seal it, and placed it between his lips. Digging in his pocket, he drew out a matchbox and lit the cigarette. He could fuel his own flame now, soon as the kid was born.

Emerald and ebony filled Nancy's vision as she stood next to Robert on a hill overlooking the valley. A crystal-clear stream divided the green meadow from the rich, black loam of a newly plowed field. She relaxed in Robert's arms. He stood behind her, his chin on her shoulder.

"I think it's time to go home," he whispered.

Nancy turned in his arms to peer into his face. "Where is home, Robert?"

He seemed surprised. "You know, I guess we do need to talk about that. I had thought we could live at my house."

"I don't even know where your home is."

"Imagine that. You were there the night we left."

"Was I?"

"Yes, we were parked in the drive for at least an hour." He pressed his lips to her forehead.

She giggled and leaned against him. "Oh, that's where we were. I wondered whose driveway we were trespassing in. For some reason, I thought you were still living with your parents."

"No, I moved into my grandparents' house in town about three years ago after I returned from college. I hope you'll like it. Of course you can make any changes you deem necessary."

"I quite like the sound of that." She moved from his embrace to look at the scenery one more time. Far below them, new spring calves cavorted in the pasture. She laughed at their exuberance, raised her arms and let her head fall back to gaze into the amazing azure sky.

Robert's deep chuckle echoed across the valley.

Nancy hugged Grandma Perry, promising to write often.

Grandma Perry dabbed at tears. "I had so wished for you to stay a bit longer. Spring is so lovely here."

Robert put his arm about her. "I know Grandma, but duty calls. I've stayed away too long as it is. We'll try to return later when the azaleas are in full bloom. I've told Nancy how beautiful they are."

The narrow lane that wound through the woods to the main road kept Nancy's interest. The beautiful weather gladdened her heart as well. But she soon grew weary of the scenery out on the main road. Robert seemed content to be quiet, but Nancy could not remain so. Too many questions crowded her brain. "Robert, how much do you know about my family?"

He slowed the car a bit to glance at her. "That's dangerous territory."

"Why? Don't you think I have a right to know?" She watched him closely.

"What I think is not important. You're putting me in a bad position." He concentrated on his driving for a few minutes while he negotiated some narrow curves.

She knew it was unfair to ask him, but it seemed the perfect time. Her curiosity had grown since he'd brought up the subject of her *other* grandfather the day he first took her out for a drive. When the road straightened out again, she ventured another question. "Are they so bad that I should have been kept even from knowing who they are?"

At least a full minute passed before Robert responded. "No, they are not that bad, Nancy. Your grandfather, Samuel Elliott, was a very good man; a decent man."

"My grandfather—the one you mentioned the other day," she said. "You knew him?"

"I knew of him. He worked for my father as a janitor for many years."

Nancy frowned. "Why have I been kept from them?"

He glanced at her again. "Nancy, don't be so quick to judge your grandmother. She had her reasons."

Nancy studied his face then turned away to peer out the window. If he had hoped to diffuse the situation, he'd been wrong. She would not be as easy to placate this time.

She laid her hand on her abdomen. "I guess I could blame it on my condition. It has changed my perspective a bit." She avoided eye contact with Robert, waiting to see if he would take the bait. No? She tried again. "I don't even remember them … my parents. I remember the flowers at the funeral and the smell of the room where they were, that's all."

"I remember them," he said. "They were elegant and were always together. I think they must have loved each other very much."

She watched his profile as he spoke. He had known her parents.

He smiled at her as he leaned in to kiss her. "Do you know how much I love you?"

"Only what I've been told."

"Hey, I've done more than tell you, you ungrateful little wretch." He grinned and jerked his attention back to the road.

She kept her eyes on him. "I love you, too, but I'm not letting you off the hook."

This time his eyes never left the road as he took her hand, lifted it to his lips, and kissed it. "Once we're home, I'll tell you all I know, which isn't much. Right now, I need to concentrate on my driving, and you look very tired."

She acquiesced. For now. But she would not forget. If he thought she would, he was sadly mistaken. "I am drowsy. How much longer do you think?"

"An hour or so, if you don't distract me."

She closed her eyes and rested, wishing for the journey to end. She did feel tired.

Dusk had nearly given up to darkness by the time they pulled in the drive. The house stood three stories tall with large windows across the front. An ample porch covered the entire front of the house, wrapping around to a side carriage entrance. Old holly trees clung to each corner of the porch and trellises on either side were covered with brown vines. There would be roses in June.

Inside, he switched on a light revealing a grand foyer, two stories high. A staircase curved around to a landing on the second floor. Warm honey-colored wood shone all around.

"Grandfather loved unstained wood. He wanted to see the natural design in everything. He had this house built with that in mind. You'll notice it especially in the study." He helped her out of her coat and hung it in a small closet near the door. Had he no servants?

He seemed to guess what she was thinking. "I only have a part-time maid right now. We'll have to look into hiring a couple more people, a full time housekeeper, and a chauffeur. Kip may be interested."

"That would be nice."

Robert put his arm around her and pulled her to him. "I'm sorry, dear. I know it's been difficult."

After a moment, she smiled into his eyes. "Show me the rest of the house."

Her new home boasted a small parlor and a grand parlor on opposing sides of the foyer. Beyond the small parlor, they entered an elongated dining room where the table took center stage. Grandma Perry's taste was evident here in the natural decor and soft colors. A swinging door opened into an ample kitchen.

Upstairs, he showed her two large bedrooms on the second floor with his grandfather's study in the middle. The study was all of paneled wood, the same honey color as the staircase. An ample bath completed their tour of that floor.

"There's another bath on the third floor, along with three smaller bedrooms traditionally occupied by servants," he told her.

Nancy stopped to examine the stained glass window on the landing. "It's obvious that so much thought went into the design. This is one thing I will never change."

He left her in their room on the second floor. "I'm sure you'll want to freshen up. I'll bring in our things."

Nancy drew a bath and spent nearly an hour soaking. When she returned to their bedroom, Robert brought tea and sandwiches. Had he prepared them himself? If so, she was impressed. They sat in two winged chairs with a small round table between them.

"You'll like the view out this window in the morning. There's an English garden and a small orchard."

"Wonderful." She suppressed a yawn. "I'm sorry. It's not the company."

He caressed her cheek. "You look very tired, love. Why don't you go to bed?"

She emptied her cup and set it aside. "You're not coming?"

He stood and began to clear away the dishes. "I'll take care of these, and then I hope to have a bath as well." He stooped to kiss her before leaving with the tray.

The bed was so high she needed a footstool to climb into it. She sank down into the cushy mattress and pressed her palms against her cheeks. She'd smiled so much her face ached. She'd never even dreamed that such happiness existed.

Robert's first order of business was to make an appointment with William Boston, who had been his mentor and closest ally for many years. After much prayer and consideration, he'd decided to confide in him.

"So what are you telling me, Robert?" William asked.

"You were right about Mr. Conners, I'm afraid. I believe he must have slipped something into her drink that night. Whatever happened, she had no memory of it, and he took no responsibility for it."

They sat in Robert's office at Woods-Sanderson, in the new leather chairs Robert had added to the decor. A bank of windows afforded a view of Main Street and enough blue sky to lighten their moods.

Robert poured coffee into Woods-Sanderson china cups and handed one to William, who took it, added two lumps of sugar, and stirred it.

"So what you're telling me," he repeated slowly, "is that Nancy is with child by Nate Conners?"

"Yes." Robert swallowed his ire. He hated to hear the words spoken aloud.

"And you—having full knowledge of this—married her?"

Robert sat back in his chair and took a sip of creamy coffee. "I think you know how I feel about Nancy. What happened is unfortunate, but it does not change my feelings for her. I acted out of love and respect for her. I certainly do not want to see her humiliated by Mr. Conners."

"Then he very nearly won," William whispered.

Robert held his cup with both hands and sat forward. "What do you mean?"

William set his coffee down on the side table and propped his elbows on the chair arms. His fingers intertwined as he concentrated his gaze on Robert. "When he found out about the will, he suddenly lost interest in her. Not too surprising. But I would be wary, Robert. He may not give up so easily."

Robert narrowed his eyes. "What can I do, or what should I do to ensure our security?"

William thought for a moment. "Are you referring to the child or your marriage?"

"I don't want him trying to use his paternity against us, either to claim the child or—"

"Use him as a means for extortion?"

"There's a good possibility of either, I'd say. I want to take whatever steps may be necessary to protect Nancy and the child."

"Well, his paternity cannot be exactly proven. He could shed doubt, of course, and people being people, you know as well as I do how that goes. But it's his word against yours, and I'd say they'd come nearer believing you. There's not much else you can do, legally, other than what you've already done. You're a good man Robert, a very good man. Nancy's lucky to have you."

"She deserves better. She's young yet, though she's grown up a lot in the last few weeks. It has been rather difficult for her." He drained his cup and set it aside.

In the silence that ensued, Robert remembered something William had said. "What did you mean earlier about Mr. Conners having very nearly won?"

William glanced up. "Amelia tried all those years—tried to keep them away—but they found a way to get to her. Right under her nose, they found a way."

Robert stared at William. Who was he talking about? Who found a way? He held his tongue and waited to see if William would continue. After several minutes of silence, it became apparent that he would not. "Who are *they*, William?"

William looked as if he had forgotten Robert's presence. "Why Georgia's family, of course."

"Georgia. Nancy's mother?"

William nodded. "Since you are now part of the family, this concerns you, too. I suppose I should tell you about it to arm you against any further trouble. Doubtless, Amelia would have, had she lived."

After taking a deep breath and releasing it slowly, William continued. "William Sanderson, when he was very young— before he met Amelia—had an affair with Georgia's mother, Liz Elliott."

As William's words sunk in, Robert's heart raced. It couldn't be.

"No, Georgia was not his child. There was no child as a result of the affair. But the woman was infuriated with him over dropping her and marrying Amelia. Of course, he married Amelia for her money, but they were well suited and did very well together. Liz waited until William and Amelia's son, Franklin was of marriageable age. I've always believed Liz saw her chance at revenge and sent her daughter after him. The girl won him, of course, very much against his mother's wishes."

"But then they were killed before Liz—Georgia's mother—could get her hands on any of the money," Robert said.

William blew out a slow breath. "Yes, they were killed, which very nearly broke Amelia's heart." After several moments, he continued. "When Liz tried to get her hands on Nancy, Amelia got a court order. She used her name and her money against the woman. For the time, Liz could do nothing. Until Nancy grew older and she found a way to get to her, without our knowledge." William gazed at Robert. "Nate Conners is the son of Liz's younger sister, Inez."

Robert froze. "But that would mean ... Nate is Nancy's cousin?"

William closed his eyes then opened them. "No. They would be, if Georgia had been Liz's natural child. But she was not. Georgia was raised by Liz. No one knew for certain who her mother was."

Robert relaxed. But his mind raced ahead. "So you believe this was all an elaborate scheme to get at Amelia's money?"

"It may not have begun that way," William answered. "They may have met quite by accident. I prefer to think that is the case."

"So when Liz found out he was seeing her, you think she got involved?"

"May have. It's all conjecture, of course. We could never prove any of it." He slapped the desk lightly and looked up at Robert. "I'm glad you stepped in when you did."

A sudden thought occurred to Robert. "How far do you think Liz would go to exact her revenge, William?"

"Why do you ask?"

"Sissy found a handkerchief beside Amelia's bed the morning she reported the death. The monogram on that handkerchief is EAE."

Chapter Twenty-One

Autumn, 1926

Nancy's clothes no longer fit her. She felt conspicuously fat and tried very hard to cover the evidence. Robert told her she was more beautiful than ever and should be proud of her condition.

"Everyone is congratulating you. They're happy for us, so you should be, too." He leaned his forehead against hers. "You're bringing new life into the world."

Nancy set her jaw. "They are all counting the months. I hear them whispering as I walk away. They're expecting me to give birth early."

"Then they'll be disappointed. We outsmarted them, remember?" He lifted her chin with his fingers and peered into her eyes. "You look for all the world like a little girl when you pout like that. A very beautiful little girl."

"Be quiet. You're just trying to make me feel better."

"Is it working?"

She smiled but made no answer.

"Oh, by the way, Mother and Dad have asked us to dinner after church on Sunday."

Nancy nodded. Church had been one of the many changes in her life since her marriage. Robert and his family always attended services. Grandmother had felt it unnecessary to attend services except on Christmas and Easter, but she raised Nancy to respect religion and the Bible. Certain scriptures were to be committed to memory, especially those that pertained to honoring your elders.

The members of the Emersons' church seemed genuine and happy. They discussed ways to help their neighbors whenever there were needs. Of course, many of the people who attended First Church were well able to help their neighbors. They also supported missionaries who lived in foreign lands throughout the world. Nancy had never even thought of such things.

This difference in their upbringings sometimes gapped in front of Nancy like a great chasm. Though Robert never talked to her about his faith, she had always known there was something different about him. An honorable man in every way, he possessed an even temper and a good nature.

She regarded him as he dressed for work. Though he seemed to give little attention to his appearance, he was always immaculate, clean-shaven, every hair in place. How different from—no, she would not allow those thoughts.

When Robert turned to face her, she made a pretense of straightening his already perfectly knotted tie. After a quick kiss good-bye, he donned his hat and coat. "I'll probably be late tonight. There's a meeting of the board at four."

She opened her mouth then closed it again.

His brow crinkled. "What?"

Dare she ask?

His face reflected a slight trace of impatience at her delay.

She pushed the words out. "Could I be copied on the minutes of the board meeting?"

"Really? They're quite boring, Nancy. Wouldn't you rather have a novel to read?" He opened the door but stood looking back at her.

"I'd like to keep up. That's all."

He touched the brim of his hat. "All right. I'll order an extra copy."

She enjoyed success for a brief moment. Why had he seemed displeased? Wasn't it her company, too? He should want her to take an interest. She rested her hand on her swollen belly as she watched him walk down the street.

They lived only a couple of blocks from Woods-Sanderson's main office, so he often walked to work. When he disappeared around the corner, her eyes were drawn to the early sunlight filtering through a large maple tree on the side lawn. Its leaves had turned a glorious golden yellow almost overnight.

After choosing a book, she strolled out to the yard. Two white Adirondack chairs, separated by a small side table, sat beneath the maple tree, Nancy's favorite spot. She'd only been there a few minutes when Kip approached carrying a blanket.

"Miss Nancy, it's a bit chilly out here. I thought you might like a cover."

He had never stopped calling her "Miss Nancy," but she didn't mind. "Thank you, Kip. I appreciate that." Perkins, the housekeeper they'd hired to replace Sissy soon followed with hot coffee.

Nancy knew these two were most likely responding to orders from Robert. She could hear him whispering, "Watch over my girl while I'm gone."

"Thank you both. I am quite comfortable, and you may tell Mr. Emerson you've done your best."

They left her to relax in the big tree's golden shade. Robert's thoughtful care for her diminished her piqued feelings somewhat. She'd wait and see if he brought her the promised meeting minutes.

Nancy had a penchant for classic novels, but today, *Jane Eyre* could not keep her attention. She set it aside and sipped her coffee. As the child moved within her, she closed her eyes and tried to imagine what it would be like to hold it in her arms. How sweet it would be to have a little girl, all dressed in cream and pink. But would she look like her father?

Nancy's eyes flew open as panic stirred in her breast. She sat forward, her heart racing, her eyes darting this way and that. She'd detected a hint of cigarette smoke on the breeze. Had she heard someone whistling? Did he watch her?

After a moment, she forced herself to breathe deeply. *Calm down.* She held her breath and listened. Birdsong filled the air. She had only imagined it. There was no one near.

John Franklin Emerson was born on the fifth of November. John, after Senator John Perry, called "Jack" by all his friends, and Franklin, after Nancy's father. When Dahlia, the nurse-midwife, laid the child in her arms, Nancy gave a satisfied sigh. The child was not the tiny embodiment of Nate that she had dreaded, but as everyone commented, very like his mother. The tuft of hair on his head shone light and fine, not dark and coarse.

Dahlia tucked the covers around her. "You want Mr. Emerson to come in now?"

Nancy couldn't take her eyes from the child's face. She nodded. How would he react now that the child was there? Her gaze flew to Robert's when he entered the room.

He pushed the door closed and crossed the space between them in two long strides. As he crouched beside the bed, his eyes held hers. "How are you?"

"I'm fine," she whispered, and dropped her gaze to the child.

Robert's eyes filled with wonder as a slow smile worked its way into his expression. He reached tentative fingers to touch the baby's face. When his eyes found hers again, they reflected love. He leaned forward and kissed her lips.

"I love you, Nancy, more than life itself. I am honored that you have given me the chance to prove it."

"Do you want to hold him?"

He held out his hands, and she placed the child in them, cupping one hand beneath his to show him how to support the baby's head. He dropped his lips to the child's forehead and breathed in. The child stirred and yawned. He and Nancy laughed.

"Hello, John Franklin Emerson," he said.

Nancy's eyes brimmed over.

"She's still asleep," someone whispered. The voice sounded familiar.

Nancy forced her eyes open. Rebecca.

As Perkins lifted the shades, sunlight spilled into the room, dazzling Nancy's still sleepy eyes. Rebecca's face floated above her. "Are you going to sleep all day, you lazy bum?"

Nancy giggled and pushed herself up onto her elbows. Pain.

Her face must have reflected it, because Rebecca drew in a quick breath. "Oh, don't hurt yourself. I can only imagine the pain, of course."

Perkins stood at the end of the bed. "Shall I call the nurse, ma'am?"

"No, not yet. I could use some extra pillows, though. And breakfast." She gazed up at Rebecca. "I'm starving."

"I'll bet you are."

She pushed herself up and forward while Perkins placed the pillows. Then she relaxed and released a shallow breath. "That's better, thank you."

After Perkins left, Nancy gazed at Rebecca. Always smartly dressed, today she wore a long-sleeved burgundy dress, gathered below the waist and adorned with exactly the right amount of lace. "Please sit down. I'm sure there's a chair about, somewhere. When did you arrive?"

"Robert called me last night with the good news. I took the early train." She plopped down on the foot of the bed and eyed Nancy. "So how is married life?"

Nancy smiled. "Better than I imagined. Robert is wonderful."

Rebecca chuckled. "You're such a newlywed. I hope you'll always be so happy. I've seen the baby. He's a little charmer."

Nancy sighed. "I barely remember him. I suppose they'll bring him around soon."

"Oh yes. Dahlia said as soon as you've had your breakfast, she'll bring him in. She said you need to practice feeding him." She shook herself. "That'll be my cue to leave."

"So you're on a first-name basis with the nurse already?"

"Of course. You know me. I've been quite chatty with all the inhabitants of the Emerson villa. Including Juliana. She's positively beaming. You'd think she'd given birth to the boy."

Rebecca stood when Perkins returned with a food-laden tray and placed it in front of Nancy. Before leaving, Perkins brought a chair for Rebecca.

Rebecca scowled at Nancy. "I guess she didn't like me sitting on the bed."

Nancy dismissed it with a wave of her hand. "She's just making you comfortable. How are you? It's been an age since I've had a letter from you."

"I've been busy, my friend. Very, very busy." She held up her hand to show off a very large, very sparkly diamond ring. Nancy almost dropped her fork.

"Oh my goodness, how do you bear the weight of that? Here, let me have a closer look." She held Rebecca's hand in hers and turned the ring to examine it. She lifted her gaze to Rebecca's. "Who is he?"

"His name is Riccardo Alverà. He's a Count."

"A Count? You'll be a Countess?"

Rebecca lifted her nose in the air. "Indeed."

After sharing a giggle with her friend, Nancy sobered. "Do you love him?"

Rebecca pulled her hand away. "He's good to me, Nancy. He loves me. I think I can love him. He's practically promised me the moon." She grinned. "I asked for a blue one."

Nancy had to laugh, though her heart ached for Rebecca. But before she could ask anything further, the door opened again.

Robert stuck his head in. "I'm sorry to disturb you two, but our son is hungry."

Nancy set the tray aside. "Of course, please bring him."

Rebecca stooped to kiss Nancy's brow. "I'll be in town a few days. We'll have plenty of time to catch up." She left the room just ahead of Dahlia's entering with the baby.

Rebecca joined Nancy for lunch two days later. Nancy hoped to delve more deeply into Rebecca's upcoming nuptials, but her friend resisted her efforts.

"I'm wondering about something, Nancy."

Nancy buttered a hot roll, observed the expression on her friend's face, and hesitated. "Seems ominous. What is it?"

Rebecca relaxed and sipped her tea. "Have you heard anything of Nate recently?"

Nancy busied her hands to hide a tremble. She finished buttering her roll, tore it in half, and took a bite. Rebecca continued to stare at her. Nancy took up her napkin and patted her lips. "Not since that night at your house."

"He visited me, not long after the announcement of your elopement."

Nancy cut into the braised beef on her plate. The savory dish was one of her favorites. "I'm sure he had an opinion about it."

Rebecca smiled. "That he did. He had doubts about the exact date, I believe."

"And do you share those doubts?"

Rebecca bit into her roll. "This is delicious. I must have the recipe."

Her smile reminded Nancy of the old days. "Rebecca?"

"Whatever doubts I may have entertained at one time have all been dissipated by the apparent joy in your marriage. You two give me hope. But don't let down your guard."

Their eyes met. "What do you mean by that?"

"Don't let him back into your life. Not in any way. Not ever. He can't be trusted."

Nancy's heartbeat quickened. "You think he'll make trouble?"

Rebecca glanced over her shoulder.

Nancy half expected to see his dark face hiding behind the curtains. She shook off the feeling.

Rebecca leaned forward. "Just keep your guard up. That's all I'm saying. He was not your best decision, Nancy. I hope we've heard the last of him. I truly do. But he had such a knack of turning up."

"Yes, he did." She eyed Rebecca and allowed a brief smile. "Are you trying to divert my attention from your future plans?"

"Ha-ha." Her voice lacked humor. "No, that is not my intention. I really am concerned about you, doll. The last time I spoke with him, he scared me a little."

"That's surprising. Not the part about Nate being scary, but I don't believe I've ever seen you rattled."

Rebecca released a pent-up breath. "Yes, well. With age comes sensibility."

Nancy grinned. "I thought it was, 'with age comes beauty.'"

Rebecca laughed out loud. "That, too." She leaned forward again and took Nancy's hand in hers. "Promise me you'll take care."

Nancy nodded and squeezed her hand. "I promise." In the back of her mind, doubt lurked. Had Rebecca guessed their secret?

Chapter Twenty-Two

The excitement of the holiday season fell far short of the former one for Nancy. So much had happened in between the two. Even shopping for a new wardrobe felt dull and lifeless. She broke down and cried when she realized she had no jewelry to wear except for the necklace Grandmother had given her for high school graduation. She was putting it on when Robert walked in, carrying a light blue box.

"I can't give you what you lost, but I can start a new collection."

Sapphires and diamonds sparkled against the white satin interior of the box, a necklace and earrings. "Oh, Robert, they're beautiful." She stood and leaned into his arms.

"Are you almost ready? We should get going."

She clipped the earrings onto her earlobes and picked up the necklace. "Yes, as soon as I have this in place."

He took it from her and fastened it then dropped a kiss on her neck. "Lovely."

She took another moment to admire her reflection before following him out of the room.

"They're all talking about us," Nancy whispered as Robert removed his jacket and hung it over the back of the bedroom chair. The Woods-Sanderson luncheon lay behind them. The DAR Holiday Dinner loomed ahead of them.

Robert loosened his tie. "Of course they are. They were talking about us last year, too. You know that." He put his arms around her. "Don't let this get to you. You're stronger than that. I've seen it." He drew back from her, his gaze threatening to penetrate her resolve. "What is it? I know something's bothering you. It's more than just that people are talking, isn't it?"

Nancy pulled away from him and sat down on the edge of the bed. "I feel … so guilty. I can't seem to shake it. And the worst is, everywhere I go, I expect to see … *him*. I'm afraid I'll see him." So great was her guilt, she could barely bring herself to look at Robert.

His shocked expression only fueled that discomfort.

A tear fell onto her arm. She swept it away.

"Nancy." He dropped down in front of her and took her hands in his. "Why did you not tell me? Why have you been carrying this alone?"

She couldn't lift her eyes to his. Worst of all, she felt the tears coming on. She didn't want to cry. She had cried enough.

"Have you seen or heard from him at all?"

She shook her head.

"Then why are you afraid? Do you suspect he may come around or cause trouble?"

"No. Not really. I just … if I saw him in public, I think I would …"

"You'd be uncomfortable, of course," Robert finished for her. "But, Nancy, he never admitted to anything. Never took responsibility at all. And Little Jack doesn't even look that much like him."

She glanced up at him. "Not that much? You think he does a little, though?"

Robert rose and sat down next to her. "Nancy, of course he does a little—a very little—and only because I know the truth. The man is his father, after all. But unless someone knew to look for it, I don't think anyone else would see it." He lifted her chin with his fingertips. "He looks too much like his mother. And in that, he is very blessed."

She gazed into his eyes, wondering what thoughts were lurking there. "Do you know what I think it is?"

He tilted his head. "What?"

"I think it's the pressure of living this lie." She'd finally managed to put it into words. Such a simple statement. The seed of all her fears. A deep, dark ball of pain inside her. Many times in her past, she'd lied—to her grandmother—to everyone. But she'd been a child then. Now it was different. She lived every day with the knowledge of her indiscretion. Robert had overlooked it, had covered it for her, but it remained in her heart, eating away at her, making her sick. How could she go on like this?

His eyes softened. "So what do you suggest we do about it?"

She heard the concern in his voice and shook her head, unable to hold back the tears. She collapsed on the bed, sobbing out all the pent-up fear and emotional pain. Robert reclined beside her to comfort her. When the tide of emotion subsided, he handed her a handkerchief and waited while she blew her nose.

When she remained quiet, he said, "What do you need from me, Nancy? What can I do to help you?"

She touched his face, caressed his strong jaw and the dimple in his cheek. "You have been so good to me. You have loved me regardless of what I have done in the past. You have accepted my son, loving him without reservation. How could I ask you to do anything more?"

He dimpled. "The king regarded Esther and said, 'Ask what you will and you shall have it, to the half of my kingdom.'"

She squeezed her eyes shut to the memory of her last conversation with Nate, when he urged her to marry Robert then to divorce him and take half of everything. An imaginary demonic face grinned at her now, taunted her.

She drew in a deep breath and forced herself to return Robert's smile. "To the half of your kingdom?"

He sat up, laid his fist over his heart, and said, "Yes, my lady, to see you smile again is worth anything."

She sat up and gazed into his eyes. She couldn't laugh, though he was in so jovial a mood. "May I have your forgiveness?"

His smile faded. "Oh, Nancy, there's nothing to forgive."

"Please, Robert. I need this."

He cupped her face in his hands. "Yes, Nancy, I forgive you. I forgive you for your part in what happened."

She relaxed against him and allowed herself to feel again, the comfort of his embrace, the touch of his lips as he kissed the top of her head. "Thank you."

Chapter Twenty-Three

Nancy kissed Jack and smoothed his hair. She tucked a warm blanket around him and then tiptoed out of the nursery and down the hall to the upstairs parlor where a woman sat knitting.

The woman looked up. "Finally asleep?"

Nancy nodded and smiled. "Yes, it's as if he knew I was trying to leave."

Sissy's cousin, Grace Boggs, had come to live with them soon after Jack's birth. A widow in her early forties, trained as a pediatric nurse, she fit well into the household. Jack adored her.

Grace set her knitting aside. "You want me to call Kip?"

"No, it's such a mild day. I think I'd like to walk."

Grace sniffed. "You just try to sneak past Kip."

Nancy smirked as she picked up a satchel. "We'll see. I'll be back before Jack's dinner."

Nancy didn't worry about Kip. She knew how to placate him. She was only going a few blocks to the house where she'd grown up. A light dusting of new snow covered the ground as she let herself out the side door. Kip was sweeping the sidewalk. He turned at Nancy's approach. "Miz Nancy, you need me to take you somewhere?"

"I thought I'd walk to the house, Kip. I can use the fresh air." When Kip's brow furrowed, his hairline rose. He'd reach up to push his hat down. The sight always made Nancy smile. She promised to let him drive her home and asked him to come for her at four.

She'd made the decision to sell her grandmother's house in the spring. Robert wanted to retain the country house, so they'd send what furnishings she wished to keep there.

The house had been empty since Sissy had gone to stay with her sister in Connecticut. A little too quiet.

She let herself in. She almost wished she'd brought Grace and Jack.

Taking a quick tour of the house, the only piece of furniture she felt she really couldn't part with was her grandmother's desk. The ancient piece of furniture had been in the Woods family for years. She tried to open the drawer. It was locked. Where would Grandmother keep the key? She rifled through papers on top of the desk, even checked the floor beneath it. As she shuffled through some things on the bookshelves, she smelled cigarette smoke. Had someone left a window open? She turned, intent on checking the windows but stopped dead.

Nate leaned against the doorjamb in his usual languid fashion, hands in his pockets, a cigarette hanging from his lips.

The wild throbbing of her heart filled her ears as panic rose in her throat. She swallowed before forcing out the words, "What are you doing here?"

He removed the cigarette then whistled and arched his brows at her. "It's chilly in here, and I'm not talking about the temperature. Not exactly the welcome I expected."

She struggled to keep her voice steady. "You have no right to be here."

He threw his head back and laughed then leveled his gaze at her. "Don't you sound like the old lady?" As he inched forward, her heart froze. He'd never frightened her ... until now. He took a long draw on the cigarette then blew a puff of smoke into the air between them. "I heard you had the baby. A fine strapping boy." He grinned. "You should be grateful to ole Nate."

Nancy coughed to rid her lungs of the foul smoke. "And why would that be?"

He stopped, several feet away from her. "Why? I gave you a son, made your present life possible. Why not, I'd say."

Nancy stood looking at him for a long moment. All the while, her mind raced. What should she do? As she considered her situation, terror sunk its claws into her heart. She grasped the notepad and pencil to hide the trembling in her hands.

"I ... I really don't ... think you should be here, Nate."

"Oh?" He took another step. "Do I ... bother you?" He licked his lips, clearly enjoying every second.

His insolence in the face of her discomfort angered her. She straightened and met his impudent gaze. "Of course not, not in the way you're thinking. You've no right to be here. I don't wish to see you anymore."

He took a long stride to stand in front of her. Then reaching around her, he crushed the cigarette out on the smooth wood of her grandmother's desk. His eyes raked over her and he grinned. "Well, you are seeing me, whether you wish to or not. I have a matter to discuss with you, and when that's done I'll leave, and not before."

She took a backward step, right into the side of the desk. But she kept her head high and forced herself to breathe. She would not give him the upper hand. "What matter?"

If only Kip would return. Or someone ... anyone. Her eyes darted about, looking for an exit, but he blocked the only way out.

He clearly had no intention of moving.

She glanced at the phone but remembered it had been disconnected.

"Nancy, sweetheart, you don't need to be afraid of me. You know I wouldn't hurt you. We've been friends a long time."

"We *were* friends, Nate. You abused that friendship. Friends don't—"

He chuckled softly and looked away for a moment, thumbing his chin. "Friends don't what, Nancy?"

He crossed to the desk, picked up a paperweight, and bounced it in his hands. "*We* had too much to drink, and *we* made a mistake. That's all. If you want to put the blame on me, that's fine. I don't mind." He grinned down at her.

This was the first time he'd ever admitted what he'd done. "This isn't about blame, Nate. This is about where we go from here. I would like never to see you again. In view of our past friendship, you should respect my wishes."

"That sounds downright unfriendly, sweetheart. I'd be willing to oblige, though—for a price."

She set the notebook and pencil on the desk and faced him. "Ah, now we get to the real reason for your visit."

"You know me, Nance. I never walk away from an opportunity. I figure my help should be worth something to you."

"Your ... help?"

"Sure, I've given you an heir. Who knows if the great Mr. Emerson can do that for you? Maybe it's why he was in such an all-fired hurry to marry you. After all, he didn't really need you to get your money, did he?"

Nancy bit back a retort. She wanted to slap him but remembered the last time she'd done that. Better not to provoke him.

Silent, he watched her. His harsh gaze erased every good memory she had of him.

"What is it you want, Nate?"

"I've always been intrigued by your natural beauty. Anger only intensifies it. I love to see the fire in your eyes." He licked his lips and took a step nearer.

Seething, Nancy searched the room for something, anything to use as a weapon against him should he advance another step.

His vile laughter echoed through the empty house. "Now there's a beautiful sight. I don't want much, Mrs. Emerson. Five hundred a month will pay for my silence."

Nancy swallowed hard. *Dear God, what should I do?* She closed her eyes for a moment, wishing Nate would simply disappear. Perhaps this was all a bad dream, a really bad dream.

"That's only six thousand a year, sweetheart. It's worth it, don't ya think? You get a beautiful baby boy, and I don't tell anybody where you were the day—or rather the night before your supposed wedding with the fine Mr. Emerson. You'd be doing him a favor, too. What would people think if they knew he'd lied about the wedding date? You see, I remember our conversation weeks following that blessed event, when you begged me to marry you. You swore you could never marry him. Yeah, Nate never forgets.

"All I want to know is how he got someone to put the wrong date on a marriage certificate. I believe that's illegal, darling." He watched her.

Had he just figured that out on his own, or had he somehow seen the wedding certificate? How was that even possible?

"Five hundred a month, sweetheart. Think of what you'll be doing for your fine husband—saving his reputation."

Nancy wrung her hands in silence, trying to concentrate. Her lips trembled as she spoke. "The only way I will agree is if I never see you again." She wouldn't look at him.

He scoffed. "Can't promise that, sweetheart. Small town, you know? But I'll do my best to avoid you, as long as the money comes promptly."

A horn sounding down below almost sent Nancy through the roof. She was all nerves and hadn't calmed any since Nate left. Now she must try to pull herself together before she went downstairs. She didn't want Kip to see her so upset. He would surely report it to Robert.

She splashed a little water on her face at the bathroom sink. At the bottom of the stairs, she slipped into her coat, gathered her purse and gloves, and took a deep breath. She let it out slowly before heading for the door.

Kip chattered away on the drive back home. Any other time, Nancy would welcome the conversation, but right now, all she wanted to think about was how to live the rest of her life with the burden that had so recently been placed on her.

She gazed out the window. People walked along the streets as if nothing had changed. Two boys rolled a hoop down an alley. The grocer stood at his door, arms akimbo, watching a younger man sweep the sidewalk. Nancy pressed her fingertips against her temples and closed her eyes.

The money was of little consequence since Robert had set up an account for her personal spending. The account grew every month with interest from Grandmother's estate. She swallowed the lump in her throat at the thought of any kind of dealings with that man. Why had this happened now, so soon after she'd finally forgiven herself?

She'd hoped and believed it was all over, but now it seemed she must go through life paying for the mistake she'd made. And she could never tell Robert. How would he react if he knew she'd seen Nate?

The scene played out in her imagination: Robert, disheveled from a sleepless night after arguing with her, shoots

Nate. Nate falls dead on the ground. Detectives Pressman and Lawson come to take Robert away to prison.

Worse yet, Nate could harm Robert. She shook her head. No, she couldn't let anything like that happen. Robert had become too important to her. She must keep the secret.

Chapter Twenty-Four

Summer, 1928

"I can hardly believe how tall Jack is," Juliana Emerson told Nancy. She and Nancy planned a garden party to raise money for the local children's ward. "Will Robert be in town for the party?"

"I hope so, but there's no guarantee. You know what his schedule's been like."

Juliana touched Nancy's cheek. "Yes, dear I know. How are you holding up?"

Nancy forced what she hoped was a brave smile. "Well enough. I'm so thankful for Florence."

"I've heard good things of her. When Robert first mentioned hiring her, I had my doubts. I thought you could better use a full-time housekeeper."

Nancy cast a sideways glance at her mother-in-law. "Should I be offended by that?"

Juliana's laughter echoed in the high-ceilinged parlor. "Please don't take that wrong. I thought it might free you from household chores. That's all."

Nancy smiled into her teacup. She seldom saw Juliana flustered. "No, this house is easy to care for, and Grace is always happy to help out when Jack is sleeping. Florence keeps my social calendar and helps keep my personal finances in order. She's a godsend."

"I suppose you're right. You do have quite a different set of responsibilities these days." She set her teacup on the tray and rose from her chair. "I'd better go. I have shopping to do, and my portion of the guest list to complete."

"Thank you, Mother. I appreciate your help with this party. Give my love to Dad."

Juliana kissed her cheek as she passed into the foyer. "I will."

As Nancy closed the door behind her mother-in-law, she heard footsteps on the stairs. She turned to see Grace descending.

"I've read so many goose tales, I'm befuddled, but the boy's finally napping."

Nancy chuckled softly. Jack loved his stories. "After your tea, I need you to help me take inventory of the pantry. The garden party is coming up."

Crinkles deepened around Grace's dark eyes. "Yes, ma'am. I'll be glad to help."

Nancy spent the next few minutes making a list of friends and colleagues so Florence could make out the invitations.

Juliana was right to worry. Nancy found it difficult to accept Robert's long absences. The business needed his strong leadership, but that knowledge didn't make her path any easier. She glanced at the calendar. He'd be leaving again in three days. She blew out a sharp breath, took up her pad and pencil, and went to join Grace in the pantry.

The garden party was a huge success. Nancy and Juliana counted nearly twenty-five thousand dollars in donations for the children's ward.

"I'll drop this off at the hospital on my way home," Juliana told Nancy. "Won't they be surprised?" She bent forward to kiss Nancy's brow. "Why don't you get some rest? You look pale."

Nancy helped Juliana gather the donations into an envelope. "Thanks for all your help, Mother. I could not have done this without you."

"I was happy to help."

Minutes after Juliana's car pulled out of the drive, Jack toddled up to Nancy and stretched his arms up.

Grace followed behind him. "Now, Jack, you come back here. Leave your momma alone. She's tuckered out."

Nancy knelt to embrace him. "Oh, he's all right. Let's go out in the yard, Jack. Would you like that?" She glanced up at Grace. "I can rest out there just as well, and Jack can play."

"All right, if that's what you want. I'll bring you some of that lemonade and a bite to eat."

"Good idea." She started out the door. Jack ran in front of her, and she had to trot to catch up. How could those short legs move so fast? They headed for the back garden, beneath an oak tree. Grace brought a quilt for Jack to play on. Nancy sat beside him in a white wicker chair. After their snack, she sipped the lemonade and read a novel. Within the hour, her active eighteen-month old had collapsed on the quilt beside her, sound asleep. The deep shade of the oak tree gave such a sense of privacy. She lay her head back and relaxed.

Her eyes were closed, and she sat in the shade, so why did she suddenly feel as if a shadow had passed over the sun? Icy fingers of dread danced up her spine as an all-too-familiar voice spoke.

"Aren't you the picture of contentment?"

She nearly fell out of her chair. "Nate?"

He stood with his back to the sun, his face in shadow. She jumped up, wanting to keep Jack's presence from him, but she was too late. Nate pushed past her to crouch beside the blanket.

She reached out her hands but stopped short of touching him. "You shouldn't come here."

He sent a scathing glance over his shoulder. "Would you keep me from ever seeing the boy, Nancy? After what your grandmother did to you?"

Her heart beat so hard she felt faint. She glanced toward the house, wishing for someone to come and rescue her. She'd never wanted Nate to see Jack, or Jack to see Nate, for that matter.

"He's a fine-looking little man. Rambunctious, too, just like his daddy."

Nancy swallowed the lump in her throat. So he'd been watching them.

He stood up and faced her. "There, there, Nancy, don't fret. I only came by to let you know I'll be needing a little more money." He chuckled at the expression on her face. "An extra hundred a month ought to do it."

"What? I can't give you more money." She closed her eyes briefly. Why couldn't she wake from this nightmare? "No, I won't do it."

Nate nodded as if he'd anticipated her refusal. He grinned at her as he pulled out a cigarette, held it between his lips and lit it. He took a long pull, removed it, and blew the smoke in her face.

"I need the extra cash to help take care of *your* grandmother."

Nancy stared back at him, speechless. What did he mean? Her grandmother was dead.

"You don't know, do you? Your fine Mr. Emerson hasn't told you about it? I'm talking about your *other* grandmother, sweetheart—your mama's mama—Elizabeth Elliott. Your husband had her put away."

Nancy's knees went weak. She gripped the back of the chair to steady herself. "Put away?"

"In an asylum … claimed she killed Amelia Sanderson."

"You don't know what you're talking about. If anything like that had happened, I would know about it."

"Well, honey, evidently you don't know everything, 'cause my Aunt Liz is in the asylum. They put her there, your husband and William Boston, all quiet-like, not wanting to cause a scandal. Now we have to take care of her, and unlike you and yours, my family doesn't have wads of money lying around."

Nancy blinked, not knowing whether to believe him. She looked down at the child he'd fathered then slowly back at him. Aunt Liz?

She didn't like his expression. He had changed over the years. Not in a good way. Something about him triggered an odd memory … a dark dream from her childhood.

He took a step nearer.

She sucked in a quick breath.

"It seems that you and I are not the only ones with a secret. What do you think of your wonderful Mr. Emerson now?"

"That's none of your business." It was the only thing she could think of to say. It sounded weak and childish to her ears.

"I got a rise out of you anyway." He narrowed his eyes and leaned close to her. "Ever wonder why he spends so much time in New York?"

"Go away, Nate. I'll pay the extra. Just go away!"

"Mama?" Jack cried, jumping up and running to her. He reached up, clearly frightened. No doubt he'd heard the tone of her voice and sensed trouble.

She grabbed him and held him tightly against her, shielding his face from this ugly man. Without a word or a backward look, she turned toward the house. She forced herself to walk, though she wanted to run.

Nancy's nerves were frazzled. She snapped at Jack then at Grace Boggs, who cast her a strange look.

"I'm so sorry, Grace," Nancy said. "I've got a terrible headache. Could you take over with Jack? I'm going up to lie down."

Grace's expression relaxed. "Is there anything I can get for you?"

Nancy drew in a shaky breath and slowly exhaled. "No, thank you. Please take care of Jack for me. I need rest, that's all."

She closed the door of her room and sat on the edge of the bed. Hard as she tried, she could not dispel Nate's words. Robert had indeed been away a lot lately. Even now, he was in New York, had been there for two weeks. Labor problems, he'd told her. That much she knew was true. It was all over the news—rioting and violence in the streets. Woods-Sanderson had never been touched by labor problems. Their employees were well paid. Now those employees were being wooed by labor unions and trouble brewed.

Robert did keep her in the loop regarding the company. After every meeting of the board, she received her copy of the minutes. One day she'd venture into one of those meetings. She looked forward to that day and seeing the looks on their faces. Especially Robert's. Would he be proud of her or would he forbid her return?

She removed her shoes and lay down on the bed. He called her every day, but still Nate's words stung her, especially after the revelation regarding Elizabeth Elliott. Why had Robert not told her?

She stayed in bed the rest of the day. When she awoke the next morning, she really did have a bad headache.

She got up and dressed to go out. She'd made up her mind to do a little detecting on her own before Robert returned from New York. Then, if he tried to lie about it, she would know the truth.

She made it as far as the front drive.

As Kip went to open the car door, Nancy fainted. She came to, lying on her bed. Grace had called the doctor.

"Kip got to you just before your head hit the ground. Poor man nearly had a heart attack."

After examining Nancy, Dr. Farber sat down opposite her. "You're expecting a baby, Nancy."

Nancy bit her lower lip. "So soon? I didn't realize. I thought I was just tired."

Dr. Farber grinned. "I'm sure you are, with an active toddler in the house." He snapped shut his medical bag then rose to go. "You should take it easy for a while. Get plenty of rest. Come and see me in about a month."

By the time Robert returned later in the evening, Nancy lay in bed, sipping warm milk.

He sat in the chair near the window, his eyes on her.

"Are you all right? Grace said they had to call Dr. Farber."

She set her cup aside and gazed into his expectant face. "Dr. Farber says I'm due in early spring."

For a moment, he said nothing. He just sat there staring at her. "You what?"

She nodded. "In the spring."

A slow smile made its way across his face. "A baby?"

She laughed out loud. "Are you in shock?"

He nodded. "I think so." He knelt beside her, took her hand and pressed it to his lips. "How do you feel?"

"A little scared."

"Scared? Why?"

"I'm not sure." She looked deep into his eyes. "What about you?"

He grinned. "Let's have a little girl."

She gave a soft chuckle. "That would be nice."

He rose and removed his jacket then went to hang it up in the wardrobe. "Grace said you've been overwrought."

Should she speak her mind? She drew a breath.

He slipped out of his shirt and laid it on the chair.

With her fingers, she traced the stitches in the quilt on their bed. "I have been tired lately."

He sat on the edge of the bed. "You'll need to take better care of yourself now."

"That's what Dr. Farber said. Not as easy as it sounds."

"That's why we have Grace and Florence. Let them take on more responsibility. It's only for a while." He reached for her hand. "Nancy, I've done everything I know to help you."

"Everything except stay home."

His crestfallen look caused her immediate sorrow. She'd answered too quickly.

He kept his voice low, but firm. "You know I have to travel. This latest ruckus with the union is the worst so far, and it's not going to go away anytime soon. Would you have me neglect the business?"

"Of course not. I'm sorry."

He leaned in to plant a kiss on her forehead. "I'll go put Jack to bed. Is there anything else I can do for you?"

She shook her head and closed her eyes. A moment later, she heard the door shut softly, and soon afterward, Jack's excited squeals.

By the time Robert returned to their room, Nancy was asleep. He sat down in the chair near the window so he could look at her. Still so beautiful, but changed.

Her words still stung him. She, of all people, should understand his business. He bent down and tugged at the laces of his shoes. After removing the shoes, he spread his toes and dug them into the carpet. It felt good to be home where he could really relax.

He leaned his head back as warmth spread through him. She was carrying his child. He tried not to think about it too much, but it was impossible to ignore for long.

He did love Jack more than he'd ever thought possible, but this would be his child, his flesh and bone. Instead of resembling someone else, this child would look like him.

Chapter Twenty-Five

Nancy needed time to think about Nate's revelation. If she confronted Robert, he'd want to know her source. She couldn't mention Nate without incriminating herself. And she'd no desire to tell another lie. So it only made sense to strike out on her own and find out what she could without Robert's help.

When she felt able to be up and about, she made an appointment with Uncle William.

"Nancy. What a wonderful surprise." William Boston greeted her and escorted her into his office. "May I have my secretary get you something? Tea or coffee?"

"No, thank you, Mr. Boston."

He cleared his throat. "I heard the good news, congratulations."

"Thank you."

He sat down at his desk. "So, why have you come?"

She began to explain what she'd heard, leaving out any reference to Nate. She kept her eyes on his face, watching for any sign of reluctance.

He sat back in his chair and gazed at her. If her discovery troubled him, he didn't show it. When she'd finished her short narrative, he wrote something on a piece of paper and handed it across the desk to her. "Most of what you have heard, my dear, is gossip."

She looked at the paper and read aloud, "Millbrooke Heights." She tilted her head and glanced back at William. "What is Millbrooke Heights?"

His eyes twinkled as he smiled. "Let's just say it's a good place for you to visit on your quest for truth."

She rose slowly from her chair. "I won't take any more of your time then."

He rose and stepped around his desk to join her. He took her hands and bent his head to meet her gaze. "Nancy, two more things, dear. First, why did you stop calling me Uncle William, and why did you not ask Robert about this? I hope you two are not having problems."

She respected him too much to be anything but honest with him. "I'm sorry, Uncle William. I thought perhaps I had outgrown the uncle thing. But apparently not." She smiled and looked down at her hands, still cradled in his. "As to why I didn't ask Robert, I suppose I hate the thought of something like this coming between us. His life is difficult enough at present."

"Yes, it is, but let me tell you something. That man loves you. Don't you ever doubt that. Don't ever, ever be tempted to believe there's someone else."

A chill lifted the hair on the back of her neck. She hadn't mentioned that to anyone. How could he possibly know? How did he always seem to discern thoughts like that? Spooky, just plain spooky.

He dropped her hands. As he opened his office door, he said, "There's nothing new under the sun, Nancy."

After her visit with Uncle William, Nancy decided to locate Millbrooke Heights. She stepped out of the Boston Emerson Law Offices, nearly running into her in-laws.

Juliana gave her a sideways hug. "Oh, Nancy. Why, we were coming to see you. How are you, dear? Robert called and gave us the news. We're thrilled."

Daniel bent to kiss her cheek. "How about lunch?"

Nancy knew exactly where they'd take her. Two doors down—to the best restaurant in town.

The Silver Spoon brimmed with suited gentlemen enjoying a leisurely lunch in the middle of the day. Nancy and her in-laws had just sat down when Robert joined them. He greeted Nancy with joy reminiscent of the old Robert. He seemed truly pleased to see her. All her doubts and fears disintegrated.

After lunch, Juliana and Daniel left, but Robert lingered over coffee. He reached across the table to take her hand in his. "It's so good to see you out, darling." His gaze burned right into her soul, as if to discern her thoughts. "I was thinking about our conversation the other night."

"I'm sorry, Robert. You know I wasn't feeling well."

He held up his hand. "No, it's all right. I have neglected you lately. Please let me make it up to you. Go with me to New York this next trip."

She sat back in her chair. Could she? "I'd like to Robert, but I wouldn't want to be in the way."

He raised her hand to his lips and kissed her fingers while gazing into her eyes. "You'll never be in my way, darling. While I'm in the meetings, you can go shopping. Then we can spend the evenings together. It'll be like the honeymoon we never had."

Heat rushed into her cheeks. With her free hand, she fiddled with the linen napkin then brushed at imaginary crumbs on the tablecloth. "Well, if we can work it out with Grace Boggs."

Robert walked her to the corner where Kip waited with the car. "I'll try not to be so late tonight," he said as he closed the door.

Nancy sat back in the plush seat and smiled. How long had it been since she'd felt so happy?

She pulled out the slip of paper William Boston had given her, folded it, and tucked it back inside her handbag. There would be plenty of time for sleuthing when she returned from New York. Nate had made it sound as if his aunt was in an asylum. But if she remembered right, Millbrooke Heights was a nursing home.

They took the train to New York. As they drew nearer the city, the number of travelers increased. Nancy watched with interest as ladies stepped into their car and found seats. It was like watching a fashion show. And the hats— she made a mental note to visit a milliner while in town. She simply must have some new hats. From the look of things, her entire wardrobe needed a serious update.

The first day out, Robert insisted she accompany him to the New York affiliate of Woods-Sanderson Associates where he introduced her to everyone. She sat in his office while he shuffled through messages and papers. "I'll only be a minute, Nancy. Then we'll go to lunch."

The minute turned into an hour, but Nancy didn't mind. She spent the hour reading *The New York Times* society column. On their way out of the office for lunch, a clerk handed Robert a message.

"Mrs. Wilcox asked that you call her as soon as possible."

Nancy arched a brow at Robert as he continued out the door. "Aren't you going to call her?"

"No." He held the door for her. She let the matter go, but couldn't help wondering about Mrs. Wilcox.

As they sat down to dinner Wednesday evening, Nancy observed an attractive redhead weaving her way through the tables. She wore a white-sequined gown, cut a bit too low. A white feather boa lay over her shoulders. The woman glided toward their table, spoke to several others along the way, finally arriving in a cloud of expensive perfume that nearly choked Nancy. She didn't think Robert had noticed the woman's approach. When he did see her, his expression reflected displeasure.

The woman seemed not to notice. "Oh, Robert, I thought you must have gone away again already, since I hadn't heard from you. Your sweet clerk told me you were in town." She looked pointedly at Nancy then back at Robert. "So why haven't you returned my call?" Her voice reminded Nancy of an oily liquid that seemed to fill the room, as all other sound receded.

Nancy sat in virtual silence observing this alien creature. When she turned back to Robert, his eyebrows were raised in something very like disgust.

"Mrs. Wilcox, allow me to introduce you to my wife, Nancy. Nancy, this is Mrs. Harvey Wilcox."

Mrs. Wilcox took a backward step. "Oh my. Your wife? I never would have guessed that. She's much too young for you." She scowled at Robert as she offered a limp hand to Nancy. "And quite beautiful. They didn't tell me you were … with your wife …" her voice faltered.

"How do you do?" Nancy returned the woman's gaze, unflinching.

After what seemed an eternity, Mrs. Wilcox gave Nancy a quick nod. "Dear, let me apologize for interrupting your dinner."

"That's quite all right, Mrs. Wilcox. I'm very pleased to make your acquaintance."

Nancy barely suppressed an outright grin when Mrs. Wilcox suddenly realized she had forgotten to do something, waved her hand in the air, and slithered away.

Robert turned his gaze on Nancy.

She leaned in close. "What … was that?"

A deep chuckle rose in his throat. "Not exactly the toast of New York society, I can assure you."

Nancy tilted her head. "Do you see her … often?"

"I am often accosted by her, yes."

Nancy relaxed in his gaze. He took her hand in his and gave it a squeeze. "But I think I've found a secret weapon. I wish I could always have you with me."

She arched an eyebrow. What would that be like? The idea gave wind to the sails of her vivid imagination. But before she drifted afar, reality tossed out an anchor. Motherhood. She could not leave her children. Her fingers slid across her abdomen soon to swell with child again. For now at least, her fantasy must wait. Robert's thumb slid across her knuckles. She focused her gaze on his handsome face. Motherhood wasn't her only anchor.

Unfortunately, Nancy spent most of the train trip home bent over a basin. Morning sickness hit hard and stayed all day.

"I'm glad I got through most of the week before it started," she told Robert in a rather weak voice as he helped her disembark from the train. Her legs were so shaky, she couldn't trust them. At home, she went to bed and stayed there for several days on the doctor's orders. Two weeks passed before she began to feel a little better.

She determined that nothing else would get in the way of her plans to visit Millbrooke Heights. She sent for Kip.

"I've just heard a friend of mine is in Millbrooke Heights. I need you to drive me there today."

His eyebrows arched then met in the middle.

Nancy bit her lip. He would not object, but the look in his eyes revealed his curiosity.

"Yes, Miss Nancy. When do you want me to bring the car around?"

Two hours later, she climbed the steps at Millbrooke. The nurse at the front desk greeted her.

"May I help you?"

"I'm here to see Elizabeth Elliott." Nancy didn't miss the almost imperceptible change in the nurse's expression.

"I'm sorry, ma'am, but only family is allowed to see Mrs. Elliott."

"I … am family. I'm her … granddaughter." Why did that feel like a lie?

"What did you say your name was?"

Nancy met her piercing gaze. She hadn't given her name. "Nancy Emerson."

"One moment, please."

Nancy found herself staring at the woman's back as she left the room. Who knew it would be so difficult to visit a patient in a nursing home?

The nurse returned a few minutes later, carrying a stack of folders, which she placed on the desk before addressing Nancy. "Please take a seat and someone will come for you shortly."

Nancy perched on a horsehair sofa, facing the double doors that opened onto the corridor the nurse had traversed a few minutes earlier. The small waiting area seemed drab at first, but as Nancy settled in, she noticed that the paintings decorating the walls were originals. She stood and crossed the room for a closer look. They were indeed originals, mostly oils.

"Aren't they wonderful?"

The nurse's question took Nancy by surprise. She glanced toward the front desk. The woman had been so formal only a few minutes earlier. "Yes, they are. Quite wonderful. Who is the artist?"

"These are done by our patients. The nicest ones are on display."

The door opened and a woman stepped through. She spoke to the nurse, who pointed to Nancy. The woman turned to greet Nancy with a bright smile.

"You're Nancy Emerson?"

Nancy stood and offered her hand. Something about the woman seemed familiar. Of average height, she had brown hair shot through with silver. Hazel eyes shone in the midst of a round face.

"I'm Bette Devereux, Mrs. Elliott's daughter. I'll take you to her." She led the way through the doors and up the steps. On the way down another long corridor, she glanced over her shoulder. "Wonderful weather we're having."

"Yes," Nancy said. *So this is my aunt?*

When they arrived outside a room at the end of the hall, Bette Devereux stopped. "Before you see her, I want to warn you. She won't know you, and she may babble on and on." Bette leveled her gaze at Nancy. "She's quite crazy."

A chill danced up Nancy's spine. "Is it all right … that I'm here?"

Bette's countenance softened. "Of course it is. I understand you must be curious. I only wish she would recognize you. She'd be pleased, though probably for all the wrong reasons."

Nancy tried to imagine what those wrong reasons would be.

After a short pause, Bette Devereux said, "Forgive me for asking, but does Mr. Emerson know you're here?"

Nancy shook her head, feeling like a schoolgirl again. "No, I came on my own."

Bette smiled. "No matter. I'm glad you've come." She opened the door and stood aside, allowing Nancy to enter.

Bright sunlight bathed the room, filtering through sheer curtains over a large window. A small bent form sat in a chair facing the window. Another woman who looked a lot like Bette sat beside her. She rose when they entered. Bette introduced them.

Agnes Miller seemed much quieter than her sister, though her brown eyes were merry. She bent toward her mother and patted her hand. "Mother, look who's come to see you. It's Georgia's girl, Nancy."

Liz Elliott slowly turned her head to look at Nancy, but no recognition lit her eyes. Her expression did not change. She turned back to the window and began to mumble.

Agnes straightened and whispered to Nancy, "I hope Bette warned you what to expect?"

"Yes." Nancy looked at the little white-haired woman. Not what she'd expected. Small-boned fingers gripped the chair arms. Tiny velvet-shod feet stuck out from under a multicolored afghan over her legs. Her dark eyes held a blank look. Her lips moved constantly, mouthing words no one understood. A single strand of faux pearls hung loosely about her neck. From time to time, she would turn her head to look up at Nancy or over at one of her daughters.

"Please sit down," Bette said, waving to a chair.

"She favors her mother," Agnes said to Bette.

"Yes, she does," Bette answered as she pulled up a chair and sat down next to Nancy. "Same lovely hair. We always envied Georgia her beautiful hair." Agnes perched on the edge of the bed.

Nancy glanced from one sister to the other. The younger of the two, Agnes, appeared older. In lieu of her sister's smooth waves and chignon, Agnes wore her silver hair in tight braids, coiled around her head and secured with turquoise and silver combs. Her lips were parted, as though she had trouble catching her breath.

Nancy intertwined her fingers in her lap trying to appear at ease.

"Can I get you anything?" Agnes asked. "Tea or coffee? They get it for you at the nurses' station."

"No, I'm fine. Thank you." So many questions buzzed around in her head. Dared she ask them?

Bette tilted her head and leaned slightly forward. "Nancy, why have you come?"

Nancy had prepared a speech for this moment. Before she could answer, Liz shouted. "Georgie, you answer your sister!"

Nancy nearly jumped out of her skin.

Agnes patted her mother's hand. "She will Mama. Give her time." Turning to Nancy, she said, "Pay no attention, dear."

Nancy raised her eyebrows and took a deep breath. That wasn't going to be easy. "I heard she was here, and I wanted to see her. I wanted to be sure … she was all right."

Bette smiled and nodded. "She's right as rain, as you can see."

Agnes scoffed. "Bette, don't be a ninny. Nancy doesn't know us well enough yet." She turned to Nancy and spoke in a low voice. "You see, dear, we make light of her condition, but she is completely off her rocker. Has been for years. Your grandmother—Miss Amelia—she took precautions to keep Mama away from you."

She sat back and looked at her mother. "Well, you can see why. She didn't want you thinking you had crazies in the family." She peered into Nancy's eyes. "It's not catching or anything. She had a nervous breakdown, brought it on herself. She was jealous as a cat of Miss Amelia. She just couldn't seem to let it go."

Bette leaned forward. "Mama loved a certain gentleman that she couldn't have, and that's what got her into all this trouble. Miss Amelia was good as gold about it, a real fine lady. She tried hard to be good to Mama. She made sure, real sure, we had all we needed. She even helped Papa get a good job with the Boston Emerson law firm—where he worked for a long time—until he died several years ago. Then Mr. Robert, he took over, and he's been a real peach."

Nancy eyed her curiously, "My husband?"

"Yes, dear," Bette said with a quick glance at Agnes. "He never told you?"

Agnes sat back in her chair. She smoothed her skirt, frowning at the floor. "Maybe he didn't want us to tell either."

Liz stiffened and jerked her head back to glare at Nancy through narrowed eyes. "Don't you tell. Don't you ever tell. If you do, I'll never bring you back here as long as you live."

Bette shook her head at her mother's ravings. "He never said not to tell Nancy. He said we mustn't tell *everyone*."

Nancy looked at Bette. "He asked you not to … tell everyone what?"

"Well," Bette hesitated and bit her lip. She looked at her sister. "We've told her this much." She turned back to Nancy. "Mr. Emerson didn't want anyone to know he was taking care of Mama's expenses, sweet man. He wouldn't let them take her to the county ward. That's where they were going to put her. The judge decided she couldn't stand trial, because she's crazy as a loon."

Agnes took her mother's hands. "Mama confessed to Miss Amelia's murder." She glanced back at Nancy. "But they didn't believe her. They think somebody else was there with her."

Nancy felt all the blood drain from her face. "What do you think happened?" She glanced from one to the other.

Agnes' face turned grim and her lips tightened. Bette shook her head and pointed to Liz. "Only Mama really knows what happened that night. But we think there must've been somebody else there with her, because she constantly refers to him."

Him. Nancy's blood turned ice cold. She forced herself to concentrate. "Do you know ... who?"

"Some things are best not to know," Agnes said.

"On the other hand," Bette leaned in to the little circle, "it is a little worrisome, knowing there may be someone still out there who killed Miss Amelia."

Agnes nodded.

Nancy began to suspect they were all crazy. She stood up, almost too suddenly, upsetting Liz, who cried out.

Nancy's hand flew to her breast. "Oh, I'm sorry. I didn't mean to upset her, but I must go. I didn't realize it was so late."

"Oh, dear," Agnes said. "I hope we haven't worried or frightened you."

Nancy shook her head. "No, I really need to get home. But may I come again, to visit?"

"Of course you may," Bette said. "Do come and see us. We're generally here of a morning. We'd love to see you again."

Agnes patted her on the back. "You've certainly turned out well—so smart and pretty—all that Mr. Emerson said you were."

Nancy spent the trip home in quiet meditation. She certainly had a lot to think about. She'd gotten some answers, but there were many more questions.

Why had Robert kept all this a secret from her? Had he simply followed in her grandmother's footsteps, keeping her mother's family in the shadows?

She remembered Bette's words, "... the judge decided she couldn't stand trial ..." Had there been a hearing, without

Nancy's knowledge? How had this happened? The more she thought about it, the angrier she became.

This wouldn't do at all. She mustn't draw any conclusions until she had all the information. But when she had it, she intended to confront Robert and find out the truth.

Chapter Twenty-Six

"I'll see you at half after eleven," Nancy told Kip. Determined to learn as much about her family as possible, she'd rearranged her regular activities to include a weekly visit with Liz Elliott and her daughters. It hadn't taken Nancy long to forge a friendship with Aunt Bette and Aunt Agnes. After only a month's acquaintance, she felt quite comfortable with them.

On this crisp October morning, she arrived to find herself alone with Liz, called "Mama Liz" by her family.

Before Nancy could retreat, the woman caught sight of her. Nancy gave her a tremulous smile as she sat down in the chair next to her. "Good morning, Mama Liz."

Mama Liz glared at her. "It's about time you got here. You better stop this always being late."

Nancy glanced around. *Is she talking to me?* "I … I'm sorry …"

Wrinkles furrowed Liz's brow. "I taught you better. Those good families don't go for that."

Nancy blinked back surprise at such a long string of words from the old woman.

Mama Liz leaned forward and pointed a trembling finger at her. "You must never tell them whose child you're carrying. You must always keep the secret."

A chill danced down Nancy's spine. She struggled for breath as she laid a hand on her expanding middle, not so noticeable, surely. Mama Liz must have mistaken her for someone else, but who? Georgia—Nancy's mother? "Mama Liz, it's me, Nancy—Georgia's *daughter*, remember?"

Mama Liz gazed at Nancy, her eyes bright and luminous. "I know who you are. You must never tell anyone the child is Nate's." She glanced over her shoulder then leaned in closer and whispered. "They'll never guess the truth." She sat back and cackled. "I told him what he must do, and he's done it." She nodded. "He's a good boy. The best one of the whole bunch."

The room spun as Nancy sat back and forced herself to breathe. Bile rose in her throat. *"I told him what he must do."*

Was she talking about Nate? Mama Liz told Nate to—

At that moment, the door swung open. Bette walked in, her eyes bright as they lit on Nancy. "You're early today." She set down a bundle of her mother's laundered clothes. Her forehead creased. "Are you all right, child? You're pale as a ghost."

Nancy forced a smile to reassure her. "Yes, I'm fine. Just a bit tired."

Bette continued to watch her through narrowed eyes. "Are you sure? You're not in pain, are you?"

Nancy shook her head. "No, really, I'm fine. I hadn't realized how tired I am, until I sat down."

Bette pulled up another chair and sat beside her. "How's Mama been this morning?"

Nancy glanced back at Liz, who stared out the window with glazed eyes. She had slipped away again. "Fine. She seemed almost lucid when I came in. I believe she recognized me."

Bette nodded. "Oh yes, she has her moments. But that's usually all they are, just moments."

Nancy stood to leave. "I had hoped to see Aunt Agnes. I hope she's well?"

"Her husband has a cold, so she stayed home today. I'll tell her you were here and asked about her." She rose to follow Nancy to the door.

"I wish you could stay a bit, but I understand. How's that boy doing?"

"He's fine. We're about to celebrate his second birthday."

"Oh, those years are so exciting. I'd love to see him, but …" She shrugged her shoulders and smiled.

"I'd love to have you, if you could come."

She patted Nancy's arm. "Oh no. We mustn't. It's in the agreement."

Nancy drew a quick breath. "What agreement?"

Aunt Bette stepped outside the door and motioned for Nancy to follow her. She glanced back at her mother then pulled the door closed. "It's in the agreement we made with your grandmother, Miss Amelia," she whispered. "Mama and Papa both signed it. We still honor it even though Miss Amelia's gone on." She smoothed Nancy's hair. "She was that good to us."

Nancy blinked, trying to clear her vision. Her mouth went dry, but she felt the need to answer Aunt Bette. "How good of all of you to honor Grandmother's wishes, even after she's gone." She raised her chin and forced a smile. "But if you ever change your mind, I would welcome you."

Aunt Bette beamed and hugged Nancy. "You're such a sweet girl. We'll see you here next week then?" Her aunt stepped back inside the room and closed the door.

Nancy's heart beat so hard in her chest its throbbing filled her senses. The information she'd received in the last few minutes would take some time to digest.

"I feel as if I am living two lives," Nancy wrote in her journal that night. "I am one person with my family here at home and quite another when I'm away. One part of me visits my long-estranged grandmother, and sees a certain ill-fated individual once a year, who continues to demand more money. The other part does her best to go on as usual with her husband and her child, trying desperately not to rock the boat. At times, the burden grows so heavy I think I will surely end up like Liz Elliott."

She closed the book and sat curled up in her chair, ruminating over all that had happened in the past few weeks. From the tiny hint given to her by her totally unbalanced grandmother, she'd constructed a story that would probably sound fantastic to any listener. Wisdom told her she should sit down with Robert and tell him the truth about everything— clear the air— "spill the beans," as they said in the movies. But how would he react? What would he say to her sneaking around behind his back?

Panic fluttered in her chest. She needed to concentrate and figure out a way to survive. She sat up, opened the journal again, and began to write. She'd write her version of the story, as she understood it. Perhaps someday, it would help her to remember.

She wrote until the child within her stirred. With a sigh, she leaned her head back and massaged her belly. Warmth flooded her heart. Robert's child. She didn't care whether it was a boy or a girl. Her lips curled into a smile as she snuggled down in the chair, dreaming of the child she would hold in her arms.

If only Robert was here now to share her joy. She closed her eyes and felt his arms about her, warming her. He would kiss the top of her head, as he often did, and she would melt in his embrace.

Robert entered a quiet house sometime later and climbed the stairs to their room where a light shone beneath the door. He pushed the door open, expecting to find Nancy reading in bed. Instead, he found her curled up in the chair, sound asleep. After loosening his tie and turning down the covers, he lifted her and laid her gently on the bed. He removed her slippers and set them beneath the bedside table.

She stirred as he pulled the covers over her.

He bent to kiss her cheek.

As he changed for bed, his eyes lit on the book, and he picked it up. He opened the cover. When he realized what it was, he set it back down again. He'd no intention of reading her private thoughts without her permission. But the lawyer side of him scratched away at his insides. What thoughts did she write there? Did she speak of him? The need to know almost overwhelmed him.

He smiled as he switched off the lamp. What she'd written in those pages was not his business. He lay down beside her and listened to her even breathing. He'd wanted so much to talk to her tonight. It seemed too long since they'd shared a quiet evening together, one not spent in the company of family or socialites.

In the morning, he'd be leaving for Minneapolis. He turned on his side and peered out the window at a quarter moon. Perhaps the approaching holidays would afford them time together as a family.

He closed his eyes and whispered a prayer.

Chapter Twenty-Seven

Nancy sang softly as she fastened the clasp of a sterling silver bracelet. They were going to spend the holidays at Perry's Landing. In the loving bosom of Robert's family, she could lay her troubles aside and have no fear of being accosted by Nate. To her profound relief, he had not shown up this year. She hoped this meant he was satisfied with the amount of money. She leaned in close to the mirror to touch her cheeks with rouge. At least that's what she kept telling herself.

She applied lipstick and blotted her lips then stood and peered at her silhouette. Robert had made most of the Christmas appearances alone, as she was a little past the official limits of social acceptance. She had no desire to be a trendsetter. The more intimate parties were perfectly safe, and she happily accompanied her husband there, but on grander occasions, he either went alone, in company with his parents, or with the Bostons.

She smiled at her reflection and made final adjustments to her hair. The beautician had talked her into a short, curly style that was so much easier to keep.

Nancy had decided to make one more trip to see Mama Liz before leaving for Perry's Landing.

After a short, but pleasant visit, she left the room and started down the stairs, where rounding the corner, she met Nate and drew up short.

He wore a dark leather jacket and knitted woolen cap. He pulled the cap off when he saw her. "Well, lookie who it is."

She pursed her lips in distaste and glared back at him. His words slurred together, and he smelled like a brewery.

Apparently unconcerned, he leaned against the corner of the wall. "Where've you been?"

She tried to push past him, but he grabbed her arm.

"Wait a minute. Let me have a look at you. Hey, I guess I was wrong about ole Robert, eh? Maybe he didn't need my help after all."

She glowered at him. "Let me go, Nate."

"Oh, don't be in such a hurry. It's been a long time." He glanced up the stairwell. "Who've you been visiting in here? Surely no one in the hoity-toity Emerson family?"

She thrust her chin forward and lifted her eyes to him. "I've been to see my grandmother."

His brow arched. "What? Your grandmother?" He relaxed his grip just enough to allow Nancy to break free. She started down the steps.

"You know who put her here, don't you?" He called to her as she slipped away. "Good ole boy you're married to, that's who. He used her to cover his guilt. Nobody ever asked where he was that night, now, did they?"

Nancy wanted to cover her ears and get out, but she couldn't escape the sound of his voice.

At the bottom of the steps, she nearly ran into Kip, who had come inside to wait for her. He glared into the stairwell. By the look in his eyes, she knew he'd heard the entire conversation.

"Are you all right, Miss Nancy?"

She covered her mouth to hide her trembling lips. "Oh, Kip, please help me to the car. Get me out of here." She didn't care what Kip thought of her, she wanted only to be gone from this place.

He kept glancing at her in the mirror, all the way home, but he never said another word. Once they arrived, he jumped out and rushed to help her into the house.

She laid her hand on his arm. "Thank you, Kip. I'll be all right now." She slipped out of her coat and laid it over the stair rail. She wanted to crumple up, right there on the bottom step, and cry. But she forced herself to climb the stairs to her room. She didn't want the servants to see her. They would worry, and they would tell Robert.

Nancy stood by as Robert lifted Jack into the saddle. Jack would ride in front of Robert for their traditional Christmas ride.

"We'll take good care of him," Robert assured her, with a jaunty smile.

Jack jabbered away, clearly excited.

Her heart ached at the sight. Robert was such a wonderful father to the boy, and such a good man. How could she ever think he could have been responsible for her grandmother's death? She crossed her arms over her chest. Nate had to be bluffing. Probably to cover his guilt.

After watching the men ride off down the bridle path, she strolled back to the house and entered through the kitchen.

Delia looked up from her work, assembling a tray of cups and saucers. "They're in the front parlor, Mrs. Emerson."

"Thank you, Delia," Nancy answered. She slipped out of her coat and hung it on a peg outside the kitchen. She crept down the hall, hoping to slip into the parlor unobserved. The two women were deep in conversation over the tiny stitches in an heirloom quilt. Nancy sank into a chair near the door.

Grandma Perry glanced in her direction. "Nancy? Are you all right, dear? You seem so distracted."

Nancy turned a smiling face to her. "I'm sorry, Grandma Perry. I'm tired, I think."

Grandma patted the sofa cushion next to her. "Come sit down with us by the fire, dear. It's so cozy here."

Nancy started to make an excuse, but the looks on their faces changed her mind. She hated to disappoint them. This was usually her favorite part of the holiday.

Seated beside them, she relaxed. How she loved this room with its warm and inviting fire on the oversized hearth. After Delia brought hot cocoa, the three women sat in contented silence for a few minutes.

"Have you been feeling all right, Nancy?"

Nancy glanced at her mother-in-law. "I've been a little down, with the holidays and everything."

Grandma Perry nodded. "It's not unusual to feel a bit down when you're expecting, especially in the latter months."

Nancy sipped her cocoa. "I suppose not."

"It'll get better, you'll see," her mother-in-law said, patting her hand.

Nancy forced a smile.

Grandma Perry set her cup aside. "What else is bothering you, dear?"

Nancy bit her lower lip and gave a shrug.

"Are you worried about something?"

"I can't really say what it is."

"I have times like that," her mother-in-law said. "Days when I have an uncomfortable feeling, but I don't know what it is. Yes, I know what you mean."

Grandma leaned forward to lay her hand on Nancy's arm. "You do know you can talk to us about anything, don't you dear?"

If only I could. Nancy smiled and nodded. "I do, Grandma Perry. Thank you for being concerned about me. I'm sure I'll be fine."

She took Nancy's hand in hers and said, "Would you mind if we pray for you right now?"

Nancy dropped her head. This, she had not expected. She breathed deep and gave them a quick nod. Grandma Perry did not delay but began at once to pray. Juliana drew near as well and took Nancy's other hand in hers. Nancy had never heard such beautiful, heartfelt words. Grandma Perry spoke as one would to a friend who sat in the room with them. How wonderful, to have such a close relationship with God.

Not wanting to disappoint them, she tried very hard afterward to seem lighthearted and carefree, though she didn't feel it. She wanted to be happy, and she longed for the peace Grandma Perry had. But in her heart she knew she would never have it. She didn't deserve it. She must pay the price for her past indiscretions.

Nancy and Jack stayed at Perry's Landing through most of January. Robert arrived from New York in time to accompany them home. He stayed overnight, and they left on the early morning train. He seemed distant, even in his dealings with Jack. When she tried to engage him in conversation, he barely acknowledged her.

She noted the dark circles under his eyes and worry lines newly etched in his forehead. *He's working too hard.* She wanted to comfort him, but his reticence kept her at a distance. Perhaps he needed space.

At home, she bathed and prepared for bed. How good it would feel to lie in her bed. She had just removed her slippers when Robert entered the room.

His face was dark, and his eyes glowered. Nancy had never seen him so angry. At first, he said nothing.

She swallowed nervously as she sat down on the edge of their bed.

Hands in his pockets, he moved to the window and turned his back to her. What was on his mind? Had something happened? Her heart beat so hard, it hurt.

Still facing the window, he spoke in a low voice. "How long have you been seeing Nate?"

Stunned, she could make no answer, just sat there looking at his back. She could almost feel the anger seething from him. Her hands began to shake so she held them together in her lap.

He turned and glared at her. "How long, Nancy?"

Tears started in her eyes as she whispered, "I ... I ... don't know what ... you mean, Robert."

"Don't lie to me. I want a straight answer from you. Kip told me he comes here, and then you saw him not long before Christmas."

Nancy covered her mouth with her hand as the tears flowed freely from her eyes.

Still seething, Robert turned toward the door. "Your silence will suffice as an answer." His dark gaze pierced her heart. "Is *this* child mine, Nancy?"

She sucked in a breath. Paralyzed, she sat in silent misery for several moments.

Robert closed the door.

She heard him descend the stairs and strained her ears to hear whether he'd leave the house. The only sound was the tick of the clock and a soft whistling of the wind outside.

She hurt too much even to cry. As the clock in the hall chimed twelve times, she gathered herself into the chair, pulled her legs beneath her, and encircled her abdomen with her arms. Then she began to sob.

Robert stood at the base of the stairs, head bowed, gulping deep breaths. He'd only meant to get information from Nancy, but by the time he'd ascended the stairs to their room, his ire had taken control. And then she'd lied to him. As he raised his head, his gaze shifted to the smooth dark wood of the door and the soft glow of the gaslight that lit the entrance. His gut clenched.

He'd gone too far in accusing her of infidelity. The expression on her face haunted him. His footsteps echoed as he paced back and forth in the parlor. This was too much to expect of any man. If there'd been nothing going on between her and Nate, she would have told him about the visits, wouldn't she?

There'd been too many secrets between them. Too many lies. He could no longer contain it. He grabbed his coat and went out to walk off his emotions. He walked until he grew weary and even then, he hesitated to return to the house.

A clear night, millions of stars twinkled overhead. He sat down on a stone bench near the entrance to their garden. Pine-scented air filled his lungs. Elbows on his knees, he dropped his head forward. A soft breeze lifted the hair on the nape of his neck, sending a chill through him. Like a voice speaking out of the darkness—a still, small voice—the breeze swept out all the doubts he'd entertained since Kip's revelation. He'd allowed them free rein, and they had grown into mountains.

What kind of man doubts the woman he loves without giving her a chance to explain herself? He'd spouted ugly accusations.

He sucked in a deep breath and released it into the darkness. He called himself a Christian, believed he could lead Nancy to trust in God. Is this how to go about it? Where was the mercy? Powerless in the face of this brutal storm, he dropped his head in his hands and prayed. Only God could bring him peace and give him strength to carry on.

Two hours later, Robert let himself back in. He hung up his overcoat and tiptoed into the parlor. Here, a gas-burner glowed, lending its feeble warmth to the large room. He stretched out on the leather sofa, gazed into the glow, and whispered one of his favorite verses, "Sorrow remains for the night, but joy comes in the morning." Surely, this too, would pass, but he had little confidence of the joy.

Just before dawn, he climbed the stairs to their room. He didn't want to give the staff reason to talk. He'd bathe, change, and then leave early for work. When he reached the top of the stairs, he saw their bedroom door standing open. Concerned, he crossed to Jack's room, thinking there may have been a problem with the boy.

Jack still slept, so Robert stepped back into the hall. He squinted into the darkness of the landing to the closed door of the guest bedroom. She'd chosen to sleep there. She didn't wish to see him.

His stomach churned as he stepped into the bathroom and began his morning routine.

Later that morning, Robert sat in William Boston's office. William heard his story with a deeply furrowed brow. "Nancy met Nate at the hospital?"

"According to Kip."

"What was she doing at the hospital?"

Robert met William's gaze. "I don't know, seeing the doctor, I suppose."

"Robert, that doesn't make sense. Do you know which hospital?"

Robert let his head fall back. He took a deep breath and blew it out. "I'm sorry, William. I made a mistake coming to your office half-cocked like this, but I felt desperate to talk to someone. You already know the worst." He frowned. "At least I hope it's the worst."

William aimed a smile at Robert and shook his head. After a moment, he paused and the smile faded. "Robert, are you sure you don't know which hospital?"

"There's only one hospital, William."

"No, actually there are two. There's County General, and there's ... Millbrooke Heights."

Robert glowered at William. "Millbrooke? How would she know to go there?" He stood suddenly and crossed to the window. "Perhaps Nate took her there?" He shook his head. "Why would Nate take her there? You'd think he'd want to stay as far from there as poss—" He swiveled back around, arching his brows at William.

William sat back in his chair. "I told her about Millbrooke, Robert."

"*You* told her?"

"She came here last summer, upset about something she'd heard. I felt I should tell her." He leveled a cool gaze at Robert. "I must admit I was a little surprised that you had not."

Robert stared back at him, struggling to piece his jumbled thoughts together. "She knew all this time about—"

"It seems to me that you two have been keeping secrets from one another. That's not necessarily a good thing."

Robert turned aside to the chair he'd vacated and sat down. He leaned forward with his elbows on his knees and stared at his hands. "I don't know what to do, William. I tried to keep her safe. I didn't do any better than Amelia."

"Perhaps it's because both you and Amelia tried to do it on your own." He got up and walked around his desk. "Robert, Nancy loves you. I'm certain of it. If Nate is coming around, I don't think it's any of her doing."

She has a funny way of showing it. "Then what do you think is happening?" Robert scoffed.

William sat down next to Robert. "Remember our talk right after your marriage, when you told me about the child?"

Robert nodded. Then his head came up suddenly. He narrowed his eyes as he recalled the conversation. "Do you think he could be blackmailing her?"

"I think it's a possibility. I certainly wouldn't rule it out." He crossed his arms over his chest and pursed his lips. "I'd check into it."

"How?" Robert said, mostly to himself.

"You have access to her bank account. That'd be the first place I'd look."

Robert rubbed his face with his hand, trying to wake himself. Missing a night's sleep was really taking its toll.

William grabbed a notebook from his desk, tore off a sheet of paper, and jotted something down. "Check the bank account. If you find anything questionable, notify me. I've got a couple of friends I can call." He handed the note to Robert. "And here's the name of an excellent private detective who can ferret out anything you need to find."

Robert glanced at the note then stuffed it into his jacket pocket. "We should have clamped down tighter on him before when we had him."

William stood. "We didn't have enough proof. You know that. If we can catch him at this, we can finally make something stick. Now I have appointments, and I'm sure you do, too, although you look as though you could use a good night's sleep."

"Right." Robert stood to go. "Thanks for your time, William. I appreciate your patience with me."

"No problem. Oh, and Robert"—he circled his desk to stand directly in front of Robert—"Take care. We don't really know what he's capable of. If our suspicions are true, and we back him into a corner …"

For a moment, their gazes locked. The possibility of violence against anyone in his family left Robert chilled to the bone. "I'll be careful, William. Thanks again, for your forbearance." He thrust his hand forward, and William gripped it in a firm handshake.

Robert strode out of the Boston Emerson law office, barely acknowledging the kind greetings of his former coworkers. He felt like kicking himself. Once he'd calmed down enough, he'd had another conversation with Kip. According to him, each time Nate came to see Nancy she'd seemed upset. She'd usually spend the rest of the day in her room. So Nate's visits had distressed her.

If his mind hadn't been so clouded by anger, he might have reasoned this out on his own. Robert stopped at a pay phone and called his office. He made an excuse for his tardiness then walked the short distance to the bank.

The manager, Jake Hammerstein, stepped out of his office to shake Robert's hand. "Mr. Emerson, it's good to see you. How can I help you?"

"I need to see one of my accounts," Robert said.

"Yes, sir." He signaled for a clerk. "Bring in the Emerson accounts."

"I really only need to see the estate account for now." Mr. Hammerstein nodded, and when the clerk returned with the books, he located the proper one and handed it to Robert.

Robert ran his finger over the neat columns of figures. Everything seemed in order. Then he caught sight of a larger sum in the withdrawal column toward the end of the prior month. He traced it back and found another at the end of the month before, in the same amount. And the same withdrawal toward the end of every month in the current year.

"Is there something in particular I can help you with?" Mr. Hammerstein asked.

Robert lifted his gaze. "Can you go any further back than this?"

"Why, yes, we can pull past years. That would take time, however—"

Robert nodded. "That's all right. If you could do that, I would appreciate it. It's a matter of great importance."

"Oh?"

"Here's what you need to look for," Robert said, leaning forward to show the bank officer the identical transactions.

"Oh, yes," he said, "I'm familiar with those. Mrs. Emerson's secretary comes in every month."

"Her secretary?"

"Yes, Miss Camden. She comes in toward the end of every month to make that withdrawal. Mrs. Emerson did it for the first year or so, though I believe it was a lesser amount. Then Miss Camden started coming. They always ask for an envelope."

Robert tilted his head. "An envelope?"

Mr. Hammerstein nodded. "Yes, Miss Camden counts the money, puts it in the envelope, and seals it, then writes something on the envelope and places it in her pocketbook. That's exactly the way Mrs. Emerson always did it."

"Thank you very much, Mr. Hammerstein." Robert got up to leave. "You've been very helpful. Oh, and by the way, I'll need proper documentation. Give me a call at the office when you have it ready." He tried to keep his voice light.

"Yes, sir. I'll get it done right away and Mr. Emerson ...?

Robert turned back. "Yes?"

"She always took a taxi."

"A taxi?" He frowned. "Going or coming?"

"Both. Came in a taxi, left in a taxi. I thought it a bit odd, sir—since I know you have a regular driver."

Nancy couldn't shake an almost overwhelming feeling of dread. She dragged herself out of bed and through the day, she tried to be chipper with Jack but finally gave up and retired to her room.

"It's much too early for the baby to come." Grace Boggs confronted her. "All this pining away is going to bring it on. Shall I call the doctor?"

Nancy shook her head. "I'm fine, or at least I will be. I just need rest." She closed the door and stood still until she heard Grace's footsteps receding.

A little later, Flo came in to get her instructions for the day. She frowned at Nancy. "You're too pale, and there are dark circles beneath your eyes. I don't know much about this sort of thing, but if it was me, I'd have Grace call the doctor."

"I'll be all right after a good night's rest." She gave Flo her orders and lay back down. The day passed in a blur. Nancy wanted to be left alone. She felt sick. She'd not been able to swallow food and her head hurt. Maybe Flo was right; maybe she should let them call the doctor. She certainly couldn't go on like this—it wouldn't be good for the baby. She looked at the clock. Nearly six, and she still hadn't heard from Robert. He must be very angry with her.

She couldn't blame him. He had every right to mistrust her. She should've confided in him long ago. How had the situation gotten so out of control? She snuggled down into the bed and squeezed her eyes shut.

They seldom had time alone together. Uncle William often told her Robert needed time off. He always gave a hundred percent to every project, though it meant he neglected his time at home.

Now a crisis had come along, and their lives fell apart.

"Put your trust in God. Spend time in the Word and in prayer every day so that when crises come in your life, you'll be able to withstand them." Nancy opened her eyes. It was an excerpt from their pastor's Sunday sermon. She'd paid little attention then, but it seemed to fit so well into this present moment.

She reached for the Bible that lay on the bedside table. Perhaps it was not too late.

Robert arrived long after everyone should have been in bed, so he was surprised to see a light shining under the bedroom door. He stood for a moment trying to decide whether to open it. In his weary state, he dreaded a confrontation with Nancy.

He inched nearer, pushed the door open a crack, and peered inside. She had apparently fallen asleep reading. He crept over, picked up the Bible, and laid it aside.

As he gazed down at her peaceful countenance, the feelings of guilt returned. He caressed her cheek with his fingers then leaned down to kiss her softly on the forehead. She stirred but did not waken. He reached to switch off the lamp then slipped out the door and crossed to the guest room. It was his turn to sleep in the doghouse.

Chapter Twenty-Eight

Nancy stirred at the sound of someone moving about in the room. Jack clambered onto her bed. "Mommy, you sleep too much."

She reached for his hand and held it in hers. "I do, don't I? I'm sorry, little man."

He lay down on his stomach and propped himself up on his elbows to look at her. "Grace Boggs says you don't feel good."

"That's right, but I'm going to get up soon. I'll come in and play with you for a while, okay?"

"All right." He rolled over and jumped down. "Can I have my hot cocoa now?"

She glanced at the clock. "Oh, I think you should wait a while. It's too close to lunchtime."

The room spun as she sat on the edge of the bed. When she reached for the bedpost to pull herself up, a hard clenching pain pierced her side. She bent forward and cried out.

Jack ran to her. "Mommy, did you hurt you-self?" He twisted to look up at her face.

Nancy reached out to him. "Go get Grace Boggs and hurry, please."

A few moments later, Grace rushed into the room. "Miz Nancy, what is it?"

"Pain."

Grace helped her back onto the bed and tucked the covers around her. "I'll call the doctor. You lie still. Jack, dear, you come with me."

Robert and Daniel Emerson strode into the hospital waiting area where Robert's mother stood with her back to them, gazing out the window. She glanced over her shoulder as they entered.

"Found him," Daniel said as he kissed Juliana's cheek.

Robert searched his mother's tearstained face. "How is she?"

She laid her hand on his arm. "I don't know anything yet, and it's been hours."

Robert rubbed the back of his neck. He'd crushed her spirit with his angry accusations. How could he have been such a brute? If she lost the baby …

A moment later, the doctor stepped into the room, caught sight of Robert, and strode toward him.

"We managed to stop the labor for the time being. She's resting now."

Relief rushed through Robert. "Then she hasn't lost the baby?"

"No, but I can't guarantee it won't happen yet. She's got six more weeks, give or take a few days. If we can keep her perfectly still for the next twenty-four hours, she's got a chance. After that, I don't know. It would be unfair for me to give you too much hope."

Robert sat down in the nearest chair and held his head in his hands. His mother knelt beside him, rubbing his back.

"Will we be able to see her?" his father asked.

"Not tonight," the doctor said, "but Mr. Robert may see her in the morning if she's stable. You should all go home and get some rest. You're going to need it."

Robert struggled to make sense of everything that had happened. He'd spent the morning talking to the police. At lunch, he'd paid a visit to Mrs. Elliott and her daughters. From there, he drove out to the Sanderson Estate then returned to find his father waiting for him.

He tried to explain the situation briefly to his father on the way home from the hospital, but there was so much he couldn't say. It came out complicated and confusing.

His father held up his hand to stop the tirade. "Put it aside for the time being, son. Better yet, let William handle it. He's equal to the task. You have more important matters that need your consideration."

Robert knew his father was right. Prioritize. He did that all the time on the job. Now he'd need to tackle his personal problems with the same strength.

Unfamiliar noises woke Nancy. For several moments, she didn't know where she was. She glanced around. A light from the hallway partially lit a corner of the hospital room. She tried to rise, but the bedclothes constricted her movement. What had happened? Had she lost the baby? Her arms were pinned to her side, so she couldn't reach her abdomen. Panic rose in her throat.

She heard low voices in the hall followed by soft footsteps. A nurse crept into the room. She took Nancy's temperature and loosened the sheets enough to check her pulse. She scribbled something on the chart at the end of her bed. "Are you comfortable, Mrs. Emerson? Is there anything you need?"

Nancy shook her head. She couldn't ask about the baby. She didn't want to hear the words. That would make it real. Final. The nurse left as quietly as she had come. Eerie shadows filled the room. Voices echoed. Nancy moved slightly and felt a sharp twinge in her lower abdomen. She remembered the intense pain she'd experienced earlier. Tears trickled down her cheeks. She'd lost the child she'd been so excited about. She'd lost her husband's trust. Nothing else mattered.

As sleep overtook her, visions of a warm, sunny place filled with the sounds of children drifted through her mind. She could see them in the distance, frolicking in the water. Two of them broke away from the game they were playing and ran to her. They smiled and pulled her up and walked with her to the edge of the water. A warm wind blew and sunlight caressed their faces as they waded along the shore. Someone whispered her name.

Nancy looked back, but she couldn't see who was calling her. She didn't want to leave this beautiful place.

Into the midst of her dream, a man came. He walked up to her and stood so near she couldn't see his face.

He told her it was time to go home.

She shook her head. "I don't want to leave."

"Go now. Your children are waiting for you." His voice became more insistent.

Nancy opened her eyes. Sunlight filtered in through the blinds. She heard voices outside her door. Turning her head to the side, she saw Robert sitting beside the bed, his head in his hands. She watched him until he lifted his eyes to hers.

He leaned forward and took her hand. "Nancy."

A lump rose in her throat and tears stung her eyes. "I … I'm so sorry."

"It's okay, darling. Don't try to talk. The doctor wants you to stay very still for a while. They were able to stop the labor, but you must be very careful for another day or so."

Her breath caught in her throat. She stared at him. What had he said? Had she not lost the child? The sheets had been loosened and she could move her arms, so she reached down and felt the evidence of the child's presence.

Flooded with relief, she began to cry.

Robert drew out a handkerchief and smoothed away her tears. He bent over her and kissed her forehead. Then his eyes sought hers. "I'm sorry, Nancy. This is my fault. I should never have said what I did. I lost my temper."

She gazed up at him, too overcome to speak. She'd been raised to hide her feelings, to never show emotion. Tears were a sign of weakness. So she gave in to the weakness.

Grandmother always said she was too much like her father. She closed her eyes, content for now to lie still with Robert holding her hand.

He stayed until they forced him to leave. As he leaned in to kiss her good-bye, she whispered, "I love you." For a fleeting moment, the dimple appeared in his cheek. And then it was gone.

Chapter Twenty-Nine

"We're not quite out of the woods yet," the doctor told Nancy and Robert. He touched Nancy's shoulder. "I want you to stay here for a while. If we can manage to keep you immobile, the baby will have a much better chance."

Nancy kept her eyes on Robert. She could sense his disappointment. He'd have to go back to work. "The company won't run itself," she'd heard Grandmother say many times. She closed her eyes as the doctor let himself out.

"I'm sorry, Nancy," Robert whispered. "I know you wanted to go home."

When she opened her eyes, his face was very near hers. His hair, usually so neatly combed, had fallen forward over his brow.

She brushed it back with her fingertips.

He took her hand in his and brought it to his lips.

She heaved a sigh. "You have to go."

He nodded. "I do." He let go of her hand and stood. "I'll be back after work."

Nancy swallowed the huge lump in her throat. "Don't worry about me. They'll take good care of me here." She drew in a shaky breath as the door closed, separating her from Robert. How would she endure the long days ahead? Endless hours with nothing to do but think.

A new worry dropped into her already overwrought mind. Would Nate find out? Would he dare to come here looking for her? Without her signature, Flo wouldn't be able to make the withdrawal, and he wouldn't get his money. What would he do?

Nancy's heart fluttered in her breast as panic rose in her throat. She tried to concentrate on other things, but she couldn't seem to let go of it.

Did she dare tell Robert everything? She covered her face with her hands. Not while Nate was still in the picture. He'd make trouble. Yes, and Nancy knew exactly how much trouble he could make for Robert.

In the second week of Nancy's confinement, Flo came to see her. Nancy asked about the monthly transaction.

"Oh, no problem." Flo gave a wave of her hand. "Mr. Emerson signed the check."

Nancy's jaw dropped. "What?"

Flo's head bobbed up and down. "Why, yes, he said for me to bring him anything that needed to be taken care of, and I did. He signed several checks so I could pay the bills. I hadn't thought about that one, but he asked me if there wasn't something more. I told him there was one other thing, and he told me to write the check and take care of it. I thought he must have spoken to you."

Nancy's hands tightened into fists. Her heart thudded against the wall of her chest. The sound of it filled her ears. Had Robert found out about the payments to Nate?

Flo moved nearer. "Miss Nancy, are you all right? Do you want me to get the nurse?"

"No. I'm all right." She took a deep breath then blew it out. She was more than all right. A great weight had lifted. Nate would not be hunting her down. "I'm fine now, thank you. And thanks for taking care of that for me."

"It's my job." She patted Nancy's hand. "You take it easy. We've got everything under control."

After Flo left, Nancy replayed the conversation in her head. She felt almost giddy. Everything is under control. Her husband had just signed a check for cash to pay for Nate's silence.

On the following day, a nurse helped Nancy into a wheelchair. "We're going to the solarium. You have a very special visitor waiting for you."

Nancy gazed up at the young woman she'd come to know as Frances. "Who is it?"

Frances smiled back. "Oh no, I'm not going to spoil the surprise."

Fearful it might be Nate, Nancy held her breath as they rounded the corner and entered an open area flanked by large windows. "Mama!" Jack dashed toward Nancy, Grace Boggs fast on his heels. Nancy couldn't hold him, but at least she could talk to him and cover his face with kisses.

He giggled as he inspected the wheelchair. "When are you coming home, Mommy?"

"As soon as I can, Jack. I miss you so much. You're growing so fast. You're almost as tall as me."

"Oh, Mommy you're funny."

She exchanged gazes with Grace. "Is everything going all right?"

"Don't you worry about a thing, Mrs. Emerson. The grandparents come several times a week. They take Jack out for a spell. Mr. Emerson, he sometimes takes Jack to the office or to the picture show. Jack likes that a lot. He's getting more attention than ever."

Nancy nodded. It seemed as though everyone was doing quite well without her.

Saying good-bye brought a baseball-sized lump to her throat. Grace must have noticed the panic in her eyes.

"Chin up," she said. "We pray for you every day. Don't we, Jack?"

He nodded and laid his head on his mother's shoulder. She stroked his hair and dropped a kiss on the top of his head.

"Thank you both for coming to see me. I hope you're planning to stop for ice cream on the way home?"

"Ice cream?" Jack left her side to jump up and down.

Grace smiled at Nancy as she took hold of Jack's hand. "Of course, we are. And then off to the park." She winked at Nancy. "I hope to wear him out real good, so he sleeps through the night."

Desperation gripped Nancy as she watched Grace lead Jack away. Could they really keep her here, if she didn't want to stay? She sat in silence, staring out the window until Frances returned. As the young nurse wheeled the chair back down the corridor, Nancy forced herself to engage in conversation. She couldn't let them think Jack's visits upset her. They might not allow it again.

"When will I be able to go home?"

Dr. Hansen glanced up from her chart. He pressed his lips together as if considering his answer. Nancy waited for several moments. He was taking too long to answer.

He tapped the clipboard with the end of his pencil. "I don't like the idea of sending you home, Nancy."

"I can stay downstairs. I have plenty of help."

"Yes, I know you do." He sat down on the end of her bed. "Nancy, this is very serious. Your baby's life is at stake." He studied her chart for another moment. "If we can manage to keep the baby in place for at least another week, it'll have a much better chance of survival."

Nancy swallowed. "Th … there's still a chance the baby won't make it?"

"If the baby's born too early, Nancy, its life could be compromised. A few do make it, but there are many complications. We want to be safe. With you here, we can keep an eye on you." He pressed his lips into a thin line while he scribbled something on her chart. Then he stepped to the end of the bed. "You're a lucky young woman. Let's not tempt fate by releasing you too soon."

He hung the chart on a hook at the foot of the bed. A moment later, he had gone, but his words still echoed in Nancy's ears.

Fate. Faith. Two very different words, though they sounded somewhat alike. Faith involved trust and belief. Fate implied that certain things in life were destined and couldn't be changed.

She swiped at tears. Was her faith enough to override fate?

Robert found Nancy staring out the window at an evening sky brilliant with color. "Nancy?"

She turned her head to look at him.

He brushed the hair away from her forehead then caressed her cheek. "Are you all right?"

"I'm fine."

Robert didn't believe her. He straightened, walked to the window, and stood looking out. He rubbed the back of his neck. There was too much going on, between his home life, the company, and trying to settle the case against Nate. Too much.

When he glanced over his shoulder at Nancy, she gazed up at him. The look in her eyes pierced his soul. He turned and knelt beside her. "Nancy—"

The door swung open. More visitors arrived.

Nancy's eyes brightened as a smile adorned her face.

He stood, forced a smile, and greeted their friends from church.

They'd brought flowers, gifts, and bustling good humor. He could not wish them gone.

After a few minutes, he excused himself to go make a phone call. Instead, he took a turn down the corridor where he found a small chapel. The cool interior provided a good refuge for him. He tried in vain to form his thoughts into prayers.

Life felt a little like a train barreling down the track. What lay ahead for them? A clear track or disaster?

His words were halting and simple. "God help me. I need … I need …"

He huffed out a breath. Nancy. He had so much he needed to say to her. She seemed so fragile right now. How could he reveal everything he'd learned?

He gripped the back of the chair in front of him, bent his head forward, and prayed again, asking for wisdom. If what he had to say upset her too much, she could lose the precious child she carried. Could he risk it?

In that moment, he knew the answer. He could not. Not yet. Perhaps never.

Chapter Thirty

The third week of her hospital stay, Nancy went into labor again. This time, they didn't try to stop it.

Amy Juliana Emerson weighed just under five pounds. Though tiny, she was healthy and possessed a good set of lungs. Everyone called her a miracle baby.

Afterwards, Nancy lay flat on her back, flooded with relief to have it over. Now she could go home. But Dr. Hansen crushed her hopes again.

"Amy is three weeks premature, Nancy. She can't possibly leave the hospital yet."

On a blustery day in mid-March, Robert escorted Nancy and their infant daughter home.

The foyer seemed crowded with people as Robert and Kip helped Nancy inside.

Grace followed along behind, carrying the baby. "We've brought the bassinet down to the parlor. That way, everyone can get a good look at her."

Robert's mother and father brought Jack downstairs. Holding his hand, Juliana approached the bassinet to let Jack get a first look at his sister. He took one glance then ran to join his mother near the fire. He climbed into her lap and laid his head against her shoulder.

"I've missed you, Mommy."

"I've missed you, too, sweetheart." She stroked his hair and allowed her gaze to follow Robert as he interacted with his parents. She envied them his smiles, his jocular manner. To her, he'd been distant, almost aloof. She suspected that in his heart he still believed the worst of her. Of course, she'd done nothing to change that. Too much time had passed with very little communication between them.

Like most men, Robert had his own interests. Perhaps he had replaced her with someone else.

Nancy drew in a painful breath and forced her gaze away from him to the embers glowing in the fireplace. If their love had dwindled and died, it was her fault.

Without a word to Nancy, Robert left the room. Nancy tried not to dwell on it.

His mother stood beside the bassinet cooing to the baby. "You are such a wonderful blessing." Amy was fast asleep, but this did not deter her grandmother. "We've never had a little girl. You're going to be so spoiled. I've made you ruffled dresses and pink satin booties. You'll be the best dressed baby girl in town."

Nancy kissed the top of Jack's head. "Mommy needs to get up now, dear."

Jack slid down from her lap.

Nancy rose from the chair. She joined her mother-in-law beside the bassinet and looked at Amy.

Her eyes still glued to the baby, Juliana said, "Oh, Nancy, she is so beautiful."

She did indeed look sweet lying amidst all the ribbons and lace. At that moment, Amy opened her eyes and looked around, as if to see where she was, then yawned and stretched and drifted back to sleep.

Juliana drew in a quick breath. "Did you see that?" She reached down to press a finger gently into the baby's cheek. "Daniel come and look."

Nancy stood aside to make room for Daniel, wondering what Juliana had seen.

He bent over the bassinet. "What's all the excitement?"

A smile lit Juliana's face. "See? She has a dimple in her right cheek—exactly like Robert's."

Robert strode into the room. "What's exactly like mine?"

His mother laid her hand on his arm. "Have you noticed the dimple in her cheek?"

Nancy's attention flew to Robert's face as he cast a glance over his mother's shoulder, but Nancy couldn't see that the news made any kind of impression on him.

"No, I haven't."

With all the attention and noise, Amy set up a howl.

"Look, there it is," his mother said.

Daniel chuckled as he stepped aside and offered an arm to Nancy. "What a lot of nonsense about a dimple." He led her to the dining room where their supper waited. "You know Mother's going to be ridiculous for several weeks, don't you?"

After everyone had gone home and Jack was asleep, Nancy and Robert were finally alone.

Robert's eyes held tenderness as he gazed at Nancy. "I guess I'd better get my two girls up to bed."

She returned his gaze. Was he happy now? Was he finally convinced the child was his?

He helped her upstairs and then went back down to bring up the bassinet. When he had everything situated, he left again.

Tears stung Nancy's eyes. He didn't want to be around her.

She was just about to lie down when he returned bearing hot cocoa.

He set the tray down and stood near the sofa. "I hoped we could have a little time together before you went to bed. Here, come sit with me."

She hesitated a moment then stepped over to the sofa and sat down. He handed her a cup.

They sat in silence while they drank. In the not-too-distant past, Nancy would welcome a companionable silence. On this night though, the air between them seemed strewn with great boulders. And the man beside her gave no indication of trouble. He sipped his cocoa and breathed.

Robert set his empty cup aside and put his arm around her. "It's so good to have you home again." He leaned sideways to kiss her forehead.

She closed her eyes and drew a deep breath, letting it out slowly. She could almost pretend nothing had ever come between them. But those hurtful words returned to mind, bringing with them the searing pain to claw at her heart. *Is this child mine?*

"Nancy," he whispered, his lips against her hair. "I want to make things right again, but I don't know how. If I could take those words back, I would. That's the trouble with words. Once they're out there, it's too late."

She swallowed the lump in her throat and forced herself to speak the thoughts so often in her mind of late. "You had a right to be angry with me. I ... I should have told you ... about the visits a long time ago."

He took the cup from her trembling hands and set it down, turned back, and encircled her in his arms.

She had longed for this. Slowly, she relaxed against him and allowed him to comfort her.

Robert pulled back to gaze into her eyes. "Nancy, was he demanding money from you?"

She bit her lip and nodded.

"And you've been paying him?"

Her breath caught in her throat. She nodded again. She squeezed her eyes shut, expecting the worst, but he pulled her even closer.

Just like the night in the parking lot at the little cafe. Just like the night they'd married.

Chapter Thirty-One

A gray sky did little to alleviate Nancy's melancholy. Dr. Hansen said it was quite common to have problems of this nature after childbirth, especially when there were difficulties.

"Get outside," he'd said. "If possible, take a walk every day. The fresh air and exercise will do you good."

Grace Boggs accompanied Nancy, pushing the baby carriage.

Jack ran ahead and then waited for them to catch up, each time saying, "Did you see me, Mommy?" When he repeated this over and over, Nancy had to smile.

They passed new construction on Elm Street where three-story brownstone houses were being built. Grace clucked her tongue. "Look at that, Miss Nancy. Why, they're building those houses so close together, you can sit at your kitchen table and say good morning to your neighbor."

Nancy kept her gaze locked on Jack lest he stray too far ahead. How she hated living with fear. She laid her hand over her heart. Worst of all, she was secretly afraid there may be some dark hereditary trait she had inherited from her mother's family. Nate's family, too. She blew out a pent-up breath and forced herself to respond to Grace's observations about the houses. "They are lovely, though. The bay windows afford a panoramic view of the park."

Grace bent forward to tend to Amy, startled awake by the pounding of a hammer. They pushed forward, crossing the street into the park. Jack made a beeline for the swings. A man in a leather jacket and dark hat stepped out of the shadows near the gazebo. Nancy's heart nearly stopped, but it wasn't Nate. The man walked right past them.

"Are you all right, Miss Nancy? You look pale. Why don't you sit down for a few minutes? I'll keep an eye on Master Jack."

Nancy smiled her thanks and strolled to a bench near the pond where ducks glided over the water. Overhead, the clouds drifted apart and the sun broke through. Its warmth stole into her heart. The muscles in her jaw relaxed, and the ache in the back of her neck ceased. She drew in a deep breath of fresh spring air and smiled at the antics of the ducks on the pond.

"Mr. Boston is here, sir."

Robert glanced up to see his secretary standing in the door.

He'd been so involved in the figures before him, he hadn't heard her entry. He nodded. "Show him in please, Martha."

William strolled into the room, and Martha closed the door. William extended his hand to shake Robert's. "Did you forget our lunch date?"

Robert shook his head. "No, but I did let the time get away from me. Trying to decide where to cut Roth's budget."

William nodded his agreement. "Not easy, is it? But necessary, if we're going to get the company through these tough times."

Robert stood, grabbed his hat and opened the door for William. "After you."

William grinned. "Age before beauty."

William's car stood out front. Robert glanced at the older man. "We're not walking?"

"I thought we'd go to the club. Hannah's cooking today."

Robert smiled as he climbed into the passenger seat. "Sure it's not an excuse to drive your new car?"

William grinned. "Well, that, too."

The *Cadillac Victoria Coupe* had been the talk of the town when William first drove it up to the courthouse. Robert removed his hat and stretched out in the cushy seat. He sucked in a deep breath of fresh spring air, tinged with diesel fuel from the truck in front of them, and relaxed.

Until they pulled into the parking lot of the country club, William kept up a steady commentary on how smoothly "his baby" drove.

Robert opened his door. He donned his hat and stood. "Looks crowded."

"News travels fast. Hannah's all the rave these days. That roasted lamb last week was amazing."

Gentlemen reclined on the veranda, smoking thick cigars as William and Robert climbed the wide steps to the door. A uniformed footman greeted them. "Gentlemen, right this way."

William winked at Robert. "I thought I'd better reserve a table."

"Good thing." The scent of well-cooked food wafted through the open door. Robert's stomach growled. Once they were seated and their glasses were filled, Robert eyed William. "What's so important we can't talk at the office?" He sat back as the waiter delivered heaping plates of food.

"Mmmm ... prime rib." William speared a forkful. "Rumblings on Wall Street." He closed his eyes and savored the taste of the food.

Robert smirked. "One would think you hadn't eaten in a week."

"Haven't. Not like this. Ever since the club stole Hannah from me."

Robert poured gravy over the silky whipped potatoes on his plate. "They hardly stole her. I heard they offered her a hefty salary. And the hours are better. One way or the other, you have to pay for your dinner. Now what's this about Wall Street? Should I be worried?"

William surveyed the room then bent his head nearer to Robert's. "It's not common knowledge, and I can't name names, but I've gotten a tip. It's not good news."

Robert sat back and eyed William. "Local or overseas?"

"Local this time." William drained the last of his tea. The waiter refilled his glass and topped off Robert's. After he'd stepped away, William continued, "Good news is, oil should be safe. Amelia got a gold mine there." He tipped his glass to Robert. "Smart woman, Miss Amelia."

"Indeed. So what are you telling me? Should we sell, hold, what?"

"Hang up the Roth deal. Then tighten up what you can. If what my man says is true, this could be bad. Worse than postwar."

Robert wiped his mouth with the napkin then returned it to his lap. "Sounds ominous."

"Could be." He finished off his potatoes and pushed his plate aside. "Now, how's Nancy?"

Robert placed his hands palms down on the tabletop. "I don't know what to do about Nancy. I've tried everything. We've all tried everything."

William glanced at Robert over the rim of his glass. After a swallow of tea, he shook his head then touched his lips with a napkin. "I think it's the snowball effect."

Robert frowned. "The snowball effect?"

"Have you thought about how much has happened to her in the last … oh, four years?"

Robert shrugged. "I *know* how much has happened. I was there, too, remember?"

"I don't think she's been able to keep up with it, son. She went from being the belle of the ball to a wife in a few short weeks. Lost her grandmother, became a mother, and that's not counting all that young rapscallion has put her through over the years. We don't know what he's been telling her. Do you know why she agreed to pay the money? Did you ever ask her?"

Robert closed his eyes. "I didn't want to upset her."

William chuckled. "Oh, how times have changed. The man so well known for his inquisitive nature cannot bring himself to interrogate his own wife." He leveled his gaze at Robert. "What are you afraid of?"

Robert pushed his plate aside. "She's so fragile right now. I don't want to hurt her. She obviously doesn't want to talk about it. Not to me, anyway."

"I could talk to her if you like. But I really believe you should do it. It might be good if the two of you could go away together."

"I've thought of that, but the timing is … not so good. Amy is too young yet."

"I suppose that's so," William said, folding his hands together.

An idea occurred to Robert. "Perhaps we could go to Perry's Landing. She loves it there. I can't take much time off, but she could stay longer."

William nodded. "I think that's a very good idea. Get her away from the regular ins and outs of home life. Your grandmother will love on her and spoil those babies, and you can bask in a little peace of mind."

William rubbed his abdomen and glanced at the waiter. "I'm going to need you to wrap up that pie." He grinned at Robert. "I'll have it for dessert after dinner."

Robert chuckled. "I give it an hour at most. That piece of pie won't make it 'til dinner."

Nancy, Grace Boggs, and the children traveled to Perry's Landing ahead of Robert. As Kip maneuvered the car down the narrow lane that led to the house, Nancy's eyes were drawn to brightly hued azaleas that bloomed among the pale green foliage of the budding trees.

Grace sighed. "It sure is a beautiful place."

Nancy caught a glimpse of Grandma Perry working in her garden. At their approach, the older woman stood and waved. She removed her work gloves and hurried to the car. Her bright eyes soon lit on the baby. "Oh, what a beautiful little girl." She hovered over Nancy to peer into Amy's face. "I can hardly wait to hold her. Come on in, everyone. Delia has supper ready to set on the table. We knew you'd all be starving."

Jack jumped up the steps one at a time as Grandma Perry led the way inside the house. With a merry giggle, she bent to kiss the top of his head. "You are growing up so fast."

He ran behind her to the door. "I'm almost four."

A bright smile lit her face as she held the screen door open for all of them to enter. "I know, only six more months to go."

Nancy laid Amy down in the bassinet when it was ready. She gave up her coat and hat to Delia as Grandma Perry carried on a constant flow of conversation.

"It's absolutely the best time of year for you to come. Everything is blooming. The runoff from the snowmelt has the creek brim full." She paused to glance back at Nancy. "Oh, I'm sorry, dear. I'm so excited you're here. You go on upstairs and get settled in. After you freshen up, we'll have dinner."

During dinner, Jack fell asleep at the table. After Grace carried him upstairs to bed, Nancy sat back in her chair. "Thank you for a wonderful meal, Grandma."

Grandma Perry beamed. "I'm glad to do it." She gave a soft chuckle as she pushed away from the table. "Of course,

Delia did most of it. Let's retire to the parlor where we can relax. Unless you need to go up to bed."

Nancy rose from her chair. "I'll sit with you a while. I need to unwind."

Once they were seated in the parlor, Grandma Perry picked up her knitting. "While you're here, perhaps you'd like to learn how to knit. I remember you mentioned it once."

"I'd like that. Thank you." She settled back in her chair, facing the fire. In the comfortable silence that followed, she heard a whippoorwill call. Farther away, a train whistle blew. Such a lonely sound.

She missed Robert.

"What's wrong, dear? Not homesick, I hope?"

Nancy shot a quick glance at the older woman. She always seemed to sense Nancy's moods. "Maybe a little."

"It'll soon pass. There's so much to do here, and I know you'll love being outdoors if the weather cooperates." She let one of the knitting needles fall into her lap and rubbed her elbow. "My aches and pains tell me we could be in for some wet weather. But that's spring for you. It won't last long. We have time on our side." She smiled and took up her work again. "That's the wonderful thing about extended visits."

Grandma Perry's achy bones held true. Nancy's first morning at Perry's Landing was overcast. Once the rain began to fall, it continued throughout the day. The back veranda provided respite, with a porch swing overlooking the valley. Nancy spent many hours there while Jack played at whatever he could find to do. The veranda wrapped all the way around the house, so he ran round and round, which irritated Grace Boggs.

"I can't abide it anymore, Miss Nancy. I'm going in to see what I can do to help Delia. If it's all right with you, that is."

Nancy glanced up from the book she was reading. Amy was being spoiled and coddled by Grandma Perry inside, so she had only Jack to tend. "You go on in. I'll keep an eye on Jack." A sudden gust of wind pelted them with rain. Jack squealed and took off in the opposite direction.

Nancy chuckled and gave the swing another push with her toe. When had she felt so relaxed? She didn't have to worry about anything. No meals to plan, no cleaning, no social events to schedule. No dread of seeing Nate.

A niggling fear scratched at her insides. What would happen if the payments ceased? What would Nate do? Would he make good on his threats? She closed her eyes and tried to shut out thoughts of him. If only Robert would come. She felt so safe when he was near.

The screen door swung open. Grandma Perry stepped out, a broad smile on her face. Nancy liked the way the skin around her eyes crinkled when she smiled. "The little lady is napping, so I thought I'd join you for a spell."

Nancy sat up to make room for her on the swing.

Grandma sat down and they set up a rhythm, swinging to and fro.

Raindrops pattered on the veranda's tin roof.

Jack scurried by, trailed by a wooden pull toy that bounced instead of rolling on its wheels.

Grandma chuckled. "Wouldn't you love to have a fraction of that energy?"

Their laughter echoed across the yard.

Grandma drew in a deep breath and sighed. "When the weather dries up, you should take Jack riding. It's so beautiful this time of year."

"That's a good idea. Jack loves to ride his pony."

"That pony's gotten fat and sassy. She could certainly use the exercise."

Nancy grinned. "Kind of like me."

Grandma Perry gazed at her for what seemed a very long time.

Nancy squirmed under the scrutiny. What was the woman thinking?

"Don't take this the wrong way, dear, but I always thought you could use a little more meat on your bones."

Nancy drew back to look at her. She'd never heard the woman utter a negative word. She crossed her arms over her chest. "A few days of Delia's excellent cooking will help with that."

Grandma cackled. "That's the truth. I hear you've made quite a few changes to the house. It needed a feminine touch."

"Yes, Robert gave me carte blanche, so I took advantage of it. It's much more comfortable now." She watched Grandma's face. "Robert told me you seldom stayed there."

Grandma sniffed. "I preferred the slower paced life out here." She glanced at Nancy. "And my presence in town would've cramped the senator's style somewhat."

Nancy tried to maintain a blank face, but it was difficult, as the meaning of Grandma's words sank in.

Grandma's tinkling laughter made it impossible. "Oh, that look is priceless." She patted Nancy's knee. "You're such a sweet girl, and Robert is a good man. Nothing like his grandfather." She sighed. "Thank God. Oh, there was a time when our marriage was important to him. He wanted me beside him during elections. But once it was over, I returned here. When he wasn't in Washington, he stayed at the house in town."

They sat in silence until the quiet penetrated Nancy's consciousness. It was too quiet. She sat forward and gazed about them. "Where is Jack?"

They both stood. Grandma headed for the back door. "I'll check with Delia and Grace, while you check the front. He's bound to be somewhere on the porch. I don't think he'd set off in this weather, do you?"

Nancy looked up. The rain was descending in sheets, straight down. "Surely not." She headed toward the front of the house. She reached the front door just as Grandma stepped out of it. Both stopped as their gazes lit on Jack, fast asleep in the big old rocker.

The rain stopped overnight. Nancy awoke to sunlight streaming through the sheer curtains of her window. It was still too wet to go out riding, so she strolled around the perimeter of the house admiring Grandma Perry's flowerbeds. By evening, the sun had dried the grass. A light breeze soughed through a stand of pine trees near the barn. Jack's high-pitched laughter rang out from the swing beneath an old oak tree where Grace tatted a lace doily and hummed "Sweet Bye and Bye." Amy cooed in her bassinet while Grandma Perry and Nancy sorted through gladiolus bulbs.

Grandma held several of the bulbs in the palm of her hand. "We'll plant the largest in the garden. These smaller ones will need more support as they grow, so I like to plant them along the fence."

A light scent reached Nancy's nose, sparking a distant memory. Someone was smoking. She was unaware of any one of Grandma Perry's household who smoked. She glanced toward the barn. Could be one of the hands. She dismissed the thought and gave her attention to Amy, who had caught sight of her.

On the morning of their third day at Perry's Landing, Nancy woke to birdsong and a light, fragrant breeze blowing in the window. After breakfast, she fed Amy then turned her over to Grace. Hand-in-hand with Jack, she headed to the stables.

Al Winston, a lanky man in his fifties, had cared for the Perry horses for years. He recommended a docile bay for Nancy to ride and brought out a speckled pony for Jack.

"There's an easy path to the river," Al told her with a nod toward the valley. "Follow this slope down through that stand of trees. From there you can cut across the pasture. There's a gate to go through then a clear path up the hill."

She'd heard Robert speak of the view from the crest of the hill but had never made the trek herself.

When she and Jack were in the saddles, she walked her horse down the hill beside Jack on his pony. He was a good little rider, thanks to Robert who'd taken the time to teach him. Jack chattered away as they rode through the pasture, his voice echoing across the valley.

Nancy drew up her horse on the crest of the hill and dismounted then helped Jack down from the pony. She could see the river snaking through the hills, its water sparkling in the morning sun. Splashes of bright spring green intermingled with the darkness of the evergreens on the hillsides.

A red-tailed hawk called overhead as it circled, looking for food.

Nancy breathed deeply, thrilling to the feel of the air that filled her lungs.

"Mommy, look," Jack said as the hawk dove into the river then back up with a wriggling fish in its claws.

Nancy knelt beside him. "He's got his lunch," she told him. "I guess we'd better get back so we can have ours. Your little sister is going to be hungry."

"Do we have to?"

"I'm afraid so, honey. But we can come back tomorrow if you like." He allowed her to help him into the saddle. She led her horse over to a rock so she could climb back on.

Jack was quiet as they made their way down the steep slope. She knew he was still upset. He was jealous of the time she spent with Amy, but it couldn't be helped. She did her best to be patient with him.

At the base of the hill, Nancy dismounted to open the gate. She waited as her son passed through then she led the bay. After refastening the gate, she climbed back on the horse, and they galloped across the pasture, Jack laughing all the way. After crossing the river, they started up along the path through the woods.

Jack's pony stopped suddenly, tossed his head, and whinnied. Nancy pulled her horse alongside.

She squinted uphill into the shadowy woods. After spending time in the bright sun, the woods seemed darker than before. A chill danced down her spine as she caught a whiff of smoke. Cigarette smoke. *Just like yesterday.*

A figure stepped out from behind a tree. At first, she thought it was Al Winston. Then her blood turned cold as she recognized Nate. He trod nearer and removed the cigarette from his mouth.

"Surprised to see me, Nancy? You shouldn't be." His eyes narrowed as he blew smoke at her. "You cut me off."

Nancy sat still, wishing she could run him over with her horse. She shot a quick glance at Jack, who sat quietly watching the man in front of them.

"I didn't cut you off, Nate," she said, struggling to keep her voice even. She didn't want to alarm her son. "Jack, you go on back to the barn."

Nate stepped in front of the pony. "You stay right there, boy. Don't you move." Jack's eyes widened as he gazed from the stranger to his mother.

Nancy slipped down from her horse and started toward the frightened boy. "Let him go, Nate, please."

Nate sneered and stepped in front of her. "He's a brave boy, Nancy. Good looking, too, like his old man. I want him to stay."

She fought rising panic. Did Nate intend to harm her son? She wanted to get between them but couldn't find a way. If only Robert would come.

For a brief moment, she pictured him riding to her rescue. But the vision was gone in a flash as reality settled in.

"If you didn't cut me off, sweetheart, who did?" He propped an elbow on the pony's side.

"Robert found out. I thought he was still sending it," she said. It sounded like a feeble excuse, but it was true. "I've been … ill … and …"

"I heard about your illness." He took a draw on his cigarette and blew smoke in her face again. "You think I care about that? Not anymore, sweetheart. Not anymore. All I want is the money." He removed his arm from the pony's back and crossed both arms over his chest. "I heard a rumor that your esteemed husband was out looking for me. What does that mean, Nancy?" He took a step nearer, his eyes boring into hers.

Nancy drew in a quick breath. "What?"

"Oh, you didn't know?" He laughed out loud. "Well, isn't that rich? Are you not married to him? Doesn't he tell you everything? What a surprise." His face was so close to hers, she could smell his foul breath. He gripped her chin as his eyes bored into hers. "I'll bet he tells his mistress in New York."

"Mommy." Jack whimpered, reaching out to her.

Nate grabbed the boy out of the saddle before Nancy could get to him.

She lurched forward, grabbing for him. "No. Please don't take him."

Nate moved farther away.

Jack began to cry.

Nate tossed his cigarette aside and tightened his grip on the boy. "What would I want with a kid? I never wanted a kid. Didn't you get that? All I ever wanted was the money." He took a couple of backward steps, still holding onto Jack, who struggled against him.

"If lover boy doesn't want to give me the money, I'll take something of his that will get his attention."

"No!" Nancy raced toward Nate. "You can't take him. I won't let you."

Nate set Jack down on the ground then straightened up slowly, his cold, dark eyes never leaving her face. "But I told you. I don't want the kid. What would I do with a kid? No, sweetheart. I came for you. Remember? We always used to talk about it. Now we can have our time together. You must be awfully tired of Mr. Perfect, Esquire by now." He reached up to grab Nancy's arm as she made a lunge for Jack.

"No! Jack, run! Run to the barn! Get help!"

Nate slapped her hard across the mouth. Tears started in her eyes. Her lips burned.

"That's enough out of you." He grabbed her around the waist, wrenched her arms back, and dragged her through the woods. She screamed and struggled against him, but to no avail. Once in the woods, he pinned her against a tree trunk and tied a bandanna through her teeth. He jerked her along the embankment to a narrow lane where a car was parked. Then he forced her into the backseat. He looped a rope around her ankles and pulled it so tight, it burned her skin. Then he slammed the door.

The car moved when he jumped into the front seat. He started the car and pulled out, scattering debris as he floored the gas pedal.

What did he intend to do with her? Jack's terrified eyes as he took off running up the hill pierced her heart. *Oh, please God, keep him safe—don't let him get lost. And my baby, oh God help me. My baby!* She stifled a sob. Amy would be hungry. She'd need to nurse, and her mommy wouldn't be coming home.

Chapter Thirty-Two

Robert stared out his office window at the noonday crush of people headed to lunch. He searched their faces for a glimpse of the man he'd not laid eyes on for almost five years. By now, Nate would have changed. He may have grown a mustache or a beard. His hair may be longer or shorter. He may have put on weight. Would Robert recognize him?

Several times, Flo had asked about the monthly withdrawal. Each time, he'd told her he would take care of it. Two weeks passed as he waited, hoping to flush out the predator.

He'd asked Flo not to say anything to Nancy before the party left for Perry's Landing. Still, he worried, his nerves painfully taut. A sharp rap at the door made his heart race.

"Mr. Emerson?" Flo called from the other side of his closed door. She knocked again.

After a moment's hesitation, he opened it and gazed down at her. "Yes, Flo?"

"I ... I was concerned about the withdrawal, sir. It's nearly two weeks since ... it was due."

"Please don't concern yourself, Flo. I told you I'd take care of it, and I will. Is there anything else you need?"

She sighed. "No, sir, I'll be going then. Everything's in order."

Robert started to close the door then thought better of it. "Flo."

"Yes, sir?"

"Thank you for all you've done. I know the last few months have been ... difficult."

Her eyes sparkled behind her spectacles. "It's been a pleasure, sir. I'd do most anything for Mrs. Emerson. She's the sweetest lady I've ever worked for."

"Yes, she is a very sweet lady."

After Flo left, Robert went back to his desk and sank into the chair, intending to get some work done, but he found it difficult to concentrate. He'd planned to keep Nancy and the children at a safe distance while the police closed in on Nate. Then he'd taken William's suggestion to stay close to home and wait for the man to show himself. So far, there'd been no sign of him.

Robert was finishing lunch when the phone jangled. His grandmother's frantic voice informed him of Nancy's disappearance. "Jack said a mean man took her. He called the man 'Nate.'"

Heart pounding with dread, Robert called his father. Ten minutes later, he jumped into his car and headed for the train station. His father and William met him there. Robert's hands shook as he paid for his ticket.

"I've called the police and informed them," William said. "Just in case he shows up around here."

His father gripped Robert's shoulder. "Your mother and I will come to Perry's Landing to take over care of the children."

He sank onto the nearest bench outside the station and dropped his head into his hands as sobs shook him. His father sat beside him on the bench rubbing Robert's back.

Robert pulled a handkerchief from his pocket to mop his eyes. "It's all my fault. I thought I could draw him out on my own. I never dreamed he'd do something like this."

His father patted Robert's knee. "No one could've predicted this."

The train whistle blew. Robert sucked in a ragged breath then rose from the bench. He reached his hand toward William.

William gave it a hearty squeeze. "We'll all be praying, Robert."

"I appreciate that."

His father caught him in a strong embrace. "Guard your heart, son."

Robert stepped onto the train. *Guard your heart.*

Robert stared out the window of the half-filled passenger car, eyes unseeing. How had Nate managed to discover Nancy's location? His breath caught in his throat. Had she spoken to Nate before she left? Surely not. She'd seemed so excited, so happy to go to Perry's Landing. He narrowed his eyes and brought them into focus but not to see the landscape passing by as the train rolled down the tracks. Perhaps she was glad to get away from him, her own husband. He sucked in a deep breath and closed his eyes. The rift between them had never completely healed. More than once, he'd caught her gazing at him with an odd look on her face. Was it possible she didn't trust him either?

His hands tightened into fists. Couldn't this train go any faster? He checked his watch for the hundredth time and tucked it back into his pocket. Finally, the depot came into view. Robert leapt from his seat, startling his neighbors. He stood on the steps of the still moving train, ready to jump down onto the platform as soon as the train stopped.

The platform was empty except for a middle-aged gentleman in a plain brown suit. He strode toward Robert and offered his hand. "Mr. Emerson? I'm Sheriff George Allen from Anglewood. How was your trip?"

Robert looked down at the shorter man, sizing him up. "Sheriff Allen." He squeezed the man's hand. "Is there any news?"

"Nothing yet. Let's head in that direction," he said with a nod toward the end of the platform and a black sedan. "Got any more luggage you need to pick up?"

"No, only this bag. I left in a hurry."

"Well, I'm afraid we've got very little to go on. We have a very sketchy description of the man, no description of the vehicle, only evidence that there was one. But we have a fine picture of the lady." He glanced sideways at Robert. "Beautiful lady, your wife."

Robert set his valise on the hood of the sheriff's car, opened the case, and drew out an envelope. "Here's all we have on Nate Conners. A photograph of him taken a few years, standing in front of an automobile—possibly the one he's driving now. We're not sure."

The sheriff pulled the photograph out of the envelope and looked at it.

Robert closed the valise. He stood with his hands on top of it, watching the sheriff. When the man lifted his eyes from the photograph, Robert said, "I'll do anything to get her back."

Sheriff Allen nodded. "I reckon he knows that."

They got into the car and the sheriff pulled away from the curb. Glancing at Robert, he said, "You right sure her disappearance was … involuntary?"

Robert swallowed an angry reply. He would have asked the same question.

"He's a right good-looking man," the sheriff went on to say. "She's a good-looking woman. It happens all the time."

"He's been blackmailing her for several years."

The sheriff's bushy eyebrows arched. "Now, that's a different colored horse altogether. Care to tell me why?"

"No," Robert said.

"All right." Sheriff Allen sent another side glance at Robert.

Robert sighed and looked out the window. "I'm sorry. I'm … a little on edge."

"I reckon you are, Mr. Emerson. I'm trying to do my job is all."

"Yes, I know." Robert's only wish was to hold his wife again. "I shouldn't have sent her here. Not by herself. I thought I was doing the best thing, by getting her away."

The sheriff glanced his way. "I'm not following you."

"My wife and I … got married a bit behind schedule."

"Ah," Sheriff Allen said. "And this guy knows about it?"

"Yes." Robert filled the sheriff in on as much as he felt necessary. No one needed to know Jack's true parentage. He hoped that would never surface.

They pulled into the drive at Perry's Landing and stopped in front of the house.

"So," the sheriff said, "we have something to go on now. We'll keep in touch. Will you be coming into town in the morning?"

Robert flinched and closed his eyes. She'd be with Nate all night. "Yes." He spoke through clenched teeth. "I'll be in first thing unless I hear from you sooner. Thanks for everything, Sheriff."

Grandma Perry opened the front door. Red-rimmed eyes beneath a brow creased with worry revealed her pain. "Oh, Robert, you're here. We've been frantic. Come inside, dear. I have coffee on."

As the sheriff pulled away, Robert followed his grandmother into the house.

Jack ran into his daddy's arms, crying.

"The bad man"—he sucked in air—"came and he wouldn't let me go with Mommy. He hurt Mommy." He buried his head in Robert's shoulder and sobbed.

Robert lifted Jack into his arms and held him. "Daddy's here now. Try to calm down." He glanced over his shoulder at Grace Boggs, who stood beside the stove, warming milk for the baby.

"He's been carrying on like that all day." She dabbed at her eyes with a corner of her apron. "We tried to get him to take a nap, but he can't be still. He's that worried. We all are, sir. I'm so sorry."

Robert kicked a chair out from under the table and sat down with Jack on his lap.

Grandma Perry brought coffee, and he took a sip before saying anything. He had to bite back the words foremost in his mind. The thought of Nancy being hurt by that man set his blood on fire.

He caught his grandmother's hand. "You're positive it was Nate?"

Before she could answer, Jack lifted his head. "She said Nate." He sat back and looked into Robert's eyes. "Mommy said, 'No, Nate, don't take him!' That's what she said. Mommy was scared, Daddy."

Robert gazed at his grandmother. "She must have thought he was going to take …" he nodded at Jack.

Grandma Perry nodded. "I think so, Robert. We think she offered herself instead."

Robert smoothed Jack's hair. "I wonder. Knowing Nate … he came for *her*."

Grandma sat down in a chair opposite Robert. Her hands shook as she twisted a handkerchief. "It's such a shame. She was beginning to perk up a little."

"Was she?"

Grandma nodded. "She was so happy to be out riding, I know she was. She couldn't wait to go with Jack. It had rained all day long the first day here, and she walked the floor."

Robert cupped Jack's chin in his palm. "Where did you go riding?"

Jack hiccupped again. "Up on the ridge, Daddy, where *we* always go. With Grandpa."

"Ah, and is that where Nate found you?"

He shook his head. "We were by the river. He was hiding in the trees, Daddy. He had a thing in his mouth. It looked like a red firebug 'til he came out of the dark. He scared Banjo."

For a moment, Robert bowed his head. If he could only get his hands on that man.

Jack squirmed. "Daddy, you're holding me too tight."

Robert relaxed his grip. "I'm sorry, Jack. I didn't mean to hurt you. Do you think you can go up to bed now?"

Jack's lower lip trembled. His eyes widened. "No, Daddy. I wanna stay with you."

"I'll go with you." Grace offered her hand. "Amy and I will be there with you, and your Daddy will be right here."

Jack sniffed. "Okay." Robert thought he sounded very grownup as he said, "I am awful tired. Will you tuck me in, Daddy?"

Robert rose and carried the boy upstairs, followed by Grace with Amy's bottle in her hand.

Robert set Jack down, and Grace went to get the boy's pajamas.

While Grace helped Jack prepare for bed, Robert scooped the baby up in his arms, holding her to him. He closed his eyes. His precious little girl. She gave him a toothless grin, revealing the dimple. He kissed her cheek and sat down on Jack's bed to hear the boy's prayers.

At the end of his long list of "God blesses," Jack said, "And please keep Mommy safe so she can come home again real soon."

Robert whispered "amen" to his son's prayer and bent to kiss him good night. He stood and passed Amy to Grace, avoiding the woman's gaze. He knew if he made eye contact with her, he'd never hold back the tears.

Desperation clawed at his breast. He needed air.

Chapter Thirty-Three

Nate drove at top speed over back roads, winding and twisting about, sometimes flinging Nancy into a heap in the floor. She would roll back up onto the seat, only to be flung down again. After several hours of driving, he stopped at a remote gas station. Before going inside, he threw a filthy old blanket over her. He gassed up the car, and they were soon back on the road.

Nancy managed to kick free of the filthy blanket when he called over his shoulder, "We're almost there, sweetheart. You're gonna like this place. It'll bring back old memories." He chuckled as he drove along. Nancy could tell he was drinking. From the way he was driving, she figured he must be plastered.

It was fully dark when he pulled the car off the road and bumped along a rough lane for several minutes before coming to an abrupt halt. He got out of the car, opened the back door, then flashed a light into her eyes. He dragged her out, pushing her roughly forward. The flash of light temporarily blinded her. Probably his intention. He loosened the bindings around her ankles, led her down an embankment, and pushed her down on the ground. She could hear him fumbling with something that sounded like metal against metal, then a loud creaking noise, like a door opening, one that had not been touched for a long while. In the few moments she sat there, she heard the flow of water and smelled the river, but there were no traffic sounds. Someplace well off the road, near a river, hours away from Perry's Landing and all she held dear.

She heard Nate returning, saw the flash of light again. He hauled her up and dragged her into the cool recesses of some kind of underground room. It had a musty smell, as if it had been closed up for a long time. The floor beneath her feet was cold and gritty. He pushed her down and left her for several minutes. She began to wonder if he was going to return. When he did, he brought more rope, which he used to bind her wrists and ankles. Then he pulled her ankles up behind her and looped the rope between her wrists. She was trussed like a turkey when he finished, lying on her side on the cold floor where the dirt and grit cut into the skin of her cheek.

"There you go, sweetheart, all fixed up. Sorry it has to be this way, but that's how it is. You can thank your husband." She heard scraping noises, like furniture being pulled over the floor. When Nate returned, he crouched down beside her. She could hear him breathing, smelled the stale alcohol and tobacco on his breath.

"Tsk, tsk, poor sweet Nancy. All this could have been avoided. Now, if your Mr. Emerson loves you, you'll get out of here. Otherwise, well ... maybe I've done you a favor." He rose to his feet and shone the light over her as if inspecting his work. "We had some fun though, didn't we, sweetheart? That's why I brought you here, so you could reminisce. I wanted you to remember how much we meant to each other at one time. Hah!" His humorless laugh grated on her nerves. He gave a soft whistle. "As if I could ever love a spoiled little brat like you. You think I didn't know you were slummin', baby?"

She heard him walking around and saw the flashlight shining here and there, as if he was searching for something. "And that snooty Miz Amelia, she was a piece of work. But in the end, she was flesh and blood just like the rest of us." She heard him chuckling softly to himself. "Ah, here it is."

It? What had he found?

"Well, this is good-bye for now, sweetheart. If all goes well, I'll be back here in two days. You'll be snug as a bug in a rug 'til then." He walked out, muttering under his breath. She heard the door shut, then metal on metal again. A metal latch?

She lay there listening for the sounds of his leaving. After several minutes, a car engine started. Then tires crunched on gravel. Tears rolled sideways, across the bridge of her nose, down the side of her face, to pool beneath her. She tried to gain control of her emotions. It was useless to cry. Panic would only wear her out. The pain of being tossed around and then tied up like an animal was excruciating. She tugged at the ropes, but they only grew tighter with the pressure.

The phone rang in the night, like an alarm in the darkness. Robert fought his way from sleep. Jumping up from the upstairs sofa where he'd finally drifted to sleep, he ran into the hall.

"Hello?" He expected to hear the sheriff's voice on the other end.

"Hello there, Robert, ole buddy. How ya doin' there? Not so good, I'll bet."

The voice was familiar, but in his groggy state, Robert couldn't place it. "Who is this?"

"Oh, Robert, you don't know me? I'm devastated."

"Nate."

"There you go. I knew you'd figure it out. You were always quick like that. But you really messed up, Mr. Big Time, I have to tell you."

"If you've hurt Nancy, I'll—"

"You'll *what*? Tell me, Mr. Lawyer Man, what will you do? Seems I'm holding all the cards here."

Robert's jaw clenched at the silly drunken banter. "What is it that you want, Nate?"

"Now let's not get in any hurry. All I want is what you owe me. I've kept up my part of the bargain. I kept my mouth shut all these years about the wedding date and that little boy. I figure you still owe me something for that. Now I've got something of yours that may mean something to you. I gotta tell you though, man, she doesn't seem to know whether you really care enough about her to pay up or not. That's no way to run a marriage.

"Let's see, what were we talking about? Oh yeah, money, money, money. I was thinking five hundred grand, Mr. Big Shot, what do you think?"

Robert pressed the heel of his hand against his forehead. "I'll need some time to come up with that."

"He doesn't even take a breath. I knew I should've asked for more. But I'm not greedy. Of course you'll need a little time. Time is what I've got. I'm in no hurry. You've got thirty-six hours. It's four in the morning now, so that'd be about right. I want small bills, too."

"How will I get it to you?"

"I'll meet you someplace dear to my heart. The ski lodge where I ... well, you know. Where little Jack got his start."

Robert closed his eyes, forced himself to ignore the goad. "The ski lodge?"

"Yeah, you know, at Sugar Creek—it's closed this time of year—nobody to bother us. By the way, if I see any cops, all deals are off."

"So, at noon day after tomorrow," Robert said, "I'll meet you at the Sugar Creek ski lodge with five hundred thousand dollars in small bills."

"And no cops, lawyer boy, or Nancy joins her grandma."

The phone went dead.

Robert stood for several moments listening to the dial tone.

"What is it, Robert, dear? I hope it's not bad news?"

Robert turned to find Grandma standing in the doorway of her bedroom holding her robe tight about her middle. Grace and Delia stood on either side of her. He set the receiver back in the cradle and faced them.

"Nate has demanded a ransom."

Chapter Thirty-Four

In the cool silence that followed Nate's retreat, Nancy fought to recover her sensibilities. She could lie here and cry all night, or she could try to figure a way of escape. She had no way of knowing if Nate really would return.

He'd referred to this a couple of times as a place she would remember. She chewed at the bandanna and tried to think what he meant. When had she ever been here?

She listened for telltale sounds that might give her a clue. The creaking sounds a house makes in the night, a branch scraping against the window, the sound of water dripping. Then, closer at hand, she heard a scurrying sound. Probably a mouse or a rat. She cringed and jerked. Pain shot up her legs as she struggled.

How long could she remain like this? If only she could fall asleep, but sleep avoided her. Hour after hour, she lay in complete misery, waiting for the dawn.

Nate was proud of himself. For once, he had the upper hand. The high and mighty Robert Emerson was down for the count. He laughed out loud while he banged the heel of his hand on the steering wheel. He pulled his car into a narrow, winding lane and followed it to a hunter's cabin belonging to his uncle. He'd get a few hours' sleep and then drive up to Sugar Creek after dark and lay low until morning.

Inside the crude cabin, he threw himself down on an old cot and lit a cigarette. After a deep draft, he blew smoke donuts and chuckled, remembering a much younger Nancy.

She'd been impressed by his ability to create such perfect circles of smoke. Poor kid, lying on that cold floor. She deserved it. After the way she'd looked down her nose at him, treated him like dirt. Now she was dirt or all but. He grinned. Nobody would ever think to look there. He should leave her to rot.

He narrowed his eyes as he fished a flake of tobacco from his mouth then reached into his shirt pocket and pulled out the gold necklace he'd given Nancy years ago. He'd dropped it on the floor of the old speakeasy a couple days before when he'd gone there to check the place out. Wouldn't Mama Liz be proud? She'd taught him how to get what he wanted out of life, and he was determined to do it.

He chuckled softly and tucked the trinket back in his pocket. Now she was living out her pitiful life in an old folks' home. Paying for a crime she didn't commit.

You'd never catch him scratching and begging like she had all of her days. With half a mil, he could go anywhere. Do anything. Be somebody. And he knew exactly where he'd go. California. Hobnob with the other big shots. He smashed out his cigarette and closed his eyes.

Maybe he could even get into movies.

After a few hours' sleep, he felt refreshed and more excited than ever. He rifled through his uncle's supplies until he found a can of beans, punctured the lid with his knife, and bent it back. He didn't even take the time to heat the beans. He ate them straight out of the can.

When he finished, he tossed the can into the cold fireplace and wiped his lips on his sleeve. "This is the last time I'm eating garbage." He swung out the door and climbed into his car.

It occurred to him along the road to Sugar Creek that the cops were liable to be out looking for him, so he took an alternate route to a nearby village. There, he pulled his car around back of a dingy little roadhouse.

He'd only stopped here once, so no one knew him. He smoothed his hair and rubbed the back of his neck. It was a little early, but he was in desperate need of a drink.

Robert left his grandmother's house before the sun came up. He'd gotten her chauffeur out of bed to drive him into town.

"You need me to wait for you, Mr. Emerson?"

Robert shook his head. "No, you go on back to Perry's Landing." He walked into the sheriff's office.

"I think it's time we called in some help," Sheriff Allen told him after hearing the story.

"He said no cops," Robert reminded him.

"I know he did, but kidnapping is a serious offense. We need help here, Mr. Emerson. We're a small town. We don't have the manpower for the hunt."

He had no sooner finished speaking when the door opened. Two men in dark suits entered the office, identified themselves as federal agents, and asked for Sheriff Allen.

One of the men stepped forward. "We're looking for Robert Emerson."

The sheriff gestured toward Robert. "This is Mr. Emerson. His wife's been abducted."

The man held out his hand to Robert. "Walter Brougham, I'm with the Federal Bureau of Investigation." He nodded his head toward the man with him. "This is my partner, Matt Stephens."

Robert shook hands with the two men. "I thought the Bureau only involved itself in organized crime."

"William Boston requested our presence. He thought we might be interested. He was right. We've been on this guy's trail for some time now." He laid a photograph on the desk. "This is your wife?"

Robert looked at the photograph. It was taken of her last summer, on the steps of their house. A lump rose in his throat. "Yes."

The man stood nose-to-nose with Robert. "I know this is tough, but I have to ask you some questions."

Robert nodded and plopped down in a nearby chair. He figured he was in for a long day.

A few hours later, Robert loaded a briefcase stuffed with tens and twenties into a borrowed sedan. He returned to Perry's Landing and pulled in behind his parents' car. His mother wrapped her arms around him. Robert allowed her to comfort him.

His father cleared his throat. "We've come to take the children back home with us."

Robert's mother released him. "Grandma, too, if she'll come."

Seated together in the parlor, Robert was subjected to his father's scrutiny. "What's the story?"

Robert kept it short, paraphrasing the phone conversation. "I believe he was inebriated, and I'm hoping that kept him from hurting her." He lifted his eyes to his father's. "Surely he won't hurt her."

His mother blew her nose then left the room to check on Grandma Perry. For a few moments, all was quiet.

Then his father spoke. "Have you had any rest at all?"

"A little last night, or rather this morning. I fell asleep on the couch upstairs. Then we got the call."

His father was silent, staring at his hands. "I know you have to do this, but be careful."

Robert gave him a wan smile as he nodded. "Detective Brougham told me they'd been following Nate since the last drop made by Florence Camden at the Southside post office. They watched him pick up the package then trailed him back to his apartment. A little while later, he went to Millbrooke Hospital where he was escorted back out again."

Robert drummed his fingers on the table and eyed his father. "He incited a loud argument between his aunts. That's what got him kicked out. And then they lost him."

"He knew he was being followed."

Robert nodded. "Undoubtedly."

"But why were they following him? Had they somehow gotten wind of the extortion?"

"No. Apparently, our Mr. Conners has another business on the side." He gave his dad a wry grin. "One that involves off-road driving ... late at night."

"Moonshine? Why am I not surprised? Well, then, he's not afraid of danger. And he may be violent. Especially if he's been imbibing that stuff. It's lethal."

Robert lowered his head in his hands.

His father rubbed his back. "I'm sorry, son. I got carried away. We're all praying. You know that."

Robert fought the desire to weep. Tears weren't going to help now. He needed to reach deep down inside himself, grasp every last drop of faith he possessed, and trust in that.

Nancy couldn't tell whether it was day or night. There was no light, so she couldn't judge time at all. Her eyes insisted on staying open, though the rest of her body was asleep and thankfully numb.

She'd managed to chew through part of the bandana. But her mouth had gone dry. She'd give most anything for a drink of water.

Drip … drip ... drip. That incessant sound—she could hear it, smell it. It was torture. But was it drinkable? Even more important, could she find it? She tried to move, but every muscle in her body objected, so she attempted a roll. She managed to drop over on one side then rocked back and forth until she was able to roll all the way over. After several minutes of total exhaustion, she started again. On the third roll, she banged into something solid. She hit her head so hard she saw stars. By pushing against the solid whatever it was, she managed to work herself into an upright position.

She took great gulps of air as her head throbbed in pain. *Concentrate. Figure out where the drip is located.* Could be an old sink or spigot. A spigot would be better. If it was low on the wall, she could reach it. She listened. It seemed to be coming from behind her, so she pressed her back against the solid thing and pushed herself around. This action brought fresh pain, as though her knees would snap in two. The pressure of moving strained her back, but the need for water would only increase. She must try to get to it if she was to survive.

Survive.

The word echoed in her tormented brain in time to the dripping.

After what seemed an eternity, she'd managed to inch her way around what she decided was some sort of cabinet. Now she knew she was very near the water source. Could even smell the rust. But rusty or not, if it was wet, she meant to drink it.

The cabinet was too high. She couldn't reach it. Instead, she collapsed in a heap on the floor and cried out in frustration and despair. When the fit of anger had passed, she willed herself to think. She had to come up with a solution.

I will get out of this!

A prayer rose within her that started out as a whisper until it dawned on her there was no one to hear her. She began to shout. She shouted out her frustration as tears flowed down her cheeks and into her mouth, soaking the bandana. She doubled over in anguish. As she did, the bandana loosened and fell in a limp ring about her neck.

"Thank You, God!" She laughed aloud and collapsed.

She lay in a stupor, halfway between sleeping and waking. Her mind began to play tricks on her. She heard voices. Grandma Perry laughed. Amy cooed. Jack called her name. "Mommy!"

She'd no idea how long she lay there. When she tried to turn over, something near her moved. She reached out with her fingers and tried to feel what it was. A board? Yes, it felt like a two-by-four. If she could get her fingers around it, perhaps she could use it.

An idea, clear as day, played like a filmstrip in her mind. She saw the two-by-four wedged beneath a dripping faucet. The water ran down the board. She could wet her tongue at the very least.

Desperation drove her to try. With great effort, she gripped the board with her fingers and pushed. Lifting took more effort, but she gave it everything she had. After several attempts, she managed to prop it against the cabinet. She gave it one final push. The board wedged against something with a force that threw her back against the floor. "Ahhhh!" Searing, almost unbearable pain jarred through her.

She opened her eyes to darkness. How long had she been out this time? No way to know.

Wait. It was quiet. Too quiet.

What was missing?

Realization broke over her like a flood. The drip had stopped. She rallied every last ounce of energy to push herself back up onto her knees then inched around, feeling for the plank. Found it.

It was wet.

"Yes!" She swung around almost too fast and nearly lost her balance. Leaning against the board, she raised herself and touched her tongue to it. The board was dirty, the water rusty, but it was wet.

It was life.

The drive to Sugar Creek took much longer than Robert had anticipated. He arrived only half an hour before the appointed time. Now it was a quarter past and still no Nate. Where was the man?

Had he misunderstood?

No, he had repeated the instructions, and Nate had confirmed them. Robert paced back and forth beside the car. After several more minutes, he stepped closer to the lodge. "Closed for the Season," the sign read. It was like a ghost town inhabited only by wildlife. Robert hunched his shoulders then loosened his neck to release some of the built-up tension. He scanned the perimeter but couldn't see anyone, though he knew the agents were in place.

Prickles ran down his spine. Had Nate seen the officers hiding in the hills? Or had something else gone wrong?

Minutes ticked away. Then the sound of an automobile brought Robert's attention back to the gravel road.

In the deep shade of the woods, he couldn't make out the color of the vehicle. At the top of the long incline, the car eased into the drive. As it approached, Robert recognized the sheriff's car.

Robert's hopes collapsed. What was that idiot sheriff doing?

The car stopped. Sheriff Allen stepped out and started toward him.

"What are you doing here? You're going to ruin—" Robert broke off at the look on Sheriff Allen's face. He swallowed. "What is it? What's happened?"

The sheriff shook his head. "He's not coming."

Robert glared at him. It was as he had feared. Nate had seen the officers. They'd spooked him off. He closed his eyes and drew in a deep breath. When the sheriff spoke, Robert opened his eyes.

"I'm sorry, Mr. Emerson. There was an accident, not fifteen minutes from here. His car left the road." He gripped Robert's arm. "Mr. Conners is dead."

Robert placed his hands on the car and leaned forward. "Dead?" *Nancy*. He jerked his head up. "Was he alone?"

The sheriff nodded. "Yes. We believe he was alone. The car flipped over several times and burned. He was thrown out. We found his body further down the incline. Looks like it happened sometime late last night."

Robert bowed his head again and moaned. "How will we ever find her now?"

Sheriff Allen reached for Robert's arm. "Come on, son. Let me drive you."

Robert shook his head. "I've got to get this other car back."

"We'll take care of it," the sheriff said. "Get the satchel."

Nancy had no idea how long she'd slept after wetting her lips and tongue with a few drops of rusty water. All she knew upon waking was that she hurt all over. Her wrists and ankles burned like fire. The pain in her knees was worse than anything she'd ever endured. The riding skirt she wore was but little protection against the grit and broken glass on the floor. Some of it had taken up residence in the skin of her knees. And the desire to straighten her legs was almost overwhelming.

She ached for Robert, to hear his voice and feel his strong arms about her, comforting her. Most of all, she wanted to see her children again. But she didn't know what to do, or how to get out of this. She couldn't even seem to cry anymore. She was too parched.

Then a new thought lodged in her brain. She wasn't sure how she knew, but she was certain. Nate wasn't coming back.

Oh, God, what am I going to do? She was going to die here, all alone. A sob caught in her throat. "Please, God, if you will get me out of this …"

Even to her ears, the words sounded lame and empty. How many chances does a person get to straighten up and live right? How many chances had she frittered away? How many times could you expect to be forgiven?

A memory echoed in her mind. "Seventy times seven." That was in the Bible. How many times was that? Four hundred and ninety. Surely she hadn't sinned that many times. Then, another memory, of another verse, "Forgive us our debts, as we forgive those indebted to us …"

She swallowed. Forgive? Forgive, Nate? No. I can't do it. I can't. Her lips stretched in agony, not physical anymore, but spiritual. She was going to die, and she couldn't forgive the one who'd done this to her.

Nancy heard voices and thought she was dreaming. When she tried to move, pain shot through her, proof she was not asleep. The voices were real. If she could hear them, would they not hear her? Perhaps if she was nearer the door. But where was the door, and how could she get close enough to call out?

How long until others came? She couldn't wait. She had to figure out a way to make herself heard. She had to get help.

It took several minutes to build up the strength. She nearly fainted from the exertion of rolling. She lay still until the pain subsided then tried again.

A woman's voice rang out. "Homer, you come back here."

Nancy thought she detected humor in the voice as the woman called again.

"I'm not finished with you, buster."

"Ain't no call for you to be yelling at me," a man answered. "Hush, now. You'll scare away all the fish."

They were fishing, so they'd probably stay a while. Nancy closed her eyes and tried to picture herself rolling in the direction of the voices. "You can do it, Nancy," she whispered. With one long draw of air to fill her lungs, she rocked herself onto her side. Stars of light flashed in her head as the pain soared. After a wave of nausea subsided, she tried again. Now on her back, she lay still and wondered how far she'd managed to roll. Six inches? A foot? Still she heard the voices. She tried to imagine their faces, to get her mind off the pain. An occasional spate of laughter convinced her they were good people. They would help her. If she could only get their attention.

After three more attempts, she rolled against something big and solid. A dead end. Tears welled up in her eyes. Then she heard the voices again. "Come on, Dora. Let's call it a day."

They were leaving. Nancy cried out and pushed against the solid object with one last show of strength. It gave a little. She pushed again, until with a loud scrape and groan, it tottered and fell.

Nancy fought back from the sudden darkness. Nausea gripped her and something warm and wet ran down the side of her face. Her arms were pinned beneath the thing on top of her. Panic threatened to steal her breath.

Then the voices returned.

"Did you hear that?" the man said. The voice sounded closer now.

"Hear what?" the woman asked.

Nancy struggled to cry out, but could only manage a gurgling noise.

"I heard a loud noise inside that building," the man said.

"Probably some varmint," the woman said. "Let's get out of here."

"No," Nancy moaned. "No, no, no!"

"No," the man echoed. "It was a loud noise, like something real heavy falling."

Someone fumbled at the door. Nancy tried to call out again, but bile rose in her throat. She sucked in a breath.

The woman's voice spoke again. "Could be somebody in there. That old place was a den of iniquity. You remember when the G-men busted it up? They put all those folks in jail and besides, I've heard tell it's haunted."

"This door's been opened recent," the man said. "Anybody in there?"

Nancy managed to cry out, "Help me!"

"There. Did you hear that?"

Someone pushed against the door. Then she heard a sound as if someone kicked it with his foot. It gave way with a loud screech.

Nancy began to sob. "Help me, please—oh God, *please* help."

"Someone's crying," she heard the woman say.

"I can't see nothing," the man said. "I've got a flashlight in the truck," he called into the pitch-black cellar. "I'll be right back."

Nancy continued to cry, praying he'd come back. "Please, please, please …"

Then the beam from a flashlight flickered. Heavy footsteps crunched in the dirt and broken glass on the floor. A bright light shone across her face.

"I found her," the man said. "Dora, get in here. I'm gonna need your help. She's over here. Leastways, I think it's a woman. Sounds like one. I need your help to lift this. Looks like part of an old billiards table. It's heavy."

Together, they managed to lift it off. The light shone in Nancy's eyes, temporarily blinding her.

Nancy tried to stop crying.

A shadow hovered over her.

"Oh my, look at this," the woman said. "We better get her into town right away."

"I was just thinking that," the man said. "Help me lift her. Look how her legs are pushed up." He was silent as he swept the flashlight beam along her legs. "Good gracious, Dora, look at this. She's all tied up."

"Mercy. Homer, do you reckon—do you think she's that one they been looking for?"

Relief flooded Nancy. Someone had been looking for her. They hadn't given up.

Together, they lifted her and managed to get her outside. The man pulled out his pocketknife and went to work on the ropes.

The woman sucked in a breath. "Lordy, that's got to hurt." She rubbed Nancy's arm and whispered words of comfort. "There, there. It won't be long now."

When he tried to straighten her legs, Nancy screamed.

Robert paced the floor in front of the fireplace, sat down on the edge of the sofa for a moment, then got up and strode to the window to gaze outside. He waited for the telephone to ring. An untouched dinner tray sat on a nearby table until the maid returned to whisk it away.

The police had questioned Nate's family and friends, looking for any possible lead as to where he could have taken Nancy. Even now, they were combing the countryside, checking every nook and cranny. Robert wanted to be with them, but they would not allow it. "Better to be home in case ..."

In case what? Would she suddenly turn up on their doorstep? He needed rest but couldn't relax. He couldn't keep his eyes closed for more than two minutes at a time without flinging them wide in a panic at the slightest noise.

He'd told Jack that Mommy was all right, that the police would find her and bring her home. Deep down in his heart, Robert believed it to be true, but this waiting was starting to get to him. Every hour, every day that passed could be crucial to her survival. He prayed constantly, "Wherever she is, Father, keep her safe."

It was four o'clock in the afternoon on the eighth day of their ordeal when the phone rang. Robert jumped to answer it.

His mother and Grace Boggs rushed in from the kitchen just in time to hear him say, "Thank God!"

Robert hung up and leaned against the desk. His legs threatened to give out. He met his mother's anxious gaze. "She's been found. She's alive." His hands shook as he pushed his fingers through his unruly hair. His mother rushed to him and threw her arms around him in a tight embrace.

Over her shoulder, Robert watched Grace cover her face with her apron and turn back to the kitchen.

With care, he pulled away from his mother. "I have to go. They're bringing her in to the hospital."

"Ours? Here? But where did they find her?"

"Hillsboro, near the river," he said on the way out the door. "I'll call you later."

Robert arrived at the hospital. He pushed through the door and rushed to the desk. The nurse directed him to a waiting room near the emergency entrance. He closed his eyes and set his jaw. More waiting.

Hours passed. The sun dipped low in the sky. Robert sat in the corner cradling his head in his hands. He raised his eyes as the door opened. A tall man in a long white coat entered.

"Mr. Robert Emerson?"

He jumped to his feet. "Yes?"

"I'm Dr. Simmons. Your wife is sleeping, Mr. Emerson, but you may see her. Don't be alarmed by the way she looks. It's not as bad as it seems."

Robert frowned. "What does that mean?"

"Well, she has some contusions to the head and face. She may have been badly beaten, or else it happened when she tried to escape, we're not certain. We've given her something to help her sleep. She needs rest so she can begin the healing process." He led the way down a long corridor and paused at the door to Nancy's hospital room.

"It's good you're seeing her now, before she's awake. That way, when she is awake, you won't react so badly. I'll let you go in alone. If you have any questions, ask one of the nurses. They'll send for me."

Robert entered the room and stood near the foot of Nancy's bed. For a moment, he thought the doctor may have directed him to the wrong room. He hardly recognized her. Her face was dark, with a swelling on one side. A white bandage covered the top of her head. Her lips were swollen and cracked. Both hands were bandaged. The portions of her forearms he could see were black and blue. He fought the desire to pull the covers away, to see how much more damage had been done.

He stepped to her side and leaned down to kiss her cheek. She gave a soft moan but did not wake.

He sat down beside the bed, watched her breathe, and wondered what she had suffered.

Too bad Nate was already dead. He should have been punished appropriately for what he had done. An old-fashioned hanging would have been Robert's choice.

A nurse tiptoed in and gestured for Robert to leave. "You may come again in the morning, sir." As she drew near, she continued. "You look as though you could use a good night's rest."

He gave her a quick nod, but even knowing Nancy was safe, he doubted he'd sleep. When he reached home, he got out of the car but stood leaning against it for a while to gather his thoughts.

He dropped his head back and gazed up at the stars. Amelia had certainly been right in all her assumptions about Nate. She'd also been right to tie up Nancy's inheritance, but it had not completely protected her. Robert had tried, but he couldn't protect her either.

Perhaps now they could get on with their lives. He prayed that it would be so. He loved Nancy, but Amelia's legacy had become a great burden to him.

Chapter Thirty-Five

Nancy stirred and opened her eyes. Was she dreaming? No, it was not a dream. As her eyes adjusted to the bright light of day, she turned her head and looked around. There was an odd pink aura to everything that she could not understand. At last, her eyes fell on the huddled figure of her husband, his elbows propped on the bed and his head in his hands. As if he sensed her gaze, he raised up. Their eyes locked.

"Nancy." He rose and bent over her.

She winced when he touched her hand. His fingers found one spot on her face that didn't feel badly bruised. She tried to smile, but her lips were still so swollen and sore, she couldn't seem to do so.

"The children?" she whispered.

"Mother and Dad have been wonderful. They've stayed right with the children since we brought them back here."

"How *ith* Jack?" She frowned. Her tongue felt swollen.

"He's doing very well. We had a time calming him down, but he's recovering quickly, as children do. He is worried about you, however. He asks about you every day." He smiled into her eyes. "We've all missed you dreadfully, darling. I'm so thankful to have you back."

She relaxed, content for the moment that everything was all right. Talking was such an effort. She didn't like the way it sounded. Lifting her hand, she reached toward Robert but was dismayed to see what the hand looked like. She drew it back again.

"I must ... look ... *tho* ... bad," she said, peering up at Robert.

"You look wonderful to me. But I'm afraid you are a little the worse for wear." He raised his eyebrows. "The doctor said the bruises will clear, in a week ... or so."

"Why ... did he leave me there?"

"You mean Nate?"

Nancy turned her head to look him full in the face. "Yes."

Robert set his jaw. "He ... left you there so he could collect a ransom."

She gazed at the ceiling for several moments before turning back to Robert. "Did you ... pay ... him?"

Robert took a breath as if he was going to answer. Then he stood and walked to the window.

Nancy watched him, wondering at his reticence. Was Nate still out there? Would he hear she was alive and return to finish the job? "Robert?"

He turned to face her. "I was set to. I went to meet him, but he never showed."

He was hiding something. She could tell. His jaw was set, brows knit, hands doubled into tight fists. All the signs were there. He released a pent-up breath and sat in the chair again. "There was an accident, Nancy. The night before he was to meet me, he ran off the road near the meeting place. He was killed."

His words hung in the air between them. A great sense of relief rushed through her, trailed by guilt. How terrible to feel this way over someone's passing, especially someone who had once been so important to her. She tried to hold back the tears, but they came on like a flood running down her face. How long had she lived in fear of Nate? Now he would no longer terrorize her. No more dread of losing Jack. No more payments every month or threat of bodily harm to herself.

Robert watched the tears stream down his wife's face. He wiped them away, but his own heart was torn. He wanted to stalk out and leave her lying there with her memories.

How could she grieve for the one who had done this awful thing to her? Could she still have feelings for the man?

After she drifted off to sleep, he left the room, nearly running headlong into Agnes Miller and Bette Devereux.

"Oh, Mr. Emerson," Bette said. "We heard they found Nancy. How is she?"

Robert glanced from one to the other. "She's fine. She's … sleeping right now." He'd asked the nurses not to allow anyone to see Nancy outside of family, so how had these two slipped in? "May I walk you out?"

Agnes Miller smiled and nodded. "Of course you may. I hope you don't mind that we've come. Mr. Boston thought she might like to see us."

Robert leveled his gaze at Agnes. "Really? Well, I appreciate your interest in her. But it's going to be at least a week, maybe more, before she's able to entertain friends."

Bette took her sister's arm. "We'd best be going, Sis. Mr. Emerson, you give her our love. She's been so good to Mama. It didn't seem right not to return such a kindness."

Robert frowned as he led the way through the labyrinthine halls of the old hospital. "I'll tell her you were here." Near the entrance, he stopped and faced them. "How is your mother?"

Bette smiled. "As ornery as ever."

Agnes glanced up at Robert. "We haven't told Mama Liz about … him. Not yet. Maybe never."

Bette nodded. "No telling what she'd do."

Robert pressed his lips together. He had no desire to speak of the man who'd brought such ruin on so many. How had these two women turned out so well despite their upbringing? He tried to lighten his demeanor, though his heart felt like a lead weight in his chest. "Maybe you can return in a couple of days. Perhaps then, she'll be able to have visitors."

"Thank you kindly, Mr. Emerson," Bette said.

Agnes smiled and nodded as Bette tugged on her arm.

Robert watched as the two left the hospital lobby. Then he set his hat on his head and strode out the door.

Robert went straight to Boston Emerson.

William popped the last bit of a ham sandwich in his mouth. He waved Robert to a chair and brushed his palms together. Robert removed his hat and sank into the offered chair across from William. "Sorry to interrupt your lunch, sir."

"Sorry I can't offer you any." He grinned and tapped his empty plate. "I ate every bite." He pushed the plate aside and sat forward. "How is Nancy?"

"She's recovering. She's the reason I'm here."

"How can I help you?"

"I wondered why you might have sent the Elliott sisters to visit her."

"Have they already come? I only meant for them to visit sometime soon. I suppose they were eager to see her."

"Why would they be? How do they know Nancy so well?"

William stood and adjusted his suspenders. "Do you two ever talk?" He strolled to a breakfront where a crystal pitcher held fresh water and poured two glasses. He offered one to Robert. "Nancy spent a great deal of time in their company before her abduction. They'd become quite close. I thought she'd like to see them."

"How is it that you know all this and I don't?

William shrugged.

Robert stared through the crystal glass William had given him, turning it to catch the light. "And you're convinced they mean her no harm?"

"Those ladies had nothing to do with what happened, Robert. In fact, they've a lot in common with Nancy. And you'll never catch them speaking evil of her. I'm sure you can't say that about our society friends." He leaned against his desk and sipped water.

"What's really eating you, Robert? Relief that it's all over?"

Robert emptied the glass and swallowed. What was eating away at his insides? He felt like a school kid, and he hated that. He stole a glance at William, who was patiently waiting for his answer. "Nancy asked me about … him. I hadn't wanted to tell her yet."

William nodded. "How did she take it?"

"Badly." *Too badly.* He turned his full gaze on William. "Is it possible she still had feelings for the man?"

William pressed his lips together as his brows met in an expression Robert had seen many times. The man must think him a fool. Maybe he was right.

"She's been through so much, Robert. I'm sure she's glad it's over."

Robert ruminated on that possibility for a moment. He massaged his temple and closed his eyes. When he looked again, William had moved to the window. He stood looking out at the street below.

A moment later, he pivoted on one foot to meet Robert's gaze. "Have you prepared a statement for the paper?"

Robert set his glass down and pushed out of his chair so he could be on a level with William. "Do you really think it necessary?"

William snorted. "Imagination oils gossip's engines. You know that as well as I do."

"I suppose you're right."

"You look tired, Robert. Why don't you let me handle it? You've got enough to worry about. I'll feed them just enough to calm their frenzy." His gaze seemed to penetrate Robert's soul. "Nothing to worry about, nothing at all."

Chapter Thirty-Six

On a sunny Wednesday morning while Robert was away on business, William Boston paid Nancy a visit.

She sat in a chair near the window, both legs propped up. As he entered, she watched his eyes for shock at her appearance but couldn't detect any.

"Nancy, it's good to see you up and looking quite well, I must say." He sat down next to her. "I heard they're going to open a new wing of the hospital for you."

She gave him a small smile. "I have been here a lot lately."

He sobered. "How are you, really?"

Nancy averted her eyes. She could never lie to him. "I'm getting better." She cast a glance at him.

Several moments ticked away as he watched her. "Right. If you say so." His warm, brown gaze calmed her nerves. He got up and crossed to the door. "I brought you something."

She watched as he stepped into the hall, amused by his demeanor. He soon returned, carrying something wrapped in a white cloth, which he set on the table in front of her. When he uncovered a familiar carved wooden box, she pressed her fingertips against her lips.

William sat down again, his eyes never leaving her face.

"Where did you find it?" She already knew the answer but had to ask.

"Nate's apartment."

Their gazes locked as she fingered the carvings on the lid of Amelia's jewelry box. "Is it ... all here?"

He cleared his throat. "All but one piece—a brooch—one of Amelia's newer purchases. I imagine the rest were too well known around here to get rid of, though he could have gone elsewhere." He smiled into her eyes. "Puzzled the detectives no end—why hadn't he sold the jewelry?"

Nancy didn't open the box. She sat back and folded her hands in her lap.

William's expression softened. "What's wrong, Nancy? I was hoping this would cheer you up."

She blinked back tears. Nervous fingers pulled at the fringe of her afghan. "I've made such a mess of things, Uncle William."

He covered her hands with one of his own. "Oh my dear, you can't possibly take the blame for all that's happened."

She shook her head. He didn't know the whole story.

He withdrew his hand and sat back in the chair. "What does Robert say?"

Much to Nancy's humiliation, she broke down and cried.

William seemed surprised at first but moved quickly to provide her with a handkerchief.

She looked up at him, wiped her eyes, and blew her nose. "I'm sorry, Uncle William. I didn't think I had any more tears. I've cried so much—"

"Well, that will be quite enough, young lady. There is no need to apologize." The glance he sent her way made her think he had something more to say.

He sat forward and gazed into her eyes. "I've something to tell you. Some of it may shock you, so you may as well sit back and make yourself comfortable."

Nancy drew back. What could possibly shock her after all she'd endured? Was it something about Robert? She bit her lower lip. Had Nate been right about him?

Her heart raced. Robert was having an affair.

William's voice was soft and low, but his words were succinct as he gave her a short history of Liz Elliott's and Amelia Sanderson's ongoing feud. She was not shocked, since she already knew about Nate's relationship to Liz Elliott, but Uncle William was not finished. Nancy watched him with a mixture of fear and dread as the man known for eloquence in the courtroom struggled for words.

"There is more to this story, more even than I previously confessed to Robert." His eyes darted to hers. "Because at the time I was still sorting it out."

Nancy maintained a respectful silence while she searched his face. What was it that troubled him so?

"Liz married out of spite, soon after your grandmother and Mr. Sanderson. She found someone she could manipulate. A pleasant enough young man, Mr. Elliott. He worked hard but had nothing. She continually pushed him to do better. He responded by drinking too much and staying away whenever he could.

Liz sought solace elsewhere. The world she frequented was filled with ... well ... let's say troubled souls. She found one such, who was at her wit's end and ready to take her own life. A rather pretty young woman who'd fallen prey to a very foolish young man. One who had no intention of marrying her. Liz persuaded this young woman to come stay at her house until the ... uh ... until her time came. Liz promised she would take care of everything. So the girl could leave and no one would be the wiser. Liz warned her never to speak of it. 'Never tell anyone who the father is,' she told the girl."

Nancy jerked to attention at the familiar statement.

William hesitated, his eyes questioning.

"I'm all right," she said with a quick shake of her head. "Do go on."

"When the child was born—a little girl—Liz kept her and raised her. The mother disappeared."

His gaze demanded her attention. He took a deep breath and exhaled before continuing. "Liz named the little girl Georgia. She was your mother."

"But, Uncle William, how ...? You said ... but that means ... Liz Elliott is not really my grandmother?"

He gave a barely perceptible nod, along with a half-smile. "Well, she did raise your mother. She expected the child to be beautiful, and she was, so she raised her to marry Franklin Sanderson. She sacrificed to put Georgia in the best schools. Trained her up to be a proper young lady. All for one purpose, to get her hands on at least a portion of the Sanderson fortune.

"As often as she could, she'd take Georgia downtown and show her the Woods-Sanderson building. Then she'd take her to your grandparents' home in town, and even out to the Sanderson estate on occasion. Anytime your father was about, she'd tell Georgia, 'this is the man that you will marry when you grow up.'"

William got up to pace around the room, as if deep in thought.

Nancy could no longer remain silent. Her mind reeled with unanswered questions. "But, Uncle William, how do you know all this if the mother disappeared as you say? Liz Elliott is hardly lucid enough to tell."

He stood with his hands behind his back looking so much more relaxed than he had been. "Liz Elliott was an avid journalist, Nancy. She wrote in her journal every day, keeping a very accurate—for the most part—record of everything. We found her journals in Nate's apartment."

She wet her lips and twisted her fingers in her lap. "So, I'm not a blood relation of Liz Elliott?"

"No, Nancy. So you need never worry about ending up in the same condition."

How did he always read her so well? Then she remembered something else. "Why would Nate have Liz's journals?"

"One only supposes, for the same reason he went after you, Nancy—money. All our suppositions about Liz's part in his designs on you, took a strange turn after these discoveries. We know now, or at least have a pretty good idea, who murdered your grandmother, although it's not completely clear why."

Nancy's heart beat faster. She'd known it all along but had never had the strength to say it. If she had uttered her suspicions long ago, so much pain could have been avoided.

"You are not to blame, Nancy. Not in any way."

"But if—"

He held up his hand. "No, Nancy. Don't try to take responsibility for any of it. If you had suspected him, you were not alone. So did I, but it took me four years to prove it. You could have done nothing different, except perhaps to tell someone that he was blackmailing you." He arched one brow as if to drive his point home.

She released a pent-up breath. "I was too afraid. Oh, Uncle William, I was so afraid he would try to take Jack."

"Yes, I know, and you certainly can't be blamed for that, dear. You did what you believed best. That's all we can do in this world, you know." He crossed the room and sat down at her side. "We also found, among his personal belongings, something we think he may have gotten hold of earlier than the night Amelia died."

Nancy held her breath.

"We found a copy of the original will—before Amelia made the final changes—in which the entire estate went to you."

Nancy put her hand to her mouth. Is that what he was after that night? Had he gone back up later, after their talk and gotten into the safe?

"H—He was in there. He startled me one night." She sat forward. "It was after one of the parties I'd attended. Grandmother called me in, and after we talked, I went into the study to put the jewelry away." She told him about the open window and Nate's interest in the safe. "How could I have been so stupid?"

"Nancy." He reached for her hand. "He was your friend. You hardly expected he would ever betray you."

She watched his expression change as a shadow seemed to pass over his face. "Uncle William, is there something else?"

He cleared his throat. "From what we've been able to piece together, Liz was in the house at least twice. It was probably Liz that Sissy heard arguing with Amelia, since we know it was not you. She was, as you remember, in the habit of going to the house. Before we had her confined, she wandered about freely. She was determined to speak with Amelia, so it was quite possible that she simply let herself in.

"Bette told us that they would often send Nate to look for her. That may have given him the idea. He was resourceful. We all know that. He could even have encouraged her to go to the house that night. He set it all up to implicate her in the murder. Everyone was aware of the enmity between Liz and Amelia. It was ingenious, in a way."

"But I don't understand why, Uncle William. Why did he want to kill Grandmother? He knew about the inheritance. He knew that night. I told him what she said to me."

"He had a copy of the original will, remember? He probably assumed she had not yet changed it and decided to get rid of her before she could."

It was all beginning to make sense, though it was as Uncle William told her, mostly conjecture. Nancy remembered Nate's reaction when she told him about the will. He had cursed her grandmother and said he knew she would pull something. So he'd slept with Nancy. Not because he'd loved her, or wanted her, but to assure a marriage with her. Nancy shook off the image of what a marriage to him would have meant, since he had later confessed he'd never really loved her. For the first time, she felt thankful to her grandmother.

With a start, she realized William was speaking again and had changed the subject. She heard him mention Robert's name.

"Nancy, you need to try to clear things up with him. He's miserable, and he's working much too hard. I don't really have the right to interfere. I hate to see two people who obviously love each other kept apart by a misunderstanding."

She scoffed. "A misunderstanding?"

He nodded. "I think he's under the presumption that you still had feelings for Nate. He has it in his head that you've been mourning that man's death."

Her jaw dropped. "Why would he think so? What would possibly give him such an idea?"

William sighed. "Who knows where men get these ideas, Nancy. To tell you the truth, men make presumptions, especially those in our profession." His eyes crinkled as he grinned at her. "Women are as unpredictable as spring weather."

He leaned forward to peer into her eyes. "Well, dear, I've no wish to overstay my welcome. I'd better go before my firm sends out the troops looking for me."

Before he could rise, Nancy reached for his hand. "Uncle William, may I ask one more question?"

"Certainly, Nancy."

"You knew her didn't you, my mother's mother?"

William gave her a wry smile. "You're very astute, Nancy. You need to use that same clarity with Robert. You would both benefit by it."

Nancy nodded. He had not really answered her question, but she supposed that would have to be enough.

He leaned forward and kissed her forehead. "There are some things best left unsaid. Someone very dear to me," he paused to steady the quiver in his voice, "could be deeply hurt by ... some of the things I have told you today."

She smiled as warmth flooded her breast. "You didn't tell me this. I figured it out on my own. I give you my solemn promise, I will never tell a soul." She leaned forward to plant a kiss on his cheek then whispered in his ear, "Grandfather."

"Oh, while we're being so candid, there's one more thing." He reached into an inner pocket and pulled something out. He held her hand palm side up, and dropped the something into it.

Her locket.

That long ago day drifted back into her mind when Nate had given her the locket. She lifted puzzled eyes to Uncle William. "How did you get this?" She hadn't seen it in years. She'd kept it hidden away in the original box, in the back corner of her lingerie drawer.

"The police recovered it. It was in Nate's pocket."

She turned it over in her hand. "I don't know why he had it. He gave it to me that Christmas. The last Christmas ..."

Something sparked in Uncle William's eyes. His right forefinger touched the gold heart locket. "Here's the interesting part, Nancy. I gave this locket to someone, long ago."

For a few moments, they stared into each other's eyes. She had a good idea how Nate had gotten it the first time. No doubt, Mama Liz had given it to him. But how had he gotten it back from Nancy? Unless he'd been in her home.

A chill danced down her spine. Uncle William brushed her cheek with his fingertips. "It's all over now, Nancy. No more secrets." He chuckled softly. "Well, except for the one."

She smiled into his eyes. "I did give you my solemn promise."

He rose from the chair and picked up his hat. "Just be sure the only soul you tell is our Robert. You may have complete confidence in him."

Chapter Thirty-Seven

Nancy stared at the closed door for several minutes after Uncle William left. Something had changed inside her. She was still the same person, but knowledge had given her insight. She'd believed herself tainted by the same blood that flowed in Liz Elliott and Nate Conners. She'd blamed her melancholy on genetics. Suddenly cold, she crossed her arms over her chest and closed her eyes.

William Boston was her grandfather. No wonder he'd stayed so close all these years. Her gaze came to rest on the wooden box. Why did it remind her of Robert? She leaned forward to run her fingers over the carved surface.

The lock had been broken. She raised the lid. Sorrow washed over her as she lifted a pearl necklace. Her grandmother's favorite. Inside one of the compartments, she found the sapphire necklace and earbobs.

She closed her eyes again, and she was back in Robert's arms, on the dance floor, New Year's Eve, 1925. It seemed like another lifetime.

Was Uncle William correct? Did Robert still love her? Sometimes, he seemed so distant and was so often away. She'd despaired of things ever becoming right for them again. Uncle William's words echoed in her mind. *I really hate to see two people who obviously love each other kept apart by a misunderstanding.*

A misunderstanding. Really? Could he really believe she had feelings for that ...? A cry caught in her throat, followed by great, wrenching sobs from deep inside her.

A nurse appeared at her side. "Mrs. Emerson, are you all right?"

She left for a moment and returned with a cool, damp cloth. She mopped Nancy's face and whispered, "It's all right. It's all right. It's good for you to cry. Get all that out of your system. It's God's cleansing."

When Nancy was calm, the nurse helped her back to bed. "You rest now, Mrs. Emerson." She pushed Nancy's hair away from her brow and laid the cool cloth there. She switched out the light and padded out, pulling the door to behind her.

"I forgive you, Nate." Nancy whispered into the empty room. Then she closed her eyes and rested. God's cleansing did feel good.

Sunlight spilled in as the morning nurse opened the blinds. "Good morning, Mrs. Emerson. Your breakfast is ready." She turned the crank to raise the bed, fluffed the pillows and handed Nancy a damp cloth to wash her face.

After the nurse had gone, Nancy ate the tepid oatmeal and drank the steaming black coffee. Everything tasted wonderful. She sipped the last of her coffee as Robert entered.

He wore a black pinstriped suit, white shirt, and burgundy silk tie. He smelled wonderful. Had he been this handsome all along? He removed her tray and replaced it with a box.

"What is this?"

He smiled. "Open it and find out."

She lifted the cover from the box and felt the blood drain from her face. "I … I don't know if I'm ready."

He sat down on the foot of her bed and gazed into her eyes. "Then save it until you are."

A girl could get lost in those eyes. Suddenly very aware of her appearance, Nancy touched her face.

He caught her hand in his. "It's not so bad, Nancy. Whenever you're ready, I'll be right here."

She nodded then lifted the handheld mirror from the box. She had never feared mirrors. In her younger days, she'd spent a lot of time in front of them. But this was different. The first glance was difficult. She nearly dropped the mirror. After a moment, she began again.

She'd been so battered, even the whites of her eyes had turned a deep red. Bruises on her face darkened from purple to black. She caught her breath. Her eyes found Robert's on the other side of the mirror. His smile gave her little comfort.

"I look like a monster," she whispered.

He tucked a strand of hair behind her ear. "You're still beautiful to me."

"How can you say that?"

"I thought I'd lost you."

She closed her eyes and allowed herself to believe that she deserved such a man. After all she'd done, and everything they'd experienced in the last few weeks, he still cared for her. She pressed her fingertips against her lips. Still sore, but at least they were beginning to heal. She met his gaze. "Thank you."

He grinned. "For bringing you a mirror?"

She shook her head as she laid the mirror in the box and set it aside. "No." For a moment, she was afraid to breathe. "I love you so much."

At first, he didn't react. Then he shook his head.

She sensed his uncertainty. Her eyes brimmed with tears. It seemed to Nancy that he moved in slow motion as his fingers caressed her cheek. A moment later, his lips brushed hers. She closed her eyes and allowed herself the luxury of a fantasy as his lips touched her brow, her eyelids, the bridge of her nose, and her mouth. If only she was well, he wouldn't have to stop. Her eyes were still closed when he spoke.

"Nancy, I think it's my turn to ask forgiveness."

She opened her eyes and gazed into his. "No, Robert."

"Yes. You have to let me do this. I didn't trust you. I withheld things. My motives were pure, but it doesn't matter why I did it. I … think the gravest infraction of all is that I couldn't protect you."

As he spoke, Nancy took his hand in hers and brought it to her lips. "I forgive you."

He gave her a wry smile. "Just like that? I was prepared to beg."

She pressed her lips together. It still hurt to smile. "There was going to be begging?"

He nodded as he leaned in close to her and spoke in a husky tone. "There was definitely going to be begging."

Nancy closed her eyes, expecting a kiss. Robert gave a soft chuckle instead. "Look who's begging now."

About the Author

Born in the Pacific Northwest, Betty Owens grew up in such exotic places as West Tennessee and San Diego, California. She lives in Kentucky with her husband. They have three grown sons living in the area, along with their daughters-in-law, four beautiful granddaughters, and two handsome grandsons.

Though she's always had an interest in storytelling, Betty's writing career began to take off in 1986. As a busy homeschooling mom, she needed an outlet for all the extra joy in the house. Now semi-retired, she spends most of her time writing, studying about writing, and critiquing other peoples' writing. She is one of twelve authors featured in the romantic novella, *A Dozen Apologies,* released Valentine's Day, 2014 by *Write Integrity Press.*

She has two fantasy-adventure novels in a second edition published by *Sign of the Whale Books*, an imprint of *Olivia Kimbrell Press.*

Betty is an active member of American Christian Fiction Writers (ACFW), where she leads a critique group, and Bluegrass Christian Writers, a lively group of Kentucky writers, who meet quarterly in a Lexington, Kentucky bookstore.

Connect with Betty online:
www.bettythomasonowens.com
www.facebook.com/betty.owens.author
https://twitter.com/batowens
google.com/+BettyThomasonOwensPMT

Other Books by the Author

A Dozen Apologies
Available on Kindle

Mara Adkins, a promising fashion designer, has fallen off the ladder of success, and she can't seem to get up. In college, Mara and her sorority sisters played an ugly game, and Mara was usually the winner. She'd date men she considered geeks, win their confidence, and then she'd dump them publicly.

When Mara begins work for a prestigious clothing designer in New York, she gets her comeuppance. Her boyfriend steals her designs and wins a coveted position. He fires her, and she returns in shame to her home in Spartanburg, South Carolina, where life for others has changed for the better.

Mara's parents, always seemingly one step from a divorce, have rediscovered their love for each other, but more importantly they have placed Christ in the center of that love. The changes Mara sees in their lives cause her to seek Christ. Mara's heart is pierced by her actions toward the twelve men she'd wronged in college, and she sets out to apologize to each of them. A girl with that many amends to make, though, needs money for travel, and Mara finds more ways to lose a job that she ever thought possible.

Mara stumbles, bumbles, and humbles her way toward employment and toward possible reconciliation with the twelve men she humiliated to find that God truly does look upon the heart, and that He has chosen the heart of one of the men for her to have and to hold.

Look for other books

published by

www.WriteIntegrity.com

and

Pix-N-Pens Publishing

www.PixNPens.com

Thank you for reading our books. If you enjoyed this one, we would greatly appreciate a brief review.